THE CONFESSION

THE CONFESSION
A NOVEL

BY

MAXIM GORKY

TRANSLATED FROM THE RUSSIAN BY
ROSE STRUNSKY

WITH AN INTRODUCTION BY THE TRANSLATOR

Fredonia Books
Amsterdam, The Netherlands

The Confession:
A Novel

by
Maxim Gorky

ISBN: 1-58963-625-2

Copyright © 2001 by Fredonia Books

Reprinted from the 1916 edition

Fredonia Books
Amsterdam, The Netherlands
http://www.fredoniabooks.com

All rights reserved, including the right to reproduce this book, or portions thereof, in any form.

In order to make original editions of historical works available to scholars at an economical price, this facsimile of the original edition of 1916 is reproduced from the best available copy and has been digitally enhanced to improve legibility, but the text remains unaltered to retain historical authenticity.

INTRODUCTION

To me Gorky has never suffered from that change it has become so fashionable for young Russia to mourn. "Since he has begun to give us doctrines, he has lost all his art," they say and shake their heads. "We can get all the doctrines we want from the platform of the Social Democratic party or from the theorists of the Social Revolutionaries — why go to Gorky? Or if it is a philosophy of life that we seek, have we not always Tolstoi, who is greater, truer and has more consummate art? Why does he not write again a *Foma Gordyeeff*, or an *Orloff and His Wife*, or a *Konovaloff!*"

I re-read *Foma Gordyeeff, Orloff and His Wife, Konovaloff* and so on, and read also *Mother, The Spy, In Prison*, and the little fables with a purpose so sadly decried, and I see nothing there but the old Gorky writing as usual from the by-ways of life as he passes along on the road. The road has lengthened and widened in the twenty-five years of his wandering, that is all. Russia has changed and grown and passed through deep-stirring experiences from the year 1890, when Gorky first published his immortal story of *Makar Chudra*, to her present moment of titanic struggle in the World War — the beginning of the year 1916.

Russia's changes were Gorky's changes. He first flung his type of hero, the people from the lowest of the low — water-rats, tramps, petty thieves — into a discouraged, disappointed and hopeless Russia. It was a Russia that had almost decided that there were no more people, that they were without courage, that the misery and degradation in which they lived was there because of their own inefficiency, their lack of idealism, their incapacity to grasp an idea and to strike and fight for it.

The Russia that thought this and the Russia that Gorky awakened from its torpor by introducing to it again the people it had almost learned to scorn, showing them with a capacity of understanding ideas, with deep emotions and great courage, was the Russia that had settled back in bitter disappointment after the sad failure of the Revolutionary movement of the eighties.

Like an eddying pool, the generations in Russia have risen to the surface, made their protest against the anachronism of autocracy and despotism, and then subsided back again into the still and inert waters of the nation. But each rising generation has made a wider and wider eddy, coming ever from a greater depth. Thus in 1825 it was merely a small group of military officers, who having learned from the Napoleonic campaigns that there were such things as constitutional law and order, that liberty and freedom were truths to fight for, broke out in revolt in Petrograd in December of that year only to be immediately crushed. Five of the leaders were hanged, and the rest, intellectuals and writers among them, were sent to Siberia.

The loss of the élite of Russia, despite the names of

INTRODUCTION

Pushkin and Lermontoff which graced that period, made great inroads in the intellectual life of the country. But in the fifties and sixties the seeming quiet was broken into by a new restlessness. This time the student youth, the young sons and daughters of the landlords and the nobles, became inspired by a passion for learning, for new conceptions of education, for new liberties of the people, for the abolition of serfdom and for a Pan-Slavism that would be democratic. It was then that the women left their homes to seek higher education and to enter new fields of work. They had to break with family tyranny which was fostered by tradition and the State, their men comrades standing valiantly by, helping them to make escapes, going through the forms of mock marriage, and conducting them safely to that Mecca of learning for the Russian youth — the medical school of Geneva. It was in this way that Sonya Kovalevsky, who later became the famous mathematician in the University of Stockholm, made her escape into the world, and the untold other heroines of Russia who were soon to return educated, free, and fired with a zeal to spread their new-found freedom to the people.

The abolition of serfdom in '61 brought with it great discontent, for the peasants had been led to believe that they would be liberated together with the land, since Russian serfdom, unlike the Western, was based on the theory that the peasant was attached to the land and that the landlord's hold on it came through his ownership of the serf. Consequently it was argued, when the Russian serf was liberated and the ancient communal

viii   INTRODUCTION

village form maintained, that all the land the serfs had owned would go to them. Of course, that was very far from what really happened. It is true that the serfs were liberated and the ancient communal form kept, but the land allotted to the village was poor and meager, the plots were scattered, and the tax on them for repayment to the landlords was so great that it took over fifty years to pay.

The peasants foresaw exactly the future that awaited them; the dearth in land, none too much to begin with, and the consequential lessening at each redistribution as the village increased in " souls," the needed " renting " from the landlord at exorbitant rates, the inability to pay and the resultant " paying in his own labor," and the eventual reestablishment of a virtual serfdom. Insurrections took place all over the country, the peasants believing firmly that the Government had treated them more kindly but that the landlords were deceiving them. However, the Government came only too gladly to the aid of the landlords, having got used to blood-baths in its drastic quenching of the Polish insurrection of '63.

The general disappointment among the youth in the Government's attitude towards both Polish liberty and peasant rights led to a stronger and more revolutionary stand on their part. Unlike the reaction that set in during the long and tyrannical reign of Nicholas I, after the outburst of the Decembrists, or the reaction that was to follow those thirty years of effort when the notes of Gorky were to sound like a clarion call to a renewed faith, the decade of the seventies rose to one of extreme

INTRODUCTION ix

and intense idealism. The generation which had gone out of Russia to gain for itself new liberties had now returned and was spread throughout the length and breadth of the vast land, making converts by the thousands where formerly there were but few. The "fathers" and "sons," though not understanding each other very fully, were nevertheless following a pretty equal tendency. Where the former had sought for new general liberties in politics and social life through education, the latter, feeling that a great deal had already been won, had decided upon propaganda of action. The movement changed from a freeing of one's self to a freeing of the people. "To the people" became the watchword of the hour. The youth of the better classes went to live among the peasants, taught them, organized them into secret revolutionary groups for "land and liberty," made several abortive attempts at peasant revolution, and finally, the Government growing more and more reactionary, ended in the wielding of a personal "terror" against the Government representatives, which culminated in the assassination of the Czar, Alexander II, in 1882.

The reprisals that set in, the wholesale exiling of the youth to Siberia, the internment for life in the fortresses of Peter and Paul and in Schlüsselberg for participation in the Party of the Will of the People, and the general opinion that however reactionary Alexander II was he was still much more ready for reforms than his successor Alexander III, gave rise to a fundamental disillusionment. The sacrifices of the youth had been too much. They had led themselves to be hanged and

INTRODUCTION

tortured only to bring in an era of still greater darkness. The people were not ready for reforms, they did not wish them. They would not have understood what to do with liberties could they have had them. There was nothing to do but sit back on one's estate, exploit the peasants as did the grandfathers and say, "We are powerless and the peasants unworthy."

This period was the more painful because it came fast upon one which was full of idealism and hope. The men who lived on in inertia, drinking tea and discussing vacuously the futility of life, had known a time when they had hoped and thought and planned otherwise. They had almost cynically to repudiate their former selves.

The writer who brought out most acutely the great anguish of this period was Anton Chekhov. He is now being recognized as the greatest artist of his time, who followed naturally the trend of the years he lived in. His humor, at first gentle and sorrowful, became later coarse and gross as the darkness around him deepened. His characters are inert, some eaten up by unfulfilled desires, others incapable even of recalling the faint echo of a former hope. A "Chekhov Sorrow" became a well-known definite phrase in Russian life.

It was before this Russia that Gorky made his appearance. Himself one of the people, he showed them again the face of the people. It had beauty and courage, it had qualities of strength long since forgotten. The effect was electrical. Gorky was hailed as one upon whom the cloak of Tolstoi was to fall, for better

INTRODUCTION xi

than Tolstoi, he did not appear as a leader of the people, but as one who disclosed the people *en masse*.

Gorky's appearance in the cultured and literary world of Russia suffering from the " Chekhov Sorrow " has an analogy in my mind to the sudden appearance of Peter Karpovitch in the fortress of Schlüsselberg. There sat the men and women for almost twenty years, cut off from all outside communication, wondering when and how their work would be carried on. One by one they had died off and only a handful remained to question if the youth would ever awake to strong purposes again. Then suddenly, in the year 1902, the big gates opened, and the student Peter Karpovitch entered. Without connection with any revolutionary group, by an instinctive feeling of the pulse of the time, he made his strike against the increasing reaction, shooting the Minister of Education, Bogolyepov, in February, 1901, for the wholesale exiling of the students into the military on the lines employed by Nicholas I.

This advance guard of the Russian Revolution was tall and handsome, with the traditional heroic figure of the Little Russian. He came to the men of the past in all his strength and beauty as a symbol of the new era. Upon his footsteps followed fast Bolmashev, the executor of Sipiagin, who this time committed his act under the direction of an organized group, the Social Revolutionaries. In two years Russia was aflame. The Governor General of Finland, Bobrikoff, was shot in June, 1904. This was followed in a few weeks by the assassination of Von Plehve and the Grand Duke

Sergei, by general labor strikes, by the demonstration in Petrograd in front of the Winter Palace which led to the terrible massacre of Bloody Sunday on January 22, 1905, by the mutinies in the Black Sea fleet and in Kronstadt, and by the nation-wide general strike in every branch of industry and life in October, 1905. Finally a Constitution and the Duma were granted to the people. The herald of the new order to the old was the tall handsome youth whose strange footsteps were heard suddenly and unexpectedly one March morning treading the hitherto silent corridors of the fortress.

Thus, as Karpovitch to the prisoners in Schlüsselberg, came Gorky to Russia at large.

He was marvelously fitted to dispel the disappointment that was felt about the people. Himself one of the people, he had merely to disclose himself to prove again their courage and nobility. The life of Gorky has been particularly tragic and particularly Russian. He was born in a dyer's shop in Nizhni-Novgorad in 1869. His real name is Alexei Maximovich Peshkov, and it is significant that when he came to write he signed himself " Maxim Gorky "—" Maxim, the Bitter." His father died when he was four and he was totally orphaned at seven. His childhood was spent in the care of his maternal grandfather, who was extremely religious and a miser. The foundation of the bitterness he was to feel was thus laid early, for the life of the lonely child with the harsh, unsympathetic old man, can be well imagined, though the peculiarly Russian setting can be had only by reading his recent book, *My Childhood*. At

INTRODUCTION   xiii

the death of his mother he was apprenticed to a shoemaker, and at eleven he decided that he had had enough of home ties and left Nizhni-Novgorad for good. He started tramping and after various vicissitudes found himself a helper to a cook on one of the Volga boats. This man had been at one time a noncommissioned officer and he carried his past culture with him in the form of a trunk full of books. It was a queer assortment, from Gogol to school manuals and popular novels, and Gorky dipped liberally into it. The result was that a craving for real learning arose in him, which would have come no doubt to the imaginative youth at this age even without the aid of that haphazard library. He left the Volga steamer and tramped to the University of Kazan, thinking that learning would be free to any one who wished it. He was bitterly disappointed, for the University demanded fees, and so instead of registering as a student he was forced to take a job as a bakery helper. This work he did for two years and it seems to have made a deep impression upon him, for there is scarcely a story of his where the hero does not spend two years baking bread in some filthy cellar among flour dust and general filth.

He left the bakeshop to wander with those tramps and "ex-men" whose poet he was later to be. The life held suffering which ate deep into the vitals of his being — hunger, privations, nights with the police for vagabondage; and finally so great became this conflict between the beauty and goodness for which his nature craved and the constant evil around him, that in 1889 at the age of twenty-one he sent a bullet through his chest. Like many of the Russian youth, whose passionate natures make impossible the compromise between their inherent idealism and the sordidness and brutality of actual existence, he had decided to be done with the mockery. Fortunately the bullet did not kill and he took up his life of vagabondage again. In 1892 he is once more in Nizhni-Novgorad, actually holding the respectable post of a lawyer's clerk. The lawyer, a man called Lanin, seems to have taken a great interest in the intelligent young man who discussed "cursed" questions and had a "live and energetic soul." He threw opportunities for study in his way, but Gorky's free and untamed youth, coupled with the taste of the "mother earth" he grew to love so, made it impossible for him to lead the well-ordered life of a professional clerk, and in a city, at that. He left Lanin, for he did not "feel at home with these intelligent people," he said, and tramped to the Caucasus, making a detour on the way from the Volga, through the Don district, into Bessarabia and Southern Crimea.

Coming to the Caucasus he found work in a railroad yard in Tiflis. His mind had already begun to digest the types of those tramps, Tartars and gipsies he met in his wanderings, for as early as 1890 his first story *Makar Chudra* made its appearance in the little paper *Kafhas* in Tiflis. It is a story of two thieves, written with great simplicity and naturalness. There is no doubt that Gorky had met them and had been true to the incidents related. It showed them strong, sensitive

INTRODUCTION

as women, with a subtle capacity of understanding each other's emotions. In a typically Russian scene, one thief unburdens his heart to the other, telling him how he had wanted to kill him and how he had nearly done so. The other listens, sympathetic, understanding fully how that state of mind came to him, and they part in great tenderness! These are no weaklings, they are personalities held by iron chains in a Greek fatalism, and the fatality is life — Russian life. Gorky had not yet come to the point where he could lay his hand on the social enemy and say "here it is." He saw only a great misery and natures torn in anguish, but not ruined as the generation before had supposed. Though this story itself, appearing, as it did, in a provincial paper, made no immediate name for him, his later stories, in which both canvas and treatment are exactly the same, brought him recognition forthwith.

Gorky left Tiflis and wandered back to the Volga and there, by happy chance, met the Little Russian writer, Korolenko, the author of *Makar's Dream* and *The Blind Musician*. As editor of *The Contemporary*, Korolenko introduced him to " great " literature, as he put it, and in a flash he was made known to all of Russia. He continued writing in the same vein he introduced in *Makar Chudra*, using the strong, outcast, rebel types in *Emilian Pibgai* and *Chalkash*, which were published in 1895 under Korolenko's editorship, and in *Konovaloff*, *Malva*, *Foma Gordyeeff* his first long novel, and in the innumerable other works which preceded the supposed " change ·" in Gorky's manner. He showed his heroes to

Russia as one shows a scene by pulling back a curtain: "this is what exists; here are men who do not conform to your laws, not because you have made outcasts of them, but because they despise you and all your smug respectability."

But he did not say so in so many words, he merely showed this canvas. The change in Gorky is the change in Russia, which grew from a silent and brooding mood to one of talk and action. As the Russian people became more self-conscious so did he, changing from a man torn hither and thither by circumstances to one who was able to analyze life and know cause and effect. His very sudden success so early in his life made it impossible for him to keep on writing and re-writing the same themes in the same manner as he had begun. He was too great and dynamic a genius for that. To him as to most Russians the art itself is not the thing, but the self-expression and the truth. Thus when Gorky swung out from the life of tramps and wanderers into the intellectual life of Russia, he found a nation organized into various groups, analyzing the cause of Russian social and political misery, finding an economic and materialistic reason for it, and setting about to remedy it. Gorky joined one of these groups, the Social Democratic Party, was one of the signers of the petition to the Czar which demanded with an amusing Russian naïveté that the Czar grant not only economic justice to the strikers in the steel works of Petrograd, but also a constitutional assembly, universal suffrage, a direct and secret ballot, and free speech, free press and freedom of

INTRODUCTION xvii

religion! For these demands and the subsequent demonstration in front of the Winter Palace which resulted in the notorious massacre of Bloody Sunday, Gorky was imprisoned in the fortress of Peter and Paul. His prominence and the fact that he was subject to tuberculosis caused a universal demand for his release. He was freed after a month and was allowed to stay in Finland and even in Petrograd for a while during the so-called days of freedom.

By this time Gorky had thrown himself entirely into the cause of the Majority Faction of the Social Democratic Party, an organization not strictly Marxian, in the sense that they did not wait for an economic development to bring about the cooperative commonwealth but believed that by mass action and general strike Russia could bring about a revolution on socialistic lines without the necessity of intermediary steps. In 1905 he left Russia and came to America, hoping to collect money for the Revolutionary cause, but his work failed entirely because of the fact that the charming and brilliant lady who came with him to America and registered as his wife was not legally so. The men of prominence, Mark Twain among them, who formed committees to help raise the funds, resigned, and Gorky's plans failed entirely. Not only was no money for the " cause " raised, but he was received nowhere, the very hotel he stayed in asking him to leave at midnight. It was supposed that agents of the Russian Government, fearing Gorky's too great success in America, sprung the trap and thus discredited him. At any rate, Gorky naturally left the shores of America in great disgust, and the dark days of Russian reaction having already set in, went to live in practical exile on the island of Capri, in Italy. Leonid Andreyeff, the Russian writer, and many revolutionary refugees generally stayed with him. It was from Capri that the longer novels, *The Spy* and this work, *The Confession,* were written. He was by this time living entirely in the cultured world, thinking earnestly and scientifically to the best of his ability about the political and social conditions around him.

The great light, the great inspiring motive power of the Russian has ever been the people. The only ray of happiness in the works of Gorky is the joy that comes to his characters when they begin to work for the people. Life is depressing, life is a quagmire, a bog wherein great and noble souls are forced to wallow, when suddenly light appears. It is in the organization for the creation of a better life. One feels just for one little instant the happiness that life can bring when this vision of the new order appears. In the novel called *Three of Them,* the pages lighten with relief when the little Social Democratic agitator appears, giving hope and courage, but she is swept out of the life of the unhappy men that fill the pages of that book as suddenly as she appeared and there is nothing for the hero to do but throw himself under a passing train and die for disappointment and impotence.

This was in the beginning when he himself first saw the meaning of the " Cause," before it had become fully part of his life. Later his works changed their scene,

INTRODUCTION xix

following the exact manner in which the Russian people themselves changed their mental attitude. The background of the same Russian people, the same giants with the same courage and the same ability, was no longer a quagmire, but a battlefield. They were struggling to win their rights. Interwoven in the pages of his later work rises the new Russia of the last decade, the self-conscious, fighting Russia. In *The Spy*, which was written in 1908, we see the Russian not yet come into his own, still living in ignorance and disorder, but his activity is different. He is in a fight. The same change is in *Mother* and in the work *In Prison*. A new pæan is sung, it is the song of the people marching *en masse*. Perhaps Walt Whitman came the nearest to this same feeling of democracy, but unlike Whitman it is not of the people that Gorky sings, but it is the people themselves that are the song-makers. They are the "creators." "In them dwells God."

The Russian who finds Gorky's later works too doctrinaire, too purposeful, never quarrels with him because he finds his theme at fault or the conclusions wrong, but because he thinks his art has failed. They say they have revised their opinion that Gorky would mean to them what Tolstoi has meant, for they still consider the latter to be more universal and truer philosopher and artist. They find it inartistic for Gorky to talk to them of what they already know. They want to hear again about the strange and beautiful types they did not know of before and to read again his beautiful lines with their exquisite descriptions of nature, which they consider unsurpassed by the greatest. However, to me Gorky's æstheticism is too one-sided. It is the æstheticism of the primitive whom only the grandiose impresses. The soft, subtle shadings leave him untouched. There is no doubt that he loves passionately his " mother earth " with the vast, undulating steppes, the tall mountains of the Caucasus, the great dome of the sky, and the living sweep of the sea. His descriptions of these scenes glow as does a Western writer over the charms of his beloved, but we miss the charms of the beloved.

In reading Russian literature, it must always be remembered that one is reading of a people whose civilization is intrinsically different from that of the West. It is the difference between action and passivity. Professor Milyoukoff would have us believe that it is the autocratic form of government which has made the Russian live so long in inactivity, that both his reasoning powers and imaginative faculties have developed far in excess of the rest of Europe's. It is true that the Russian is never afraid to go to the end of a thought, to fight for freedom far in excess of that already attained in the Western world, and to ask continually the fundamental questions of " Why," and " Wherefore," and " Where am I going," and " Where does this lead me to? " The knife of Russian literature discloses as surely a cross-section of Russian civilization as does that of Guy de Maupassant, Flaubert, Zola and other realists of the French school disclose the French. And yet this cross-section of Russian civilization is difficult to grasp without a more intimate knowledge of both the history and

INTRODUCTION

the people. It is difficult for me now to remember my conceptions of Russian life as I got them from the Russian writers before my visit to Russia ten years ago. America, California, all the activities of our Western life made the characters and problems in Turgeneff, Dostoyeffsky and Gogol seem vague and unreal, made them move about in a nebulous society where one asked embarrassing personal questions and were always answered with a truth that had rudeness in it.

I had a coward's entry into Russia. There were rumors of riots and disorders, for it was in the year of general strikes and barricades, and as the train moved farther into the interior, the guards who shoveled the snow off the track seemed to me soldiers under arms, standing there to protect us from some infuriated mob. My heart beat with fear at that great and uncouth stranger to me, the Russian people. But as my stay in Russia was prolonged, my kinship with the people grew. The common man appeared to me as a gentle protector and friend. The drivers of the droshkies, the peasants, the workingmen, the conductors on the trains, all became kindly elder brothers, who set one on one's right path or made a friendly remark as one passed along. Every one talked to every one, and although the great interest of the time was the Duma and the political situation, there lurked always a personal understanding and a personal relation behind each discussion. All classes had this attitude, and though the educated had more facts at their resources, for they knew history and the outside world, they had the same outlook and the same manner as the others. I became so much at one with the people around me, that when I left Russia eighteen months later, I felt this time fearful at going away, as if now truly I were going from home into a strange land. As the train came into the Western world, as I found myself in Poland and out again into Austria, I was again alone, a solitary and detached individual who was to stand on guard against the ill-turn which would be given me if I were not watchful. Outside of Russia, the people, " the God-creators," as Gorky calls them, fell apart into millions of various atoms, each struggling for his own life. It was in Russia that I left them still unspoiled, unadventitious, united in a great simplicity of faith and love. It is therefore that the last chapter of this book is distinct and real to me, and I can almost see with my own eyes that vast, surging procession of the people, showing their loving strength and giving of their strength to the weak.

To-day, when all ideals and hopes have gone smash in the hurly-burly of this World War, Gorky has taken his side with his country and is again living in Russia. In the interim, before he can pick up the gauntlet to fight on for a new and better order, he has gone back to his former theme, writing as before of the tramps and " ex-men " and gipsies he knew in his youth, and Russia is pleased with him once more.

Rose Strunsky.

New York, February, 1916.

THE CONFESSION

CHAPTER I

LET me tell you my life; it won't take much of your time — you ought to know it.

I am a weed, a foundling, an illegitimate being. It isn't known to whom I was born, but I was abandoned on the estate of Mr. Loseff in the village of Sokal, in the district of Krasnoglinsk. My mother left me — or perhaps it was some one else — in the landlord's park, on the steps of the little shrine under which the old landlady Loseff lay buried and where I was found by Danil Vialoff, the gardener. He was walking in the park early in the morning, when he saw a child wrapped in rags lie moving on the steps of the shrine. A smoke-colored cat was walking stealthfully around it.

I lived with Danil until I was four years old, but as he himself had a large family, I fed myself wherever I happened to be, and when I found nothing I whined and whined, then fell asleep hungry.

When I was four I was taken by the sexton Larion, a very strange and lonely man; he took me because of his loneliness. He was short of stature, round like a toy balloon and had a round face. His hair was red, his voice thin like a woman's, and his heart was also like a woman's, gentle to everybody. He liked to drink wine and drank much of it; when sober he was silent, his eyes always half-closed, and he had an air of being guilty before all, but when drunk, he sang psalms and hymns in a loud voice, held his head high and smiled at every one.

He remained apart from people, living in poverty, for he had given away his share to the priest, while he himself fished both summer and winter. And for fun he caught singing birds, teaching me to do the same. He loved birds and they were not afraid of him; it is touching to recall how even the most timid of little birds would run over his red head and get mixed up in his fiery hair. Or the bird would settle on his shoulder and look into his mouth, bending its wise little head to the side. Then again Larion would lie on a bench and sprinkle hempseed in his head and beard, and canaries, goldfinches, tomtits and bullfinches would collect around him, hunting through his hair, creeping over his cheeks, picking his ears, settling on his nose while he lay there roaring with laughter, squinting his eyes and conversing tenderly with them. I envied him for this — of me, the birds were afraid.

Larion was a man of tender soul and all animals recognized it; I can't say the same for men, though I don't mean to blame them for I know man isn't fed by caresses.

It used to be rather difficult for him in winter; he had no wood and he had nothing to buy it with, having drunk up the money. His little hut was as cold as a cellar, except that the birds chirped and sang, and the two of us would lie on the cold stove, wrapped in everything possible, listening to the singing of the birds. Larion would whistle to them — he could whistle well — looking like a grossbeak, with his large nose, his hooked bill and his red head. Often he would say to me: "Well, listen, Motka" (I was baptized Matvei). "Listen!"

He would lie on his back, his hands under his head, squinting his eyes and singing something from the funeral Liturgy in his thin voice. The birds would then become quiet, stopping to listen, then they themselves would begin to sing one after the other. Larion would try to sing louder than they and they would exert themselves, especially the canaries and goldfinches, or the thrushes and starlings. He would often sing himself up to such a point that the tears from his eyes would trickle from out his lids, wetting his cheeks and washing his face gray.

This singing sometimes frightened me, and once I said to him in a whisper:

"Uncle, why do you always sing about death?"

He stopped, looked at me and said, smiling,

"Don't get frightened, silly. It doesn't matter if it is about death; it is pretty. Of the whole church service the funeral mass is the most beautiful. It offers tenderness to man and pity for him. Among us, no one has pity except for the dead."

These words I remember very well, as I do all his

words, but of course at that time I could not understand them. The things of childhood are only understood on the eve of old age, for these are the wisest years of man.

I remember also that I asked him once, "Why does God help man so little?"

"It's none of His business," he explained to me. "Help yourself, that's why reason was given to you. God is here so that it won't be so terrible to die, but just how to live, that is your affair."

I soon forgot these words of his, and recalled them too late, and that is why I have suffered much vain sorrow.

He was a remarkable man! When angling most people never shout and never speak so as not to frighten the fish, but Larion sang unceasingly, or recounted the lives of the saints to me, or spoke to me about God, and yet the fish always flocked to him. Birds must also be caught with care, but he whistled all the time, teased them and talked to them and it never mattered — the birds walked into his traps and nets. The same thing as to bees; when setting a hive or doing anything else, which old bee-keepers do with prayers, and even then don't always succeed, the sexton, when called for the job, would strike the bees, crush them, swear profanely, and yet everything went in the best way possible. He didn't like bees — they blinded a daughter of his once. She found herself in a bee-hive — she was only three at the time — and a bee stung her eye. This eye grew diseased, and then blind, and soon the other eye followed. Later the little girl died from headache, and her mother became insane.

Yes, he never did anything the way other people did, and he was as tender to me as if he were my own mother. They did not treat me with much mercy in the village. Life was hard, and I was a stranger, and a superfluous one. . . . Suddenly and illegally to be eating the morsel that belonged to some one else!

Larion taught me the church service, and I became his helper and sang with him in the choir, lit the censer, and did all that was needed. I helped the watchman Vlassi keep order in the church and I liked doing all this, especially in winter. The church was of brick, they heated it well, and it was warm inside it.

I liked vespers better than morning mass. In the evening the people were purified by work and were freed of their worries, and they stood quietly and majestically, and their souls shone like wax candles with little flames. It was plain then, that though people had different faces their misery was the same.

Larion liked the church service; he would close his eyes, throw back his red head, stick out his Adam's apple and burst forth into song, losing himself so that he would even start off on some uncalled for hymn and the priest would make signs to him from the altar: "Where is it taking you?" He also read beautifully. His voice was singsong and sonorous, and had tenderness in it, and emotion and joy. The priest did not like him, nor did he like the priest. More than once he said to me:

"That, a priest! He is no priest, he is a drum upon whom need and force of habit beat their sticks. If I were a priest, I would read the service in such a way that not only would I make the people cry, but even the holy images!"

It was true — the priest did not suit his post. He was short-nosed and dark as if he had been singed by gun-powder. His mouth was large and toothless, his beard straggly, his hair thin and bald on top, his arms long. He had a hoarse voice and he panted as if carrying a load that was too much for his strength. He was greedy and always in a bad humor — for his family was large and the village was poor, the land of the peasants bad and there was no business.

In summer, even when the mosquitoes were thick, Larion and I spent our days and our nights in the woods to hunt for birds or on the river to catch fish. It happened that he would be needed unexpectedly for some religious ceremony and he would not be there, nor would any one know where to find him. All the little boys in the village would scatter to hunt for him, running like hares and crying, "Sexton! Larion! Come home!" He would hardly ever be found. The priest would scold and threaten to complain, and the peasants would laugh.

CHAPTER II

LARION had a friend, Savelko Migun, a notorious thief, and a habitual drunkard. He was beaten more than once for his thieving and even sat in jail for it, but for all that he was a remarkable person. He sang songs and told stories in such a way that it is impossible to remember them without wonder.

I heard him many times, and now he stands before me as if alive; he was dry, lively, had a sparse beard, was all in tatters; with a small phiz and a wedge-shaped, large forehead underneath which often twinkled his thievish, merry eyes like two dark stars.

Often he would bring a bottle of vodka, or Larion would insist on buying one, and they would sit opposite each other at the table, Savelko saying:

"Well, sexton, roll out the litany."

Then they drank . . . Larion, a bit abashed, would nevertheless begin to sing, and Savelko sat as if glued to the spot, trembling, his little beard twitching, his eyes full of tears, smoothing his forehead with his hand and smiling or wiping the tears from his cheek with his fingers.

Then he would bounce up like a ball, crying:

"Most superb, Laria! Well, I envy the Lord

God — beautiful songs are made for Him! But for man, Laria? What's man anyway, no matter how good he be or how rich his soul? It isn't hard for him to go before the Lord. But He, what does He do? Thou givest me nothing, Lord, and I give Thee my whole soul!"

"Don't blaspheme!" Larion would say.

"I blaspheme?" Savelko would cry; "I never even thought of such a thing! How am I blaspheming? In no way at all! I am rejoicing for the Lord, that's all. And now I am going to sing you something."

He would stand up, stretch out his arm, and begin to chant. He sang quietly and mysteriously, opening his eyes wide and moving his dry finger continually on his outstretched arm, as if it were hunting for something in space. Larion would lean up against the wall, rest his hands on the bench, and look on in open-mouthed wonder. I lay on the stove with my heart melting within me with sweet sadness. Savelko would grow black before me, only his little white teeth would glisten and his dry tongue would move like a serpent's while the sweat would rise on his forehead in thick drops. His voice seemed endless and it flowed out and shone like a stream in a meadow. He would finish, stagger a bit, wipe his face with the back of his hand, then both would take a drink and remain silent a long time. Later Savelko would ask —

"And now Laria, 'The Ocean Waves.'"

THE CONFESSION 9

And in this way they cheered each other up all evening as long as they were not yet drunk. When that happened, Migun began to tell obscene stories about priests, landlords, and kings, and my sexton would laugh and I with them. Savelko without tiring produced one story after another, and each one so funny that he almost choked with laughter.

But best of all he sang on holidays in the wineshop. He stood up in front of the people, frowning hard so that the wrinkles lay deep on his temples. To look at him, one would think the songs came to his bosom from the earth itself and that the earth showed him the words and gave strength to his voice. Around him stood or sat the peasants, some with heads bowed chewing a piece of straw, others staring into Savelko's mouth, and all were radiant, while the women even wept as they listened.

When he finished they said:

"Give us another, brother."

And they brought him drinks.

The following story was told about Migun. He stole something in the village, and the peasants caught him. When they caught him, they said:

"Well, that finishes you! Now we are going to hang you, we can't stand you any longer."

And he, the story goes, answered:

"Drop it, peasants, that's a nasty job you've begun. You have already taken from me the things I've stolen, so that you have lost nothing. Anyway, you can always get new things, but where will you get such a fellow as I? Who will cheer you up when I'm gone?"

"All right," they said, "talk on."

They took him to the wood to hang him and he began to sing on the way. When they first started out, they walked fast, then they slowed up. When they came to the wood, though the rope was ready, they waited, until he should finish his last song. Then they said to one another:

"Let him sing another song. It will do for his Last Communion."

He sang another and then another, and then the sun rose. The men looked about them; a clear day was rising from the east. Migun stood smiling among them awaiting his death without fear. The peasants became abashed.

"Well, fellows, let him go to the devil," they said. "If we hang him, we might have all kinds of sins and troubles on our heads for it."

And they decided not to touch Migun.

"We bow to the ground before you for your talent," they said, "but for your thieving we ought to beat you up, all the same."

They gave him a light beating, and then they all went back in a body with him.

All this might have been made up, but it speaks well for human beings, and puts Savelko in a good light. And then think of this: if people can make up such good stories, it follows they are not so bad, and in this lies the whole point.

Not only did they sing songs together, but Savelko and Larion carried on long conversations with each other — often about the devil. They did not give him much honor.

Once I remember the sexton saying:

"The devil is the image of your own wickedness, the reflection of your own dark soul."

"That means, he is my own foolishness?" Savelko asked.

"Just that and nothing else."

"It must be so," Migun said, laughing. "For were he alive, he would have snatched me up long ago!"

Larion didn't believe in devils at all. I remember him discussing in the barn with the Dissenters and he shouting:

"It is not devilish, but brutish! Good and evil are in man. When you want goodness, goodness is there; if you want evil, evil is there, from you and for you. God does not force you by His Will either to good or evil. He created you free-willed, and you are free to do both good and evil. Your devil is misery and darkness! Good is really something human, because it springs from God, while your evil doesn't come from the devil, but from the brute in you."

They shouted at him:

"Red-haired heretic!"

But he kept on.

"That's why," he said, "the devil is painted with

horns and feet like a goat's, because he is the brute element in man."

Best of all Larion spoke about Christ. I always wept when I pictured the bitter fate that befell the Holy Son of God. His whole life stood before me, from the discussion in the Temple with the wise men, to Golgotha, and He was like a pure and beautiful child in His ineffable love for the people, with a kind smile for all and a tender word of consolation — always like a child, dazzling in His beauty.

"Even with the wise men of the Temple," Larion said, "Christ conversed like a child, that is why in his simple wisdom He appeared greater than they. You, Motka, remember this, and try to conserve the child-like throughout your whole life, for in it lies truth."

I would ask him:

"Will Christ come again soon?"

"Yes, soon," he would say, "soon, for it is said that people are again looking for Him."

As Larion's words now come back to me, it seems to me that he saw God as the great Creator of the most beautiful things, and man as an incompetent being, who was lost on the by-ways of the world. And he pitied this talentless heir to the great riches left to him on this earth by God.

Both he and Savelko had one faith. I remember that an ikon appeared miraculously in our village. Once, very early on an autumn morning a woman came to the well for water, when suddenly she saw

THE CONFESSION 13

something glow in the darkness at the bottom of the well. She called the people together. The village elder appeared, the priest came, and Larion ran up. They let a man down into the well and he brought up the ikon of the "unburnt bush." They performed mass right on the spot and then they decided to put up a shrine above the well, the priest crying:

"Orthodox, give your offerings."

The village elder lent his authority and gave three rubles himself. The peasants untied their purses and the women earnestly brought pieces of linen and grain of all sorts. There was rejoicing in the village and I, too, was happy, as on the day of Christ's holy Resurrection.

But even during mass I noticed that Larion's face looked sad. He glanced at no one, and Savelko ran about like a mouse through the crowd and giggled. At night I went to look at the apparition. It stood above the well, giving forth an azure glow like a vapor, as if some one unseen was breathing on it tenderly, warming it with his light and heat; it gave me anguish and pleasure.

When I came home I heard Larion say sadly,

"There is no such Holy Virgin."

And Savelko drawled out the following, laughing:

"I know, Moses lived long before Christ. Why! the scoundrels! A miracle, what? Oh, but you peasants are queer!"

"For this the elder and the priest ought to go to jail," Larion said in a very low voice. "Let them not kill the God in man just to slack their own greed."

I felt uneasy at this conversation and I asked from the stove:

"What are you talking about, Uncle Larion?"

They were silent, then they whispered to each other; evidently they were disturbed. Then Savelko cried:

"What is the matter with you? You yourself complained that the people were fools, and now you are shamelessly making a fool of Matveika! Why?"

He jumped over to me and said:

"Look, Motka, here are matches. I rub them between my hands, see? Put out the light, Larion."

They put out the lamp, and I saw Savelko's two hands glow in the darkness with the same blue phosphorescence as the miraculous ikon. It was terrible and offensive to see.

Savelko said something, but I crouched in a corner of the stove, closed my ears with my fingers, and remained silent. Then they crawled in by my side, took vodka along, and for a long time they took turns in telling me about true miracles and of the faith of man sacrilegiously betrayed. And so I fell asleep while they talked.

After two or three days, many priests and officials arrived, arrested the ikon, dismissed the village elder from his post, and the priest, too, was threatened with a law-suit. Then I believed the whole thing had been a fraud, though it was hard for me to admit that it was done for the purpose of getting linen from the women and some pennies from the men.

When I was six years old, Larion began to teach me the abcs in the Church-tongue and when two winters later a school was opened in our village, he sent me there. At first I grew somewhat apart from Larion. I liked to study, and I took to my books zealously, so that when he asked me my lessons, as sometimes happened, he would say, after hearing me,

"Fine, Motka."

Once he said:

"Good blood boils in you. It's plain your father was no fool." And I asked,

"But where is he?"

"Who can know!"

"Is he a peasant?"

"All one can say for sure is that he was a man. His caste is unknown. However, he could hardly have been a peasant. By your face and skin, not to mention your character, he seems to have been from the gentry."

Those casual words of his sank deep into my mind and they didn't do me much good. When they called me a foundling at school, I balked and shouted to my comrades:

"You are peasant children, but my father is a gentleman!"

I became very firm about this. One must protect

oneself somehow against insults, and I had no other protection in my mind. They began to dislike me, to call me bad names, and I fought back. I was a strong youngster and could fight easily. Complaints grew about me, and people said to the sexton:

"Quiet that bastard of yours!"

And others without bothering to complain, pulled my ears to their hearts' content.

Then Larion said to me:

"You may be a son of a general, Matvei, but that isn't of such great importance. We are all born in the same way and therefore the honor is the same for all."

But it was too late. I was twelve years old at the time and felt insults keenly. Something pulled me away from people and again I found myself close to the sexton. All winter we wandered together in the wood, catching birds, and I became worse in my studies.

I finished school at thirteen, and Larion began to think what he should do with me. I would go rowing with him in a boat, I at the oars and he steering, and he led me in his thoughts over all the paths of human fate, telling me of the various vocations in life.

He saw me a priest, a soldier, an employee, and nowhere was it good for me.

"What should it be then, Motka?" he would ask.

Then he would look at me and say, laughing,

"Never mind, don't get frightened. If you don't

fall down, you will crawl out. Only avoid the military. That's a man's finish."

In August, soon after the Day of Assumption, we went together to the lake of Liubushin to catch sheat-fish. Larion was a bit drunk and he had wine along with him. From time to time he sipped from the bottle, cleared his throat and sang so that he could be heard over the whole water.

His boat was bad, it was small and unsteady. He made a sharp turn, the bow dipped, and we both found ourselves in the water. It was not the first time that such a thing happened, and I was not frightened. I rose and saw Larion swimming at my side, shaking his head and saying to me:

"Swim to the bank and I'll push the damned tub there."

It was not far from the bank and the current was weak. I swam tranquilly, when suddenly I felt as if something pulled at my feet, or as if I had struck a cold current, and looking back, I saw that our boat was floating bottom up, and Larion was not there. He was nowhere.

Like a stone striking my head, terror hit my heart. A cramp seized me and I sank to the bottom.

An employee from the estate, Yegor Titoff, who was crossing the field, saw how we capsized. He saw Larion disappear and when I began to drown, Titoff was already on the bank undressing. He pulled me out, but Larion was not found until night.

His dear soul was extinguished, and immediately it became both dark and cold for me. When they buried him, I was sick in bed, and I could not escort the dear man to the cemetery. When I was up, the first thing I did was to go to his grave. I sat there, and could not even weep, so great was my sorrow. His voice rang in my memory, his words lived again, but the man who used to lay his tender hand on my head was no longer on this earth. Everything became strange and distant. I sat with my eyes closed. Suddenly somebody picked me up. He took me by the hand and picked me up. I looked and saw Titoff.

"You have nothing to do here," he said. "Come." And he led me away. I went with him.

He said to me:

"It seems you have a good heart, youngster, it remembers the good."

But this did not make me feel any better. I was silent. Titoff continued:

"Even at the time when you were abandoned, I thought to myself, I shall take the child to me, but I came too late. However, it seems it is God's wish. Here He again puts your life into my hands. That means you will come to live with me."

It was all the same to me then, whether to live, not to live, how to live or with whom. . . . Thus I passed from one point in my life to another without realizing it myself.

CHAPTER III

AFTER a time I began to take interest in all that surrounded me. Titoff was a silent man, tall in stature, with his head and cheeks shaved like a soldier's, and he wore a long mustache. He spoke slowly and as if he were afraid to say one word too many, or as if he were in doubt himself of what he was saying. He held his hands in his pocket or crossed them behind his back, as if he were ashamed of them. I knew that the peasants of the village and even those of the neighboring district hated him. Two years before, in the village of Mabina, they beat him with a stake. They said that he always carried a revolver with him.

His wife, Nastasia, was handsome, tall and slender. Her face was bloodless, with two feverish, large eyes. She was often sick. Her daughter, Olga, who was three years my junior, was also pale and thin.

A great silence reigned about them. Their floor was covered with thick carpet, and not a footstep could be heard. Even the clock on the wall ticked inaudibly. The lamps, which were never extinguished, burned before their holy images. There were prints stuck on the walls, showing the Last Judgment and the Martyrdom of the Apostles and of Saint Barbara. In one corner, on the low stove, a large cat, the color of smoke, looked out of its green eyes on the surroundings and seemed to guard the silence.

In the midst of this awful stillness it took me a long time to forget the songs of Larion and his birds.

Titoff brought me to the office of the estate and showed me the books. Thus I lived. It seemed to me that Titoff watched me and followed me about in silence as if he expected something from me. I felt depressed and unhappy. I was never gay, but now I became almost morose. I had no one to speak to, and, moreover, I did not wish to speak to any one. When Titoff or his wife asked me about Larion I did not answer, but mumbled something. A feeling of unhappiness and sadness weighed upon me. Titoff displeased me by the suspicious stillness of his life.

I went almost daily to the church to help the watchman, Vlassi, and also the new sexton, a handsome young man, who had been a school teacher. He was not interested in his work, but he was a great friend of the priest, whose hand he always kissed and whom he followed about like a dog. He continually reproved me, for which he was in the wrong, because I knew the holy service better than he did and always did everything according to rule.

It was at this time, when life became difficult for me, that I began to love God. One day when I was placing the tapers in front of the image of the Holy Virgin and her Child, before mass, I saw that they

THE CONFESSION

looked at me with a grave and compassionate expression. I began to weep, and, falling on my knees, I prayed for I do not know what — for Larion, no doubt. I do not know how long I remained there, but I arose consoled, my heart warm and animated. Vlassi was at the altar and he mumbled something incomprehensible. I mounted the steps, and when I was near him he looked at me.

"You look very happy," he said. "Have you found a kopeck?"

I knew why he asked that question, for I often found money on the ground. But now these words left an unpleasant impression on me, as if some one had hurt my heart.

"I was praying to God," I said.

"To which one?" he asked me. "We have more than a hundred here. And the living One, the true One, who is not made of wood, where is He? Go and find Him."

I knew the value to attach to his words. Nevertheless, they appeared offensive to me at this time. Vlassi was a decrepit old man, who could hardly walk. His limbs stuck out at the knees and he always tottered as if he were walking on a rope. He had not a tooth in his mouth, and his dark face looked like an old rag, from which two wild eyes stuck out. He had lost his reason and had commenced to rave even some time before Larion's death.

"I don't watch the church," he said. "I watch cattle. I was born a shepherd and shall die a shepherd. Yes, soon I shall leave the church for the fields."

Every one knew that he had never watched cattle.

"The church is a cemetery," he would say. "It is a dead place. I wish to deal with something living. I must go and feed cattle. All my ancestors have been shepherds, and I also up to my forty-second year."

Larion used to make fun of him. One day he said to him laughingly:

"In olden times there was a god of cattle who was called Voloss. Perhaps he was your great-great-grandfather."

Vlassi questioned him about Voloss; then he said:

"That's right. I have known that I was a god for a long time, only I am afraid of the priest. Wait a little, sexton; don't you tell it to him. When the right time comes I will tell him myself."

It was impossible to get the idea out of his head. I knew that he was crazy, yet he worried me.

"Take care," I said to him. "God will punish you."

And he muttered: "I am a god myself."

Suddenly my foot caught on the carpet and I fell, and I interpreted it as an omen. From that day I began to love passionately all that pertained to the church. The ardor of my childish heart was so great that everything became sacred for me — not only the images and the gospels, but even the chandeliers and the censer, whose very coals became precious in my eyes. I used to touch these objects with joy and with a feeling of great respect. When I went up the steps of the altar my heart would cease beating, and I could have kissed the flagstones. I felt that I was under One who saw everything, directed my steps and surrounded me with a supernatural force; who warmed my heart with a dazzling and blinding light, and I saw only myself. At times I remained alone in the darkness of the temple, but it was light in my heart; for my God was there, and there was no place for childish troubles, nor for the sufferings which surrounded me — that is to say, the human life about me. The nearer one comes to God, the farther one is from man. But, of course, I did not understand that at that time.

I began to read all the religious works which fell into my hands. Thus my heart became filled with the divine word. My soul drank avidly of its exquisite sweetness, and a fountain of grateful tears opened within me. Often I went to the church before the other faithful ones, and, kneeling before the image of the Trinity, I wept lightly and humbly, without thinking and without praying. I had nothing to ask of God and I worshiped Him with complete self-forgetfulness. I remembered Larion's words:

"When you pray with your lips you pray to the air and not to God. God thinks of the thoughts, not the words, like man."

I did not even have thoughts. I knelt and sang in silence a joyful song, happy in the thought that

I was not alone in the world and that God was near me and guarded me. That was a happy time for me, like a calm and joyful holiday. I liked to remain alone in the church, when the noise and the whisperings were over. Then I lost myself in the stillness and rose up to the clouds, and from that height man and all that pertained to man became more and more invisible to me.

But Vlassi bothered me. He dragged his feet on the flagstones, he trembled like the shadows of a tree shaken by the wind, and he muttered with his toothless mouth:

"I have nothing to do here. Is it my business? I am a god, the shepherd of all earthly cattle. To-morrow I am going away into the fields. Why have they exiled me here in these cold shadows? Is this my work?"

He troubled me with his blasphemies, for I imagined that his profanity sullied the purity of the temple and that God was angry at his being in His house.

People began to notice my piety and my religious zeal. When the priest met me he grunted and blessed me in a special way, and I had to kiss his hand, which was always cold and covered with sweat. Although I envied his being initiated into the divine mysteries, I did not love him and was even afraid of him.

Titoff's little, dull eyes, like buttons, followed me with increasing vigilance. Every one treated me

THE CONFESSION

carefully, as if I were made of glass. More than once little Olga would ask me, in a low voice:

"Will you be a saint?"

She was timid even when I was kind, when I told her religious stories. On winter nights I read aloud the Prologue and the Minea. Gusts of snow blew over the country, groaning and beating against the walls. In the room silence reigned and no one stirred. Titoff sat with head bowed, so that his face could not be seen. Nastasia, who was sleepy, sat with her eyes fixed on me. When the frost crackled she trembled and glanced about her, smiling gently. When she did not understand the meaning of a Slavic word she would ask me. Her sweet voice resounded for an instant, and then again there was quiet. Only the flying snow sang plaintively, wandering over the fields seeking repose.

The holy martyrs, who fought for the Lord and celebrated His greatness by their life and by their death, were especially dear to my soul. I was touched also by the merciful and pious men who sacrificed everything for love of their neighbors. But I did not understand those who left the world in the name of God and went away to live in a desert or in a cave. I felt that the devil was too powerful for the Anchorites and the Stylites, that he made them flee before him. Larion had denied the devil. Nevertheless, the life of the saints forced me to recognize him. And, besides, the fall of man would be incomprehensible if one did not admit the existence of the devil. Larion saw in God the one and omnipotent Creator, but then from where came evil? According to the life of the saints, the author of all evil is the devil. In this rôle I accepted him. God, then, was the creator of cherries, and the devil the creator of burrs; God the creator of nightingales and the devil the creator of owls. However, although I accepted the devil, I did not believe in him and was not afraid of him. He was useful to me in explaining the existence of evil; but at the same time he bothered me, for he lessened the majesty of God.

I forced myself not to think of this problem, but Titoff continually made me think of sin and of the power of the devil. When I read, he questioned me curtly, without raising his eyes.

"Matvei, what does that last word mean?"

And I explained it.

Then after a second of silence, he would say:

"Where can I hide before Thy countenance? Where can I flee before Thy wrath?"

His wife would sigh deeply and look at him, still more frightened, as if she expected something terrible. Olga blinked her blue eyes and suggested:

"In the forest."

"Where can I flee before Thy wrath?" he repeated.

This time I remember he took his hands from his pockets and twirled his long mustache, and his eyebrows trembled. He hid his hands and said:

"It was King David who asked, 'Where can I

THE CONFESSION

flee?' Yes, he was a king and he was afraid. You see that the devil was stronger than he. He was anointed of God and the devil conquered him. 'Where can I flee?' To hell — that is certain. We lesser people, we have nothing to hope for if the kings themselves go there."

He frequently returned to this subject. I did not always understand his words; nevertheless, they produced a disagreeable impression upon me.

People began to speak more and more about my piety. One day Titoff said to me:

"Pray zealously for my whole family, Matvei. I beg of you, pray for us. You will thus repay me for having gathered you to me and treated you like a son."

But what did that mean to me? My prayers were without object, like the song of a bird which he pours out to the sun. Nevertheless, I began to pray for him and for his family, and especially for little Olga, who had become a very pretty young girl, sweet and tender. I borrowed the words of the Psalms of David and all the other prayers which I knew. I liked to repeat the sing-song and cadenced phrases, but from the time when I said in praying for Titoff: "Lord, in Thy grace, have pity on Thy servant, Yegor," my heart closed. The spring of my prayers became dry, the serenity of my joys was disturbed. I was ashamed before God and could not continue. Lowering my eyes before the countenances of the holy saints I arose, overcome with a feeling of anger and embarrassment. It troubled me. Why should I feel like that? I tried to understand it, but could not, and I was sorry for the joy which had been destroyed on account of this man.

CHAPTER IV

THE people about me began to notice me, and I took notice of them, too.

On holidays when I walked through the streets I was stared at with much curiosity. Some greeted me earnestly while others mocked, but all looked after me.

"Here goes our prayer-book," was heard. "Say, Matvei, are you going to become a saint?"

"Don't laugh at him, friends; he is not a priest and he does not believe in God for the sake of the money."

"Have there not been peasants who became saints?"

"Oh, we have all kinds of men, but that does not help us much."

"Who said he is a peasant? He has got gentleman's blood in him — but that's a secret."

And thus they talked, and some praised and some jeered.

As for myself, I was then in a peculiar state of mind. I wished to be at peace with all and wanted all to love me. However, try as I would to live up to it, their insults prevented me.

Of all who persecuted me, Savelko Migun was the

worst. He fell on his knees when he saw me and prostrated himself, declaiming aloud:

"Your Holiness, I bow to the ground before you. Pray for Savelko, I beg of you. God may do the right thing by him then. Teach me how to please the Lord God. Must I stop stealing, or must I steal more and burn him a wax candle?"

The crowds laughed at Savelko's jokes, but they made me feel queer and hurt me.

He would continue:

"Oh, ye Orthodox, prostrate yourself before the Righteous One. He fleeces the peasants in his office and then reads the gospel in church. And God cannot hear how the peasants howl."

I was sixteen and could easily have broken his face for his insults. But instead, I took to avoiding him. When he noticed this he gave me no leeway at all. He composed a song, which he sang in the streets on holidays, accompanying himself with his balalaika.

> "Oh, the squires embrace the maidens,
> And the maidens all grow big;
> From these gentlemanly doings
> Come out dirty cheats as children.
> They are thrown upon the masters
> Who refuse to feed them gratis;
> And they put them in their office,
> To the peasants' great misfortune."

It was a long song and everybody was mentioned in it, but Titoff and I had the biggest share of all.

It got to such a point that when I caught sight of Savelko with his little thin beard, his cap on his ear and his bald head, I trembled all over. I felt like springing on him and breaking him into bits.

Though I was young, I could hold myself in with a strong hand. When he walked behind me, jingling, I did not move a muscle to show that it was hard to bear. I walked slowly and made believe I did not hear.

I began to pray more zealously, for I felt that I had no protection except prayers, which, however, were now filled with complaints and bitter words.

"Wherefore, O Lord, am I to blame that my father and mother abandoned me and threw me like a kitten into the brush?"

I could find no other sin in me. I saw men and women placed on this earth without rhyme or reason; saw each one so accustomed to his business that the custom became law. How was I to know right off why and against whom this strange force is directed?

However, I began to think things over, and I grew more and more troubled as things became insufferable to me.

Our landlord, Constantine Nicolaievitch Loseff, was rich and owned much land, and he hardly ever came to our estate, which was considered unlucky by the family. Somebody had strangled the landlord's mother, his father had fallen from a horse and been killed, and his wife had run away from him here.

I only saw the landlord twice. He was a stout man, tall, wore spectacles and had an officer's cape and cap, lined with red. They said he held a high position under the Czar and that he was very learned and wrote books. The two times he was on the estate he swore at Titoff very thoroughly and even shook his fist in his face.

Titoff was the one absolute power on the estate of Sokolie. There was not much land, and only so much grain was sown as was necessary for the household. The rest of the land was rented to the peasants. Later there came an order that no more land should be rented and that flax should be sown on the whole estate. A factory was being opened nearby.

In addition to myself, there sat in a corner of the office Ivan Makarovitch Judin. His soul was half dead and he was always drunk. He had been a telegraph operator, but he had lost his position on account of his drunkenness. He took care of the books, wrote the letters, made the contracts with the peasants, and was remarkably silent. When he was spoken to, he only nodded his head and coughed a little. At most he answered, "All right." He was short and thin, but his face was round and puffy, and his eyes could hardly be seen. He was entirely bald and he walked on his tip-toes, silently and unsteadily, as the blind. On the Feast of the Virgin of Kazin, the peasants made Judin so drunk with vodka that he died.

THE CONFESSION

I was alone now in the office, did all the work, and received a salary from Titoff of forty rubles a year. He gave me Olga as an assistant.

I had noticed for a long time that the peasants walked around the office as wolves around a trap. They see the trap, but they are hungry, and the bait tempts them, so they begin to eat.

When I was alone in the office and became acquainted with all the books and plans, I realized, even with my poor understanding, that our whole arrangement was nothing more than theft. The peasants were head over ears in debt and worked, not for themselves, but for Titoff. I cannot say that I was either very much surprised or ashamed at this discovery. And even if I did understand now why Savelko swore at me and insulted me, still I did not think it was right of him. Was it then I who had originated this stealing?

I saw that Titoff was not quite straight even with the landlord, and that he stuffed his pockets as much as he dared.

I became bolder toward him, for I realized that in some way I was necessary to him. And now I understood why. I had to hide him, the thief, from the Lord God. He now called me his "dear son," and his wife did so too. They dressed me well, for which, of course, I was grateful.

But my heart did not go out toward them, and my soul was not warmed by their goodness. I became more and more friendly with Olga, however. I liked her wistful smile, her low voice and her love of flowers.

Titoff and his wife walked before God with sunken heads, like a team of horses, and behind their timid glances seemed to be continually hiding something which must have been even greater than theft.

I did not like Titoff's hands. He always hid them in a manner which made me suspicious. Perhaps those hands had strangled some one; perhaps there was blood on them. They kept asking me, he as well as she:

"Pray for our sins, Motia."

One day I could stand it no longer. I asked them:

"Are you then more sinful than others?"

Nastasia sighed and went away, and he turned on his heel and did not answer.

In the house he was thoughtful and spoke very little, and then only on business. He never swore at the peasants, but he was always haughty with them, which was worse than swearing. He never conceded a point and stood his ground as firmly as if he were sunk to the waist in the earth.

"One should give in to them," I said to him once.

"Never," he answered. "Not an iota must you give in, or you are lost."

Another time he ordered me to count false, and I said to him:

"You can't do that."

"Why not?"

"It is a sin."

"It is not you who are forcing me to sin, but I you. Write as I tell you. No one will ask any account of you, you are only my hand. Your piety will not suffer by it; have no fear. For ten rubles a month neither I nor anybody else can live honorably. Do you understand that?"

"Oh, you scoundrel!" I said to myself. But aloud I said to him: "That is quite enough. Things must end right here. If you don't stop this swindling I will tell the village all about your deals."

He pulled his mustache up to his nose, lifted his shoulders to his ears, showed his teeth and stared at me with his round, bulging eyes. We measured each other.

"You will do that, really?" he said to me in a low voice.

"Yes."

Titoff burst out laughing, and it sounded as if some one had thrown silver pieces on the ground.

"All right, my holy one, that is all that I needed. From now on we will manage this affair differently. We won't bother any more with kopecks. We will deal with rubles. If the thief's dress is too tight, he becomes honest."

He went out, slamming the door so that the panes in the windows rattled.

It seemed to me that Titoff was a little more cross

after that. Still I was not quite sure of it. But he left me in peace from then on.

He was a terrible miser, and though he did not deny himself anything, nevertheless he knew how to value a penny. He ate well and was very fond of women, and as he had the power in his hands, there was not a woman in the village who dared to refuse him. He let the young girls alone, and only went to the married women. He made my blood hot once or twice.

"What is the matter, Matvei?" he asked. "Are you timid? To take a woman is like giving charity. In the country every woman yearns for love. But the men are weak and worn out, and what can the women expect from them? You are a strong, handsome young fellow; why not make love to the women? You would get some pleasure out of it yourself."

He followed every villainy, the low rascal. Once he asked me:

"Do you think, Matvei, that a pious man is of much value in the eyes of God?"

I did not like such questions. "I don't know," I answered.

He remained doubtful for a minute and then he said:

"God led Lot out of Sodom and saved Noah; but thousands perished by fire and water. Still it says, 'Thou shalt not kill.' Often it seems to me that these thousands perished because among them there were a few pious and virtuous people. God saw that despite the stringent laws which He gave, there were several who could lead a righteous life. If there had been no pious men in Sodom, God would have seen that it was impossible to observe His commandments and He might have lightened them without putting to death thousands of people. They call Him the All-merciful One. But where is His mercy?"

I did not understand then that this man was only seeking license to sin. Nevertheless, the words angered me.

"You are blaspheming," I said. "You are afraid of God, but you don't love Him."

He drew his hands out of his pockets, threw them behind his back, and his face turned gray. It was plain that he was in great wrath.

"Whether it is so or not, I don't know," he answered, "but it seems to me that you pious ones use God as a ruler by which you mark off the sins of others. Without such as you, God would have a hard time measuring sins."

He took no notice of me for a long time after that. But an insufferable hatred rose in my soul against this man. I avoided him even more than I did Savelko. If at night I mentioned his name in my prayers, an ungovernable anger possessed me. It was at this time that I said my first spontaneous prayer:

"I do not wish to seek grace for a thief, O Lord.

I ask that he be punished. May he not rob the poor without being punished."

And I prayed to God so ardently that Titoff be punished that I grew frightened at the terrible fate that awaited him.

Soon after this I had another encounter with Migun. He came to the office for lime-bast[1] when I happened to be alone. I asked him:

"Why do you always make fun of me, Savel?"

He showed his teeth and stared at me with his piercing eyes.

"I haven't much business here," he said. "I only came for lime-bast."

My legs trembled beneath me and my hands clenched of themselves. I clutched his throat and shook him lightly.

"What have I done?"

He was not frightened, nor was he angry. He simply took my hand and pushed it from his throat as if it were he, not I, who was the stronger. "When you are choking some one, he cannot speak well," he said. "Let me alone," he continued; "I have received beatings enough, and I don't need yours. Besides, you mustn't strike any one. It is against the commandments."

He spoke quietly and mockingly, in a light tone. I shouted:

"What do you want here?"

"Some lime-bast."

[1] A vegetable fiber made from the bark of the lime tree.

THE CONFESSION

I saw that I could make no headway with him by words, and my anger was already gone. I now only felt hurt and cold.

"You are all beasts," I said. "Can you make fun of a man because his parents abandoned him?"

He threw his words at me as if they were little stones:

"Don't be a hypocrite. We know you by your actions. You eat stolen bread and others suffer want."

"You lie!" I said. "I work for my bread."

"Without work you can't even steal a chicken. That is an old story."

He looked at me with a devilish smile in his eyes and said pityingly:

"Oh, Matvei, what a good child you used to be. And now you have become learned, despite God, and like all thieves in our country, you found a religion based on God's truth that all men have not equally long fingers."

I threw him out of the office. I did not want to understand his play on words, for I considered myself a true servant of God and valued my own opinion more than any one else's.

I felt strange and fearful, as if the strength of my soul was vanishing. I had not sunk so low as to whine before God against man, for I was no Pharisee for all that I was a fool. I knelt before the holy Virgin of Abalatzk and looked up at her countenance and at her hands, which were uplifted to heaven. The little fire in the holy lamp flickered and a faint shadow spread over the ikon. The same shadow fell on my heart and something strange and invisible and oppressive rose up betwixt God and myself. I lost all joy in prayer, and I became wretched and even Olga was no longer a comfort to me.

But she looked at me all the more kindly. I was eighteen at this time, a well developed youth, with red curly hair and a pale face. I wanted to come nearer her, yet was embarrassed, for I was innocent before women then. The women in the village laughed at me for it, and it even seemed to me at times that Olga herself smiled at me in a queer way. More than once the enticing thought came to me: "There, that's my wife."

Day in, day out, I sat with her in the office in silence. When she asked me some questions about the business I answered, and in that lay our whole conversation.

She was slender and white, like a young birch, and her eyes were blue and thoughtful. To me she seemed pretty and tender in her quiet, mysterious wistfulness.

Once she asked me:

"What makes you so sad, Matvei?"

I had never spoken about myself with any one before, nor had ever wished to. But here suddenly my heart opened and I poured out all my misery to her. I told her of the shame of my birth, of the abuse that I suffered for it, and of the loneliness and

THE CONFESSION 41

wretchedness of my soul, and of her father. I told her everything. I did not do it to complain. It was only to unburden myself of my inmost thoughts, of which I had amassed quite a quantity — all worthless, I suppose.

"I had better enter a monastery," I ended.

She became depressed, hung her head and did not answer. I was pleased at her distress, but her silence hurt me. Three days later she said to me softly:

"It is wrong to watch people so much. Each one lives for himself. To be sure, now you are alone, but when you will have your own family, you will need no one and you will live like the rest, for yourself, in your own house and home. As for my father, don't judge him. I see that no one loves him, but I can't see wherein he is worse than the rest. Where does one see love anyway?"

Her words consoled me. I always did everything impetuously, and so here, too, I burst forth:

"Would you marry me?"

She turned and whispered:

"Yes."

CHAPTER V

IT was done. The next day I told Titoff, just the way it happened.

He smiled, stroked his mustache and began again to torture me.

"You want to become my son. The way is open for you, Matvei; it is the will of God and I make no objections. You're a serious, modest, healthy young man. You pray for us, and in every way you are a treasure. I say that without flattery. But in order to have enough to live on, one must understand business, and your leanings that way are very weak. That's the first thing. The second, you will be called to military service in two years and you will have to go. Should you have some money saved up by then, say some five hundred rubles, you might buy yourself off. I could manage that for you. But without money you will have to go and Olga will remain here, neither wife nor widow."

He struck me in the heart with these dull words. His mustache trembled and a green fire burned in his eyes. I pictured military life to myself. It was terrible and antipathetic to me. What kind of a soldier would I make? The very fact that I would have to live with others in the barracks was enough, and then the drinking and the swearing and the brawls! Everything about the service seemed inhuman to me. Titoff's words crushed me.

"That means," I said to him, "that I become a monk."

Titoff laughed.

"It is too late. They don't make you a monk right away, and novices are recruited as well as laymen. No, Matvei, there is no way to bribe fate but with money."

"Then give me the money," I said to him; "you have enough."

"Aha," he said, "what a lucky thought of yours! Only, how would I fare by it? Perhaps I earned my money by heavy sins; perhaps I even sold my soul to the devil for it? While I wallow in sin you lead a righteous life. And you want to continue it at the expense of my sinning. It is easy for a righteous one to attain heaven if a sinner carry him in on his back. However, I refuse to be your horse. Better do your own sinning. God will forgive you, for you have already merited it."

I looked at Titoff and he seemed to have suddenly grown yards taller than I, and I was crawling somewhere at his feet. I understood that he was making fun of me, and I stopped the discussion.

In the evening I told Olga what her father said. Tears shone in the girl's eyes, and a little blue vein beat near her ear. Its sad beating found an echo in my heart. Olga said, smiling:

"So things aren't going as we want them to?"

"Oh, yes, they will go," I said.

I said these words thoughtlessly, but with them I gave my word of honor to her and to myself, and I could not break it.

That day an unclean life began for me. It was a dark, drunken period, and my soul flew hither and thither like a pigeon in a cloud of smoke. I was sorry about Olga and I wanted her for my wife, for I loved her. But above all I saw that Titoff was more powerful than I, and stronger-willed; and it was insufferable to my pride. I had despised his villainous ways and his wretched heart, when suddenly I discovered that something strong lived in him, which looked down on me and overpowered me.

It became known in the village that I had proposed and had been refused. The girls tittered, the women stared at me, and Savelko made new jokes. All this enraged me and my soul became dark within.

When I prayed I felt as if Titoff were behind me, breathing on the nape of my neck, and I prayed incoherently and irreverently. My joy in God left me and I thought only of my own affairs. What will become of me?

"Help me, O Lord," I prayed. "Teach me not to wander from Thy path and not to lose my soul in sin. Thou art strong and merciful. Deliver Thy servant from evil and strengthen him against temptation, that he may not succumb to the wiles of his

THE CONFESSION 45

enemies nor grow to doubt the strength of Thy love for Thy servant."

Thus I brought God down from the height of His indescribable beauty and made Him do service as a help in my petty affairs, and having lowered God, I myself sunk low.

Olga in her sorrow shrunk from day to day, like a burning wax candle. I tried to imagine her living with some one else, but could not place any one beside her except myself. By the strength of his love, man creates another in his image, and so I thought that the girl understood my soul, read my thoughts and was as indispensable to me as I to myself. Her mother became even more depressed than before. She looked at me with tears in her eyes and sighed. But Titoff hid his ugly hands, walked up and down the room and circled silently around me like a raven over a dying dog, who is about to pick out his eyes the moment death came.

A month passed and I was at the same point where I left off. I felt as if I were on the edge of a steep ravine which I did not know how to cross. I was disgusted and heavy-hearted. Once Titoff walked up to me in the office and said in a whisper:

"You have an opportunity now. Take it if you want to be a man."

The opportunity was of such a nature that if it succeeded the peasants would lose much, the estate profit a bit and Titoff make about two hundred rubles. He explained it and asked:

"Well, you don't dare?"

Had he asked it in some other way, I might not have fallen into his clutches, but his words frenzied me.

"Not dare to steal? You don't need daring for that, but just meanness. All right, let's steal."

Here he laughed, the scoundrel, and asked:

"What about the sin?"

"I'll take care of my own sins," I answered.

"Good," he said, "and know that from now on each day brings you nearer the wedding."

He enticed me, fool that I was, like a wolf with a lamb in a trap.

And so it commenced. I wasn't stupid in business, and I had always had enough audacity in me. We began to rob the peasants as if we were playing a match. I followed each move he made with a bolder one. We said not a word, only looked at each other. There was mockery in his eyes and wrath burned in mine. He was the victor, and since I lost all to him, I did not want to be outdone in wickedness by him. I falsified the weights in measuring flax, I did not mark the fines when the peasants' cattle strayed on the landlord's pastures, and I cheated the peasants out of every kopeck I could. But I did not count the money nor gather in the rubles myself. I let everything go to Titoff, which, of course, did not make things easier either for me or the peasants.

In a word, I was as if possessed, and my heart was

THE CONFESSION

heavy and cold. When I thought of God I burned with shame. Nevertheless, I threw reproaches at Him more than once.

"Why dost Thou not keep me from falling with Thy strong arm? Why dost Thou try me beyond my strength? Dost Thou not see, O Lord, how my soul is being destroyed?"

There were times when Olga seemed strange to me, and when I looked at her and thought of her hostilely.

"For your sake, unhappy one, I am selling my soul."

After such words I grew ashamed of myself before her and became kind and gentle — as gentle as possible.

But, of course, it was not out of pity for myself nor for the peasants that I suffered and gnashed my teeth in wrath; but for sheer chagrin that I could not conquer Titoff and that I had to act according to his will. When I remembered the words he often used against pious people, I became cold all over; and he saw the situation through and through and triumphed.

"Well, my holy one," he said, "it is time to begin thinking of your own nest. You will be too crowded here when you have a wife. You will have children, of course."

He called me "holy one." I did not answer. He called me that more and more often; but his daughter became all the more loving, all the more tender to me. She understood clearly how heavy my heart was.

Then Titoff begged from the landlord, Loseff, when he went to pay his respects to him, a little piece of land for me. They gave him a pretty place behind the manor building, and he began to build us a little house.

And I continued to oppress and to cheat.

Things began to move quickly. Our pockets swelled. The little house began to be built and shone bright in the sun, like a golden cage for Olga. Soon the roof was to be put on, and then the stove had to be built, and in the fall it would be finished for us to move into.

One evening I was going home from the village of Jakimoffka, where I had gone to take the cattle from some peasants for their debts. Just as I stepped out of the wood which lay before the village, I saw my house in the sunset burning like a torch. At first I thought it was the reflection of the sun surrounding it with red rays which reached up to heaven. But then I saw the people running and heard the fire crackle and snap, and my heart suddenly broke. I saw that God was my enemy. Had I had a stone then, I would have thrown it against heaven. I saw how my thievish work was going up in smoke and ashes, and saw myself as if on fire, and said:

"Thou desirest to show me, O Lord, that I have

THE CONFESSION

burnt my soul to dust and ashes. Thou desirest to show me that. I do not believe it; I do not wish Thy humiliation. It was not through Thy will that it burned but because the peasants through hatred of me and Titoff set fire to it. I do not wish to believe in Thy wrath, not because I am not worthy of it, but because this wrath is not worthy of Thee. Thou didst not wish to lend Thy help to the weak in the hour of his need, so that he could withstand sin. Thus, Thou art the guilty One, not I. As in a dark wood, which was already full grown, so I stepped into sin. How could I then have kept myself free from it?"

But these foolish words could neither console me nor make me right. They only awoke in my soul an evil obstinacy. My house burned down more quickly than my wrath. For a long time I stood on the edge of the wood, leaning against the trunk of a tree and haggled with God, while Olga's white face, bathed in tears and drawn with pain, rose up before my eyes. And I spoke to God boldly, as to one familiar:

"Thou art strong. So will I be also. Thus it should be for justice' sake."

The fire was quenched and all became quiet and dark. Only a few flames thrust their tongues out into the night, like the sobs of a child after it has stopped crying.

The night was cloudy and the river shone like a

flaming sword which some one had lost in the field. I could have clutched at this sword and swung it high in the air to hear it ring over the earth.

Toward midnight I reached the village. At the door of the house were Olga and her father. They awaited me.

"Where were you?" Titoff asked.

"I stood on the hill and watched the fire."

"Why didn't you come to put it out?"

"Can I perform miracles? Would the fire have gone out if I had spat on it?"

Olga's eyes were swollen with tears and she was black with smoke and soot. I laughed when I saw her.

"You worked hard?" I asked.

Her eyes filled with tears. Titoff said gloomily:

"I don't know what will happen now."

"You must begin the building anew," I said.

Such wrath took possession of my soul then that I could have dragged the logs myself and have begun building unaided, until the house should be ready again. If it was not possible to go against the will of God, it was at least possible to find out whether God was for me or against me.

And again the roguery began. What ruses and wiles I thought out! Formerly I spent the nights in praying, but now I lay without sleep and worried how I could put one more ruble into my pocket. I threw myself entirely into these thoughts, although I knew how many tears flowed on account of me; how

THE CONFESSION 51

many times I stole the bread from the mouths of hungry ones; and how, perhaps, little children were starving to death on account of my avarice. Now, at the memory of it, I feel abhorrence and disgust and I laugh bitterly at my foolishness.

The faces of the saints no longer looked down at me with pity and goodness, as before. But instead they spied on me, as Olga's father did. Once I even stole a half ruble from the office of the village elder. So far had it gone with me.

Once something special happened to me. Olga went up to me, put her delicate arms on my shoulders, and said:

"Matvei, as surely as God's alive, I love you more than anything in the world."

She spoke these holy words wonderfully simply, as a child would say, "Mother." Like the hero in the fairy tale, I felt myself grow strong, and from that hour she became indescribably dear to me. It was the first time she had said she loved me, and it was the first time that I had embraced her and kissed her, so that I lost myself in her and forgot myself — as when I used to pray with all my heart.

Toward October our house was finished. It looked like a plaid where the logs showed blackened by the fire. Soon we celebrated the wedding, and my father-in-law became duly drunk and laughed with a full throat, like Satan at some success. My mother-in-law was silent and smiled at us through her tears.

"Stop crying!" Titoff roared at her. "What a son-in-law we have! Such a righteous one!"

Then he swore at her thoroughly.

We had important guests — the priest was there, of course, and the land commissioner, and two district elders, and various other pike among the carp. The village people had assembled under our windows, and among them Savelko made himself popular, for he was gay up to his last days. I sat at the window and heard the jingling of his balalaika and his thin voice pierced my ear. For though he was afraid to make his jokes too loud, still I heard him sing distinctly:

> "Hurry and drink till you burst,
> Eat yourself full till you split."

His jokes amused me, though I had something else to think about then. Olga nestled up to me and whispered:

"If only all this eating and drinking were over!"

The gluttony went against her, and to me, too, the sight of it was disgusting.

When we were alone we burst into tears, sitting and embracing each other on the bed; we wept and laughed together at our great unforeseen happiness in our marriage. All night we did not sleep, but kissed each other and planned how we would live with each other. We lit the candle in order to see each other better.

"We will live so that all will love us. It is good to be with you, Matvei."

We were drunk with our unutterable happiness, and I said to Olga:

"May the Lord strike me dead, Olga, if on account of me you should weep other tears."

But she said to me:

"I will bear everything from you. I will be your mother and your sister, my lonely one."

CHAPTER VI

WE lived together in a dream. I worked automatically, saw nothing and did not wish to see anything. I hurried home to my wife and walked with her in the fields and in the woods.

My past came back to me. I caught birds and our home became light and airy with the cages which were hung on the walls and the singing of the birds. My gentle wife loved them, and when I came home she told me how the tomtit behaved and how the cherry-finch sang.

In the evening I read Minea or the Prologue, but more often I spoke to my wife of my childhood and of Larion and Savelko; how they sang songs to the Lord and how they talked about Him. I told her about crazy old Vlassi, who was dead by this time. I told her everything that I knew, and it seemed that I knew very much about man and birds and fish. I cannot describe my happiness in words, for a man who has never known happiness and only enjoys it for a little time, never can describe it.

We went together to church and stood next to each other in a corner and prayed in unison. I offered prayers of thanks to God in order to praise

Him, though not without secret pride, for it seemed to me that I had conquered God's might and forced Him, against His will, to make me happy. He had given in to me and I praised Him for it:

"Thou hast done well, O Lord," I said, "but it is only just and right, what Thou hast done."

Oh, the miserable paganism of it!

The winter passed like one long day of joy. One day Olga confided to me that she was to become a mother. It was a new happiness for us. My father-in-law murmured something indistinctly and my mother-in-law looked with pity at my wife.

I began to think of bettering my condition a little; I decided to have a beehive, and I called it "Larion's Garden," so that it should bring me luck. Also, I planned to have a vegetable garden, and to breed song-birds, and I thought of doing things which would bring no harm to man. One day Titoff said to me, quite harshly:

"You have become so sugar-coated, Matvei; see that you do not get sour. You will have a child in the summer. Have you forgotten that?"

I had already wished to tell him the truth as I understood it then, so I said to him:

"I have sinned as much as I wished. I have become like you in sins — just as you desired. But to become worse than you, that I will not."

"I do not understand what you mean," he answered. "I only want to explain to you that seventy-two rubles a year for a man and a family is not much; and I will not permit you to squander my daughter's dowry. You must consider things well. Your wisdom is in reality hatred of me because I am more clever than you. But that will help neither you nor me. Each one is a saint just so long as the devil doesn't catch him."

I could have beaten him well, but out of consideration for Olga I restrained myself.

In the village it was known that I did not get on well with my father-in-law, and the people began to look at me in a friendlier way. As for myself, happiness had made me more gentle, and Olga, too, was mild and good of heart.

In order to save the peasants from loss I began to give in to them here and there; helped one and spoke up for another. The village is like a glass house, where every one can look in, and so pretty soon Titoff said to me:

"You again wish to bribe God."

I decided to drop my work in the office and said to my wife:

"I earn six rubles a month, and with my birds I can make more."

But the poor child became sad. "Do whatever you want," she answered, "only let us not become beggars. I am sorry for my father," she added. "He wanted to do the best by us, and has taken many sins upon his soul for our sakes."

"Ah, my dear one," I thought, "his well-wishing weighs heavily enough on me."

THE CONFESSION

Some days later I told my father-in-law that I was going to leave the office.

"To become a soldier?" he asked, smiling ironically.

I was hurt to the quick. I felt that he was ready to do anything against me, and it would not be difficult for him to harm me, considering who his acquaintances were. If I became a soldier I would be lost. Even for the love he bore his daughter he would not save me.

My hands became more and more tied. My wife wept in secret and went about with red eyes

"What is the matter, Olga?" I asked her.

And she answered: "I do not feel well."

I remembered the oath I had made to her, and I became ashamed and embarrassed. One step and my problem would be settled, but I pitied the beloved woman. Had I not had Olga on my hands I would have even become a soldier to get out of Titoff's clutches.

Toward the end of June a son was born to us, and again for some time I was as if dazed. The travail was difficult, Olga screamed, and my heart almost burst with fear. Titoif looked into the room gloomily, though most of the time he stood in the court and trembled. He leaned against the staircase, wrung his hands, let his head hang and muttered to himself:

"She will die. My whole life was useless. O Lord, have mercy! When you shall have children,

Matvei, then you will know my pain and you will understand my life; and you will cease to curse others for their sins."

At this moment I really pitied him. I walked up and down the court and thought:

"Again Thou threatenest me, O Lord. Again Thy hand is raised against me. Thou shouldst give me time to better myself and to find the straight path. Why art Thou so miserly with Thy grace? Is it not in Thy goodness that all Thy strength and power lie?"

When I remember these words now I grow ashamed at my foolishness.

My child was born and my wife became changed. Her voice was louder, her body taller, and in her attitude toward me there was a change, too. She counted every bite she gave me, although she was not exactly stingy. She gave alms less and less often and always reminded me of the peasants' debts to us. Even if it were only five rubles, she thought it worth while to remind me of it. At first I thought, "that will pass."

I became more and more interested in the breeding of my birds. I went twice a month to town with my cages and brought five rubles or more each time I returned. We had a cow and a dozen hens. What more did we want?

But Olga's eyes had an unpleasant light in them. When I brought her a gift from town she reproached me:

THE CONFESSION

"Why did you do that? You should rather have saved the money."

It was hard to bear, and in order to get over it, I worked the harder among my birds. I went into the woods, laid the net and the snares, stretched myself out on the ground, whistled low and thought. My soul was quiet; not a wish stirred in me. A thought arose, moved my heart and vanished again into the unknown, as a stone sinks into the sea. It left ripples on my soul; they were feelings about God.

At such times I looked upon the clear sky, the blue space, the woods clothed in golden autumn garments or in silvery winter treasure, and the river, the fields and the hills, the stars and the flowers, and saw them as God. All that was beautiful was of God and all that was of God was related to the soul.

But when I thought of man, my heart started as a bird does when frightened in its sleep. I was perplexed and I thought about life. I could not unite the great beauty of God with the dark, poverty-stricken life of man. The luminous God was somewhere far off, in His own strength, in His own pride. And man, separated from Him, lived in wretchedness and want.

Why were the children of God sacrificed to misery and hunger — Why were they lowered and dragged to the earth as worms in the mud? Why did God permit it? How could it give Him joy to see this degradation of His own work?

Where was the man who saw God and His beauty? The soul of man is blinded through the black misery of the day. To be satisfied is considered a joy; to be rich a happiness. Man looks for the freedom to sin; but to be free from sin, that is unknown to him. Where is there in him the strength of fatherly love, where the beauty of God? Does God exist? Where is the God-like?

Suddenly I felt a hazy intuition, a slight thought. It encircled and hid everything. My soul became empty and cold, like a field in winter. At this time, I did not dare express my thoughts in words, but even if they did not appear before me clothed in words, still I felt their power and dreaded them, and was afraid, as a little child in a dark cave. I jumped up, took my hunting traps with me, and hurried from the house. To rid myself of my sickly fear, I sang as I hurried along.

The people in the village laughed at me. A catcher of birds is not especially respected in the country, and Olga sighed heavily many times; for it seemed to her, too, that my occupation was something to be ashamed of. My father-in-law gave me long lectures, but I did not answer. I waited for autumn. Perhaps I would draw a lucky number and not have to serve in the military, and so escape this terrible abyss.

My wife became with child again, and her sadness increased.

"What is the matter, Olga?" I asked.

THE CONFESSION 61

At first she evaded the question and made believe that nothing was troubling her. But one day she embraced me and said:

"I shall die, Matvei — I shall die in childbirth."

I knew that women often talk thus, still I was frightened. I tried to comfort her, but she would not listen to me.

"You will remain alone again," she said, "beloved by none. You are so difficult and so haughty toward all. I ask you for the sake of the children, don't be so proud. We are all sinners, before God, and you also."

She spoke this way often to me, and I was wretched with pity and fear for her.

As to my father-in-law, I had made a sort of truce with him, and he immediately made use of it in his own way:

"Here, Matvei, sign this," or "Do not write that."

Things were coming to a climax. We were close to the recruiting time, and a second child was soon expected. The recruits were making holiday in the village. They called me out, but I refused to go, and they broke my windows for me.

The day came when I had to go to town to draw my lot. Olga was already afraid at this time to leave the house, and my father-in-law accompanied me and during the whole way he impressed it upon me what trouble he had taken for me, how much money he had spent and how everything had been arranged for my benefit.

"Perhaps it is all in vain," I said.

And so it was. My number came along the last, and I was free. Titoff could hardly believe my luck and he laughed at me gloomily.

"It seems really that God is with you."

I did not answer, but I was unspeakably happy. My freedom meant everything to me — everything that oppressed my soul. And above all, it meant freedom from my dear father-in-law.

At home Olga's joy was great. She wept and laughed, the dear one; praised and caressed me as if I had killed a bear.

"God be praised," she said; "now I can die in peace."

I poked fun at her, but at the bottom of my heart I felt badly, for I knew that she believed in her death — a ruinous belief, which destroys the life force in man.

Three days later her travail began. For two long days she suffered horrible agony, and on the third day it was ended, after giving birth to a still-born child — ended as she had believed, my dear, sweet one.

I do not remember the burial, for I was as if blind and deaf for some time afterward. It was Titoff who woke me. I was at Olga's grave, and I can see him now as he stood before me and looked into my face, and said:

"So, Matvei, it is for the second time that we meet near the dead. Here our friendship was born. Here it should be strengthened anew."

I looked about me as if I had found myself on earth for the first time. The rain drizzled, a mist surrounded everything, in which the bare trees swayed and the crosses on the tombstones swam and vanished. Everything looked dressed, garbed in cold, and in a piercing dampness which was difficult to breathe, as if the rain and the mist had sucked up all the air.

"What do you want? Go away from here," I said to Titoff.

"I want you to understand my pain. Perhaps because I hindered you from living out your own life God has now punished me by taking away my daughter."

The earth under my feet was melting and turned into sticky mud, which seemed to drag down my feet. I clutched him, threw him on the ground as if he were a sack of bran.

"Damn you!" I shouted.

A mad, wild period began for me. I could not hold my head up. I was as if struck down by some strong hand and lay stretched out powerless on the ground. My heart was full of pain and I was outraged with God. I looked up at the holy images and hurried away as fast as I could, for I wanted to quarrel, not to repent. I knew that according to the law I had to do penance and should have said:

"Thy will be done, O Lord. Thy hand is heavy, but righteous; Thy wrath is great yet beneficent."

My conscience did not let me say such words. I remained standing, lost in my thoughts, and was unable to find myself.

"Has this blow fallen upon me," I thought, "because I doubted Thy existence in secret?"

This thought terrified me and I found excuses for myself:

"It was not Thy existence that I doubted, but Thy mercy; for it seemed to me that we are all abandoned by Thee without help and without guidance."

My soul was unbearably tortured; I could not sleep; I could do nothing. At night dark shadows tried to strangle me. Olga appeared before me. My heart was overcome with fear and I had no more strength to live.

I decided to hang myself.

It was night. I lay dressed on my bed. I glanced about me. I could see my poor, innocent wife before me, her blue eyes shining with a quiet light and calling me. The moon shone through the window and its bright reflection lay upon the floor and only increased the darkness in my soul.

I jumped up, took the rope from my bird snare, hammered a nail into the beam of the roof, made a noose and fixed the chair. I had already taken off my coat and torn off my collar, when suddenly I saw a little face appear indistinctly and mysteriously on the wall. I could have screamed with fear, though

THE CONFESSION

I understood that it was my own face which looked back at me from Olga's round mirror. I looked insane — so distracted and wretched, with my hair wild, my cheeks sunken in, my nose sharp, my mouth half open as with asthma, and my eyes agonized, full of a deep, great pain.

I pitied this human face; I pitied it for the beauty that had gone out of it, and I sat down on the bench and wept over myself, as a child who is hurt. After those tears the noose seemed something to be ashamed of, like a joke against myself. And in wrath I tore it down and threw it into the corner of the room. Death was also a riddle, but I had not yet answered the riddle of life!

What should I do? Some more days passed. It was as if I were seeking peace. I must do penance, I thought, and I gritted my teeth and went to the priest.

I visited him one Sunday evening, just as he and his wife were at table drinking tea. Four children sat around them. Drops of sweat shone on the dark face of the priest, as scales on a fish.

"Sit down," he said, good-naturedly, "and drink some tea with us."

The room was warm and dry; everything was clean and in order. It occurred to me how negligent this priest was in the performance of his church duties, and the thought came to me, "This, then, is his church."

I was not sufficiently humble.

"Well, Matvei, you suffer?" the priest asked.

"Yes," I answered.

"Ah, then you must say the Forty-Day prayers. Does she appear in dreams to you?"

"Yes."

"Then only the Forty-Day prayer will help you. That is certain."

I remained silent. I could not speak before the wife of the priest. I did not like her. She was a large, stout, short-winded woman, with a broad, fat face. She lent money on interest.

"Pray earnestly," the priest said to me. "And do not eat your heart. It is a sin against the Lord. He knows what He does."

"Does He really know?" I asked.

"Certainly. Oh, oh, my young man, I know well that you are proud toward people, but do not dare to carry your pride against the laws of God. You will be punished a hundredfold more severely. This sour stuff which ferments in you comes from the time of Larion, does it not? I know the heresies which he committed when he was drunk — remember this!"

Here the priest's wife interrupted:

"They should have sent that Larion to a monastery, but the father was too good and did not even complain about him."

"That is not true," I answered. "He did complain, but not on account of his opinions, but because of his negligence, for which the father himself was to blame."

We began to quarrel. First he reproached me for my insolence, and then he began talking about things which I knew just as well as he, but the meaning of which, in his anger, he changed. And then they both began, he as well as his wife, to insult me.

"You are both rascals," they cried, "you and your father-in-law! You have robbed the church. The swampy field belonged to the church from time immemorial, and that is why God has punished you."

"You are right," I said. "The swampy field was taken from you unjustly. But you yourself had taken it away from the peasants."

I rose and wanted to go.

"Stop!" cried the priest, "and the money for the Forty-Day prayer?"

"It is not necessary," I answered.

I went out and thought: "Here you have found comfort for your soul, Matvei."

Three days later, Sasha, my little son, died. He had mistaken arsenic for sugar, and eaten it.

His death made no impression on me. I had become cold and indifferent to everything.

CHAPTER VII

I DECIDED to go to a town, where an archbishop lived — a pious, learned man, who disputed continually with the Old Believers about the true faith and was renowned for his wisdom. I told my father-in-law that I was going away and that he could have my house and all that I possessed for a hundred rubles.

"No," he answered, "that is not the way to do business. You must sign me a note for half a year for three hundred rubles."

I signed it, ordered my passport and began my trip. I walked on foot, for I thought that thus the confusion in my soul would subside. But although I walked to do penance, still my thoughts were not with God. I was afraid and angry with myself. My thoughts were distorted and they fell apart like worn-out cloth. The sky was dark above me.

With great difficulty I reached the Archbishop. A servant, a pretty, delicate youngster, who received the visitors, would not let me enter. Four times he sent me back, saying:

"I am the secretary. You must give me three rubles."

"I won't give you a three-kopeck piece," I said.

THE CONFESSION

"Then I won't let you in."

"All right. Then I'll go in myself."

He saw that I was determined not to give in to him.

"Well, then, come in," he said. "I was only joking. You are a funny fellow."

He led me into a little room, where a gray old man sat coughing in a corner of a divan, dressed in a green cassock. His face was wrinkled and his eyes were very stern and set deep in his forehead.

"Well," I thought, "he can tell me something."

"What do you want?" he asked me.

"My soul is troubled, father."

The secretary stood behind me and whispered:

"You must say 'your reverence.'"

"Send the servant away," I said. "It is difficult for me to speak when he is here."

The Archbishop looked at me, bit his lip and ordered:

"Go behind the door, Alexei. Well, what have you done?"

"I doubt God's mercy," I answered.

He put his hand on his forehead, looked at me for some time and then muttered in a singing voice:

"What? What's that? You fool!"

There was no need to insult me, and perhaps he did not mean it in that way. Our superiors insult people more out of habit and foolishness than from ill will. I said to him:

"Hear me, your reverence."

I sat down on a chair. But the old man motioned with his hands and shouted:

"Stand up! Stand up! You should kneel before me, impious one!"

"Why should I kneel? If I am guilty, I should kneel before God, not before you."

He became enraged. "Who am I? What am I to you? What am I to God?"

I was ashamed to quarrel with him on account of a bagatelle, so I knelt. He threatened me with his finger and said:

"I will teach you to respect the clergy!"

I lost my desire to talk with him, but still, before the desire had entirely gone, I began to speak, and I forgot his presence. For the first time in my life I expressed my thoughts in words, and I was astonished at myself. Suddenly I heard the old man cry out:

"Keep still, wretched one!"

I felt as if I had suddenly come up against a wall while running. He stood over me, shaking his hands threateningly at me, and muttered:

"Do you know what you are saying, you crazy fool? Do you appreciate your blasphemies, wretched one? You lie, heretic! You did not come to do penance. You came as a messenger from the devil to tempt me!"

I saw that it was not wrath, but fear that played in his face. He trembled, and his beard and his hands, which were held out to me, were shaking. I, too, was frightened.

"What is your reverence saying?" I asked. "I believe in God."

"You lie, you mad dog!"

He threatened me with the wrath and the vengeance of God, but he spoke in a low tone, and his whole body trembled so that his cassock flowed like green waves. He placed before my spirit a threatening, gruesome God, severe in countenance, wrathful in spirit, poor in mercy, and like the old God Jehovah in sternness. I said to the archbishop:

"Now you, yourself, have fallen into heresies. Is this then the Christian God? Where have you hidden Christ? Why do you place before man the stern Judge instead of the Friend and the Helper?"

He clutched my hair and shook me to and fro, saying, haltingly:

"Who are you, crazy one? You should be brought to the police, to prison, to a monastery, to Siberia!"

I came to myself. It was clear to me that if man called in the police to protect his God, then neither he nor his God could have much strength, and much less beauty. I arose and said:

"Let me go."

The old man fell back and spoke breathlessly.

"What are you going to do?"

"I will go away, I can learn nothing here. Your words are dead and you kill God with them."

He began to speak about the police again; but it was all the same to me. The police could not do anything worse than what he had already done. "Angels serve for the glory of God, not the police," I said; "but if your faith teaches you something else, then stick to your faith."

His face became green, and he jumped at me. "Alexei," he called, "throw him out!"

And Alexei threw me out on the street with great vigor.

It was evening. I had spent fully two hours talking with the old archbishop. The streets were in semi-darkness, and the picture was not joyful. Everywhere there were noisy crowds, talk and laughter. It was holiday time, the feast of the Three Wise Men. Weakly I walked along and looked into the faces of the people. They angered me and I felt like shouting out to them:

"Hey, you people, what are you so satisfied about? They are murdering your God. Take care!"

I walked along in my misery as one drunk, and did not know where I was going. I did not want to go to my inn, for there there was noise and drinking. I went out into the farthest suburb. Little houses stood there, whose yellow windows looked out upon the fields, and the winds played with the snow about them, and whistled and covered them up.

I wanted to drink — to get very drunk; but alone, without people. I was a stranger to all and was guilty before all. "I will cross this field," I thought, "and see where it leads to."

Suddenly a woman came out of a gate, dressed in

a light dress and with a shawl as her only protection against the cold. She looked into my face and asked:

"What is your name?"

I understood that she was guessing her future husband.

"I will not tell you my name. I am an unhappy man."

"Unhappy?" she asked, laughing. "Now, in the holiday season?"

I did not like her gaiety.

"Is there no inn here in the neighborhood?" I asked. "I would like to rest and warm myself a bit. It is cold."

She looked at me searchingly and said in a friendly tone:

"There, farther on, you will find an inn. But if you wish, you can come to us and get a glass of tea."

Indifferently and without thinking, I followed her. I came to the room. On the wall in the corner burned a little lamp, and under the holy images sat a stout old woman, chewing something. A samovar was on the table; everything seemed cozy and warm.

The woman asked me to sit down at the table. She was young, with red cheeks and a high bosom. The old woman looked at me from her corner and sniffed. She had a large, withered face, almost, it seemed, without eyes.

I was embarrassed. What was I doing here? Who were they? I asked the young woman:

"What do you do?"

"I make lace."

True. On the wall were hung bunches of bobbins. Suddenly she laughed boldly and looked me straight in the face, and added:

"And then, I walk some."

The old woman laughed coarsely: "What a shameless hussy you are, Tanka!"

Had the old woman not said that, I would not have understood Tatiana's words. Now I knew what she meant, and became ill at ease. It was the first time in my life I had seen a loose girl, near-to, and naturally I did not think well of such women. Tatiana laughed.

"See, Petrovna, he blushes," she said.

I became angry. "And so I have fallen in here — from penance right into sin," I thought. I said to the girl:

"Does one boast of such an occupation?"

She answered boldly: "I boast of it."

The old woman began to sniff again: "Oh, Tatiana, Tatiana!"

I did not know what to say or how to go away from them. No excuse came to me.

I sat there silent. The wind rattled on the windows, the samovar sang and Tatiana began to tempt me.

"Oh, it's hot," she said, and unbuttoned the collar of her waist.

She had a pretty face and her eyes attracted me in spite of her bold expression. The old woman put vodka on the table, a bottle of " ordinary," and also some cherry brandy.

"That's good," I thought to myself. "I will drink some, pay and then go."

"Why are you so miserable?" Tatiana asked suddenly.

I could not restrain myself and answered:

"My wife is dead."

Then she asked very low: "When did she die?"

"Only five weeks ago."

The girl buttoned her waist and became more reserved. It pleased me. I looked into her face and said to myself:

"Thank you."

Though my heart was heavy, yet I was young and was used to women. I had two years of married life behind me. But the old woman said, gasping:

"Your wife is dead — that is nothing much. You are young and there are women enough. The streets are full of them."

Here Tatiana said to her sternly:

"Go to bed, Petrovna. I will escort our guest and will lock up."

When the old woman was gone, she asked me earnestly and in a friendly way:

"Have you relatives?"

"None."

"And friends?"

"No friends."

"What are you going to do then?"

"I do not know."

She became thoughtful, stood up and said:

"Listen. I see that you are in despair. I advise you, don't go out alone. You followed me in here at my first word. You might have fallen in somewhere where you could not get out so easily. Better remain here over night. There is a bed here. Spend the night here, in heaven's name. If you do not wish to do it for nothing, give something to Petrovna — as much as you wish; and if I am in your way, then say so frankly and I will go."

I liked her words and also her eyes. I could not suppress a feeling of joy and I said to myself, smiling:

"Oh, that archbishop!"

"What archbishop?" Tatiana asked, surprised.

I was confused and did not know what to say.

"That is just an expression of mine," I answered. "That is, not really an expression; only very often there is an archbishop who appears in my dreams."

"Well, good night," she said.

"Not yet," I answered quickly. "Don't go away, I beg of you. Remain here a little longer, if it is no trouble to you."

She took her place again and smiled.

"Very gladly. It is no trouble."

She asked me if I would drink a glass of vodka or tea, and whether I wished to eat. Her sincere friendliness brought the tears to my eyes, and my heart became as happy as a bird on a spring morning when the sun rises.

"Excuse me for my plain words," I said, "but I would like to know if it is true what you told me about yourself a little while ago? Or did you wish to joke with me?"

She frowned and answered: "Yes, I am one of them. Why do you ask?"

"It is the first time in my life that I have seen such a girl, and I am ashamed."

"What are you ashamed of? I am not sitting naked." And she laughed low and caressingly.

"Not on your account," I answered. "I am ashamed on my own account — because of my stupidity."

And I told her frankly my opinion of her class of girls. She listened quietly and attentively.

"There are various kinds among us," she said. "There may be some who are even worse than you think. You believe people altogether too readily."

I could not get the thought out of my head how such a girl could sell herself, and I asked her again:

"Do you do it from necessity?"

"At first," she answered, "I was deceived by a handsome young fellow. To spite him I got another one, and so I fell into the play. And now it happens many times that I do it for the sake of a piece of bread."

She said it quite simply and there was no pity for herself in her words.

"Do you go to church?" I asked.

She started and became red all over. "The way to the church is forbidden to no one."

I felt that I had offended her and added hurriedly:

"You misunderstood me. I know the gospels; I know of Mary Magdalene and of the sinner through whom the Pharisees tempted Christ. I only wished to ask you whether you were not angered against God for the life that you were leading; whether you did not doubt His goodness."

She frowned again, remained thoughtful, and said, surprised:

"I do not know what God has to do with it."

"How then?" I asked. "Is He not our Shepherd and our Father in whose mighty hand the destiny of man rests?"

And she answered: "I do no harm to people. What am I guilty of? And whom can it hurt that I lead an unclean life? Only myself."

I felt that she wished to say something good and true, but I could not understand her.

"I alone am responsible for my sins," she said, bowing to me and her whole face lighting up in a smile. "Besides, my sins do not appear so great. Perhaps what I am saying is not quite right, but I am speaking the truth. I go to church gladly.

Our church has just been built, and it is so bright and sweet. And how our choir sings! Sometimes they touch the heart, so that I must weep. In the church the soul gets a rest from all worries."

She remained silent for some time, and then added:

"Of course, there are other reasons. The men see you there."

I was so astounded by what she said that she told me I had drops of sweat standing on my temples. I could not understand how all these things came together in her so simply and harmoniously.

"Did you love your wife very much?" she asked me.

"Yes, very much," I answered, and her naïveté pleased me more and more.

I began to tell her of my spiritual state, of my wrath against God, because he did not hold me back from sins and then unjustly punished me by the death of Olga. She became now pale and depressed, now red all over with eyes on fire, so that she excited me. For the first time in my life I let my thoughts sweep over the whole circle of human life as I saw it, and it appeared to me as something incoherent and wasteful, shameful in its evil and helplessness, its groaning and moaning and wailing.

"Where are the Godlike?" I asked. "People sit on each other's backs, suck each other's blood, and everywhere there is the brutal struggle for a piece of bread. Where is there room for the Godlike? Where is there room for goodness and love, strength and beauty? Although I am young, I was not born blind. Who is Christ, the God-child? Who has trampled the flowers which His pure heart has sown? Who has stolen the wisdom of His love?"

I told her of the archbishop and how he had threatened me with his black God and how he, to protect his God, wanted to call in the police to help him.

Tatiana laughed. I, too, found the archbishop quite laughable now. He looked to me like a green grasshopper who chirps and jumps about as if he were doing something, heaven knows how important, but when one examines more closely, then one sees that he himself does not believe in the truth of his work.

She laughed at my words. Then the brow of the good girl became clouded.

"I did not understand everything," she said. "Still, some of the things you said were terrible. You think so boldly about God."

"One cannot live without seeing God," I said.

"True," she answered. "But you seem to be having a hand-to-hand fight with Him. Is that allowed? That the life of man is difficult is true enough. I myself have thought at times, 'Why should it be?' But listen to what I am going to tell you. Right here in the neighborhood is a nunnery where a hermitess, a very wise old woman, lives. She speaks beautifully about God. You ought to visit her."

"Why not?" I asked. "I will go to her. I

THE CONFESSION

am going everywhere — to all righteous people, to seek peace."

"And I will go to sleep," she said, giving me her hand. "You, too, go to bed."

I pressed her hand, shook it warmly, and said to her from the fulness of my heart:

"I thank you; what you have given me I do not yet know how to value, still I feel that you are a good girl, and I thank you."

"For heaven's sake, what are you saying?" she asked. She became embarrassed and blushed all over. "I am so glad," she went on, "that you feel better."

I saw that she was truly pleased. What was I to her? And yet, she was happy for having made a stranger feel better.

I put out the lamp, lay down on the bed, and said to myself:

"I fell into a real holiday celebration quite unexpectedly."

Though my heart was not much lighter, nevertheless I felt that something new and good was born within me. I saw Tatiana's eyes, which now looked enticingly, now earnestly, but from which there spoke more of the human heart than of the woman, and I thought of her in pure joy. And to think so about any one — is it not to make holiday?

I decided that to-morrow I would buy her a gold ring with a blue stone, but later I forgot about it. Thirteen years have passed since that day, and when

I think of the girl I always regret that I did not buy her the ring.

In the morning she knocked on the door.

"Time to get up."

We met as old friends and sat down to drink tea together. She urged me to go to the hermitess and I promised to do so. Saying farewell to each other heartily, we went together as far as the gate.

CHAPTER VIII

I FELT as alone in the city as in the wide steppes. There were thirty-three versts to the monastery, and I immediately started on my way to it and on the next day I said early mass there.

Around me were nuns, a whole black crowd, as if a mountain had fallen apart and its broken pieces were lying about in the church.

The monastery was rich. There were many sisters, all rather heavy, with fat, white, soft faces, as if made of dough. The priest said mass energetically, but a little too hurriedly. He had a good bass, was large and broad and seemed well fed.

The nuns in the choir were every one of them pretty, and sang wonderfully. The tapers wept their white tears and their flames trembled with pity for men.

"My soul struggles to reach Thy temple, Thy holy temple," their young voices sang out humbly.

Out of habit I repeated the words of the litany, but my eyes wandered and I tried to pick out the hermitess. There was no reverence in my heart, and it hurt me to admit it, for I had not come here to play. My soul was empty and I tried to collect myself. Everything in me was confused and my thoughts wandered, one after the other. I saw a few emaciated faces, half-dead old women, who stared at the holy images and whose lips moved but made no sound.

After mass I walked around the church. The day was bright and the white snow reflected the glistening rays of the sun, while on the branches the tit-mice piped and sent the hoar-frost from the twigs. I walked to the churchyard wall and looked out into the distance. The monastery stood on the mountain, and before it Mother Earth was spread out, richly dressed in its silvery blue snow. The little villages on the horizon looked sad, the wood was cut through by streams, and the pathways wound in and out like ribbons which some one had lost. Over all, the sun sent its slanting winter rays and stillness, peace and beauty were everywhere.

A little later I stood in the cell of Mother Fevronia. I saw a little old woman with browless eyes, who wept constantly. On her face, with its myriad wrinkles, a good-natured, unchanging smile trembled. She spoke low, almost in a whisper, and in a singsong tone.

"Do not eat apples before the day of the Lord. Wait till the Lord in His love has made them ripe; until the seeds are black."

"What does she mean by that?" I thought to myself.

"Respect your father and mother," she continued.

THE CONFESSION

" I have no father or mother," I said.

" Then pray for the peace of their souls."

" Maybe they are still alive."

She wiped the tears from her eyes and looked at me with a pitying smile. Then again she began shaking her head and continued in her singsong:

" The Lord God is good; He is righteous toward all and covers all with His rich bounty."

" That is just what I doubt," I said.

I saw that she started, her arms sank, and she remained silent, while her eyes continued to sparkle. Then she controlled herself and sang on, quite low:

" Remember that prayers have wings which fly even faster than birds and reach the throne of the Lord. No one has yet entered heaven on his own horse."

This much I understood: that she represented God to herself as some noble lord, good natured and lovable, but still, according to her opinion, bound by no law. She expressed all her thoughts in allegories which, to my disappointment, I could not understand. I bowed and went my way.

" Here they have broken the Lord God into many pieces," I thought to myself, " each one to his own need. One makes Him good-natured, the other stern and dark. And the priests have hired Him as their clerk and pay Him with the smoke of incense for His support. Only Larion had an infinite God."

Several nuns passed me, drawing a sleigh full of snow, and tittered. My heart was heavy and I did not know what to do. I went out from the gate. All without was still. The snow sparkled and shone, the frost-covered trees stood motionless, and heaven and earth seemed sunk in thought and looked in a friendly manner at the quiet monastery. A fear arose in me lest I break this stillness with my cries.

The bells called to vespers — what sweet chimes! They were soft and coaxing, but I had no desire to enter the church. I felt as if my head were full of sharp little nails. Suddenly I made the resolution:

"I shall enter a monastery with severe regulations. There I shall live alone in a solitary cell; will reflect and read books, and perhaps I shall in this loneliness become the master of my scattered soul."

A week later I found myself before the Abbot of the small monastery of Sabateieff. I liked the Abbot. He was a good-looking man, gray headed and bald, with red, firm cheeks and a promising look in his eyes.

"Why do you flee the world, my son?" he asked me.

I explained to him that the death of Olga disturbed the peace of my soul, but further I did not dare say anything. Something seemed to hold me back from speaking.

He pulled at his beard, looked at me searchingly and said:

"Can you pay the initiation fee?"

"I have about a hundred rubles with me."

"Give them to me. Now go into the guest room.

THE CONFESSION

To-morrow, after the noonday service, I will speak to you."

The care of strangers fell to the lot of Father Nifont, and him, too, I liked.

"Everything is very simple in our monastery," he said. "It is democratic. We all work equally in serving God, not as in other places. True, we have a gentleman here, but he does not mix with any one or bother us in any way. You can find peace and rest for your soul here and attain blessedness."

By the following day I had examined the monastery well. In former times it must have stood in the center of the wood, but now everything around it was hewn down. Only here and there in front of the gates a few tree trunks stood out from the ground. Toward the side the wood reached up to the very walls of the monastery and embraced, as with two black wings, the blue-domed church and the monastery. Nearby lay Blue Lake under its ice cover, formed like a half moon. It was nine versts from end to end and four versts wide. Behind it one could see the land on the other side, and the three churches of Kudejaroff, and the golden cupola of St. Nicholas of Tolokontzeff. On our side of the lake, not far from the monastery, was the hamlet of Kudejaroff, with its three and twenty little huts, and around it lay the mighty forests.

All was beautiful, and a quiet peace filled my soul. Here I would hold communion with the Lord; would unfold before Him my innermost soul, and would ask Him with humble insistence to show me the way to the knowledge of His holy laws.

In the evening I attended vespers. The mass was said severely and according to rule, and with ardor. But the singing did not please me; good voices were lacking.

"O Lord, forgive me if my thoughts about Thee were too bold," I prayed. "I did not do it out of lack of faith, but because of love and passion for the truth, as you know, O Omniscient One!"

Suddenly the monk who stood near me turned and smiled at me. Evidently I had spoken my repentant words too loud. As he smiled I looked at him. Such a handsome face! I let my head sink and closed my eyes. Never, either before or since, have I seen so handsome a face. I stepped lightly forward, placed myself next to him and looked into his wonderful countenance. It was as white as milk and framed in a black beard sprinkled here and there with gray. His eyes were large, and they had a soft mellow light and a bright expression. His figure was well built and tall; his nose a little bent like an eagle's, and his whole bearing was distinguished and noble. He made so deep an impression on me that even at night he stood before me in my dreams.

Early in the morning Father Nifont woke me.

"The Abbot has assigned you some test work. Go to the bakery. This worthy brother here will

THE CONFESSION

take you there. He will be your superior in the future. Here, take your cloistral robes."

I put on a monk's garb. They fitted me well, but were worn and dirty and the sole from one boot was loose.

I looked at my superior. He was broad-shouldered and awkward, with his forehead and cheeks full of pimples and pockmarks, from which sprouted little bunches of gray hair; his whole face looked as if it were covered with sheep's wool; he would have been laughable were it not for the deep folds on his forehead, his compressed lip and his little, dark, blinking eyes.

"Hurry up!" he said to me.

His voice was harsh and cracked, like a broken bell.

"This is Brother Misha." Father Nifont introduced him, smiling. "Well, go, and God be with you."

We walked out into the court. It was dark. Misha stumbled over something and swore horribly. Then he asked me:

"Can you knead dough?"

"I have seen the women knead," I answered.

"Women!" he muttered. "You're always thinking about women! Always women! On account of them the world is accursed, don't you forget that!"

"The mother of God was a woman," I said.

"Well?"

"And also there are very many virtuous women."

"If you speak like that the devil will surely drag you to hell."

"Anyway, he is a serious man," I thought to myself.

We arrived at the bakery and he made the fire. There were two large kneading troughs covered with sacks, a large flour bin nearby, a big sack of rye and a bag of wheat. Everything was dirty and filthy, and cobwebs and gray dust lay over all. Misha tore the sack off from one of the troughs, threw it on the earth, and commanded:

"Well, come and learn! Here is the dough. Do you see those bubbles? That means it is ready — it has already risen."

He took a sack of flour as if it were a three-year-old youngster, bent it over the edge of the trough, cut it open with his knife and cried as though at a fire:

"Pour four pails of water here and then knead!"

He was white like a tree with hoarfrost.

I threw off my cassock and rolled up my sleeves. He shouted:

"Not that way! Take off your trousers! With your feet!"

"I haven't taken a bath for a long time," I said.

"Who asked you about that?"

"How can I, then, with dirty feet?"

"Am I your pupil," he roared, "or are you mine?"

He had a large mouth, and strong, broad teeth,

and long arms, which he waved angrily in the air.

"Well," I thought, "the devil take you; I don't care."

I wiped my feet with a wet cloth, stepped into the kneading trough and began to work the dough, while my teacher ran here and there, grumbling.

"I will teach you to bend, my little mother's son. I will teach you humility and obedience!"

I kneaded one trough, began another, and when that was done, started on the wheat, which is kneaded with the hands. I was a strong fellow, but was not used to the work. The flour filled my nose, my mouth, my ears and eyes, so that I became deaf and blind; and the sweat kept dropping from my forehead into the dough.

"Haven't you a piece of cloth," I asked, "to wipe the sweat off?"

Misha became raging mad. "We will get you velvet towels. The monastery has been standing 230 years, and has only been waiting for your new orders."

I had to laugh, unwillingly. "I am not kneading the dough for myself," I said. "There are others who have to eat the bread."

He walked up to me, bristling like a porcupine and every part of him trembling.

"Take a sack and wipe yourself, if you are so tender. But I will tell the Abbot about your impudence."

I was so surprised at this man that I could not be

angry at him. He worked unceasingly, and the heavy two-hundred sacks were like little pillows in his hands. He was covered with flour, grumbled, swore and urged me on continually.

"Hurry! Hurry!"

I hurried till my head swam.

CHAPTER IX

THE first days of my cloistral novitiate were not easy. The bakery was in the cellar under the refectory; the ceiling was low and vaulted, and its one window was nailed tightly. The air was suffocating. The dust from the flour hung in the cellar like a thick mist, in which Misha trotted back and forth like a bear on a chain. The flame in the oven burned unclearly; it was a nightmare, not work.

Only we two were down there, for it was seldom that any one was sent as a punishment to help us.

There was no time even to attend religious services.

Day after day Misha preached his sermon to me, and I felt as if I were being bound with stout ropes. He was all aflame and burned with wrath against the world, while I breathed in his words and I felt that my inmost heart was covered with soot.

"You have nothing more to do with man," he said. "They continue to commit sins out there in the world, but you have left the world forever. If you separated from it with your body, then you must also flee it in spirit. You must forget it. If you think of man, you think unwillingly of woman. And through woman the world has sunk into darkness and sin and is bound eternally."

I wanted to say something, but no sooner did I open my mouth than he shouted at me:

"Keep still! Listen attentively to what an experienced man has to say, and respect your elders! I know you were going to blab something about the mother of God again. But it was just on account of her that Christ died on the crucifix — because He was born of woman, and did not descend holy and pure from heaven. He was altogether too good to that nasty woman all his life, and he should have pushed the Samaritan into the well instead of conversing with her. And He should have been the first to throw a stone at the sinner. Then the world would have been free."

"That is not a church thought," I said.

"Again I tell you, keep still. The church is entirely in the hands of a pale clergy, who are slaves to all sorts of debauchery and who themselves go around in silk clothes like women in petticoats. They are all heretics. They should dance quadrilles, not dictate religious laws. Moreover, is it possible for a man with a wife to think upon God-like things with a pure heart? No, he cannot, for he is committing the terrible sin on account of which the Lord drove him out of the Garden of Eden. And because of this sin we are damned to eternal punishment; sentenced to howl and to gnash our teeth, and we are blinded by it so that we cannot see the countenance of God from one eternity to another. The clergy themselves help spread this sin, for they have children with women

THE CONFESSION 95

and encourage the world to follow their bad example. And thus they change all the laws of God to justify their violations of them."

This man made me feel as if I were surrounded by a stone wall, which came closer and closer around me. He brought the roof of the cellar sinking upon my head. I was oppressed and stifled by the dust of his words.

"But," I said, "did not the Lord say, 'Multiply and increase'?"

Here my superior became blue in the face, stamped his feet on the ground, and roared like a beast:

"He said! He said! How do you know what he meant by it, you blockhead? He said: 'Be fruitful and multiply and people the earth. I leave to you the power of Satan, and may you be damned now, and forever and through all eternity.' That is what he said. And these cursed debauchees who call themselves the servants of God turned these words into a law of God. Do you understand their deceit and their vileness?"

He fell on me like a mountain which crushed me and darkened everything about me. I could not believe him, yet I could not contradict his bigotry, and he confused me by the violence of his attacks. If I quoted a passage from the Scriptures he quoted three others and disarmed me. The Scriptures are like a field of many-colored flowers. If you desire red flowers you can find red ones; if white, they, too, are to be had.

I remained silent, oppressed by his torrent of words, while he triumphed and his eyes glowed like a wolf's. And all the time we toiled hard at our work. I kneaded and he rolled the dough, pushed the loaves into the oven, and took them out when they were ready. But I had to put them on the shelves, which burned my hands.

I was all sticky with dough and covered with flour; I was blind and deaf and did not understand from sheer weariness what was said to me.

Sometimes the monks came to visit us, said something mockingly and laughed. Misha barked at them all angrily, and drove them out of the bakery, and I felt scorched. I was wretched, for I did not like this being together with Misha, whom I not only did not love, but even feared. Many times he asked me:

"Do you see naked women in your dreams?"

"No," I answered, "never."

"You're lying! Why do you lie?"

He became enraged, showed his teeth and threatened me with his fist.

"You're a liar and a rascal," he shouted.

I was only astonished. What is he saying there about naked women? A man works from three o'clock in the morning till ten at night and then lies down to sleep with bones aching like a beggar's in winter — and he talks of women. Such were my thoughts.

Once I went into the ante-room for yeast. It was

a dark room in the cellar, opposite the bakery. I found the door unlocked and a lantern burning. I opened the door and saw Misha crawling on the ground on his stomach, and crying out:

"Send them away, I implore Thee, Lord! Send them away! Deliver me!"

Of course, I immediately went out, but I could not guess what it was about.

He always spoke hatefully and insultingly about women, called all womankind vulgar and in real peasant fashion spat at them, clutching the air with his fingers as if in his mind's eye he were tearing and pulling a woman's body apart.

I could not bear to hear him talk. I remembered my own wife and our happy tears the first night of our marriage, and the quiet, inner wonder with each other, and our great joy. Is it not Thy sweet gift to man, O Lord? I remembered Tatiana's good heart and her simplicity, and I was hurt to tears for womankind. I thought to myself:

"When the Abbot will call me for an interview, I shall tell him everything."

But he did not call me. The days passed one after another, like blind people in a wood along a narrow path, each one stumbling upon the other, and still the Abbot did not call me. Darkness was within me. At that time, in my twenty-second year, my first gray hair came.

I wanted to speak with the handsome monk, but I saw him rarely and only for an instant. Now and then his proud countenance came before me and then vanished and my longing for him followed him like an invisible shadow. I asked Misha about him.

"Oh," Misha cried, "that one! That animal! He was sent away from the military for gambling in cards and from the seminary for his scandals with women. A learned one, yes! He fell into the seminary from the military, cheated all the monks in the monastery of Chudoff; then came here, bought himself in with seven and a half thousand rubles, donated land and so won great respect. Here, too; they play cards. The Abbot, the steward and the treasurer, they all play with him. There is a girl who visits him — oh, the pigs! He has a separate apartment, and there he lives just as he pleases. The great filth of it!"

I did not believe him; I could not. One day I asked the steward, Father Isador, to help me gain an interview with the Abbot.

"An interview about what?"

"About faith."

"What do you mean, 'about faith'?"

"I have various questions."

He looked me over from head to toe. He was a head taller than I, thin, angular, with wise, smiling eyes, a long, crooked nose and a pointed beard.

"Speak plainly; your flesh masters you?"

Always of the flesh! Though I did not want to, nevertheless I told him of some of my doubts in a few words. He frowned, then smiled.

"For this, my son, you should pray. By means of prayer you can heal the suffering of your soul. Still, in consideration of your love for labor, and because your request is so unusual, I will place the matter before the Abbot. Wait."

The word "unusual" surprised me. I felt that the expression was frivolous and there was hostility in it toward me.

Then I was summoned to come before the Father Abbot, and he looked at me sternly as I bowed before him. He said in a tone of authority:

"Father Isador told me of your desire to discuss the faith with me."

"I did not mean to argue," I said.

"Do not interrupt the speech of your elders. Every discussion which two people have about a subject is an argument, and every question is a seducer of thought, unless, of course, it is a subject which concerns itself with the daily life of the brotherhood — some commonplace subject. Here we have a working community. We work to subjugate the flesh, so that the soul, which lives in it temporarily, may devote itself wholly to the Lord, and thus pray and receive His mercy for the sins of the world. Our lot is not to gain cleverness, but to work. Cleverness is not necessary to us, only simplicity of soul.

"Your discussions with Brother Misha are known to me, and I cannot approve of them. Limit the boldness of your thought so that you do not fall into temptation, for the aimless thoughts which are not bound down by faith are the keenest weapons of the devil. The mind comes from the flesh; bold thoughts from the devil; but the strength of the soul is a part of the spirit of God, and open-heartedness is given the righteous through meditation.

"Brother Misha, your superior, is a strict monk, a true ascetic and brother, beloved by all for his work. I will punish you with a penance. After your day's labor is done read the Acathistus to Christ at the altar on the left in front of the Crucifixion, three times during the night, for ten successive nights.

"Added to this, you will also have to have interviews with the penance monk, Mardarie. The time and the number will be told you later.

"You were a clerk on an estate, were you not? Go in peace. I will think about you. It seems that you have no relatives on this earth. Well, go, I will pray for you. We will hope for the best."

I returned to the bakery and began to weigh his words in my mind. That was easily done. Perhaps the mind does become scattered in its search. Still, to live like a sheep is hardly worthy nor right for man. At that time I understood "meditation in prayer" as a sinking into the depths of my own soul, where all the roots lay, and from which thoughts strove to grow upward, as fruit trees. I could not find anything in my soul which was hostile or not to be understood. All that was not to be understood

THE CONFESSION

I felt was in God, and all that was hostile was in the world — that is — outside of me.

That the brothers loved Misha I knew to be absolutely untrue, for although I kept myself apart from all and did not mix in their conversations, still I noticed everything and saw that the vested monks as well as the novices disliked Misha and feared him and abhorred him.

I saw also that the monastery was laid out on a purely business basis. They sold wood, they rented land to peasants and the right to fish on the lake; they had a mill, vegetable gardens, large orchards, and sold apples, berries and cabbages. Seventy horses stood in the stables, and the brotherhood was composed of a little over fifty men, all strong and hard workers. There were a few old men — only for parade — to show off before the pilgrims. The monks drank wine and mixed much with women. The young ones spent their nights in the village; and women came to the cells of the older ones, ostensibly to wash the floors; and of course the pilgrims were made use of also.

But all this was not my affair and I could not judge them. I saw no sin in it, only a disgusting lie.

Many novices came to the monastery, but the tests were so difficult that they could not endure them and deserted. During the two years that I spent in this holy place, eleven brothers escaped. They remained one or two months and fled. It seemed the life in the monastery was too difficult.

For the pilgrims who came to the monastery there were, of course, all kinds of attractions. There were the chains of the deceased pious brother Joseph, which were a cure for rheumatism, and his little cap which, when put on the head, cured headaches. And there was a very cold spring in the wood, whose water was good for sickness in general. An image of the Assumption of the Virgin contained all kinds of wonders for believers, and the pious penance brother, Mardarie, could foretell the future and comfort the unhappy. Everything was as it should be, and in the spring, in the month of May, the people streamed here in crowds.

After my conversation with the Abbot, I wanted to find another monastery, which would be simpler and where I need not work so hard, and where the monks would stand nearer to their real task — the understanding of the sins of this world. But several things happened which kept me back.

One day I made the acquaintance of a novice named Grisha, who was employed in the office of the monastery. I had noticed him before. He walked quickly and noisily among the brothers, wore smoked glasses, had an insignificant face, an under-sized body, and walked with his head bent forward, as if he wanted to see nothing but his own path.

The day after my conversation with the Abbot, Grisha came into the bakery. Misha had just gone to the brother treasurer to give his accounts. Grisha came in, greeted me low, and asked:

THE CONFESSION

"You were at the Abbot's, brother?"

"Yes."

"Did you talk with him?"

"No."

"He sent you away?"

"Why should he?"

Grisha fixed his glasses, became confused and said.

"I beg your pardon, in Christ's name."

"Did he ever send you away?" I asked.

He nodded affirmatively and sat down on the edge of the flour bin, bent forward, coughed dryly and beat the bin with a hook while I told him what the Abbot had said to me. Suddenly he jumped up, straightened to his full height as if on springs, and began to speak in his loud, plaintive, excited voice:

"Why do they call this a place for the salvation of the soul when everything here is based upon money; when we live here for money, just as in the world outside? I fled to save myself from the sin of business, and again I fell upon business here. Where shall I flee now?"

His whole body trembled, and he told me quickly the history of his life. He was the son of a merchant who owned a bakery, had graduated from a school of commerce, and was placed by his father in his business.

"Were it some little nonsense," he said, "then, perhaps, I could deal in it. But with bread it was unpleasant and shameful to me. Bread is indispensable to all. One should not own it to make it the means of trade for human need. Perhaps my father would have broken me had his avarice not broken him. I had a sister, an academy student, gay and proud, who read books and was friendly with all the students. Suddenly my father said to her:

"'Stop your studying, Elizabeth. I have found a husband for you.'

"'I don't want him,' she answered.

"But my father pulled her hair until my little sister gave in. The bridegroom was the son of a rich tea merchant — a cross-eyed, large man, vulgar and continually boasting of his wealth. Liza, next to him, looked like a mouse next to a dog. He disgusted her. But my father said:

"'You fool, he has shops in many cities on the Volga.'

"Well, they were married, and during the wedding supper she went to her room and shot herself in the breast. I found her still living, and she said to me:

"'Good-by, Grisha. I want to live very much, but it is impossible! It is terrible! I can't! I can't!'"

I remember that he talked very, very fast, as if he were running away from the past, while I listened and looked at the stove. Its brow was before me and it looked like some ancient and blind face whose black mouth licked with flames ate up the whistling and hissing wood. I saw Grisha's sister in the fire and thought bitterly:

"Why do people violate and destroy one another?"

THE CONFESSION 105

Grisha's thick words fell one upon the other like dry leaves in autumn:

"My father almost went out of his senses. He stamped his feet and cried: 'She has insulted her parents! Her soul is lost.' Only after the burial, when he saw that all of Kazan followed Liza's body and laid wreaths upon her tomb, did he come to himself. 'If all the people are for her,' he said, 'it means that I behaved like a scoundrel toward my child!'"

Grisha wept and dried his glasses, and his hands trembled.

"Even before this misfortune befell us I wanted to enter a monastery, and I had said to my father:

"'Let me.'

"But he swore at me and beat me. Nevertheless, I said firmly:

"'I will not do business. Let me go.'

"He was frightened by Liza's death and gave me freedom, and now, in these four years, I have lived in three monasteries, and everywhere there is barter, and I have no place for my soul. They sell God's earth and God's word, His honey and His miracles. I cannot stand it any longer!"

His story awoke my soul again, for I did little thinking while I lived in the monastery. I was so worn out by my labors, that my rebellious thought slumbered. Suddenly his words woke me. I asked Grisha:

"Where, then, is our God? There is nothing

around us but the arbitrary and mad foolishness of man; nothing but the petty deceptions from which misfortunes arise. Where, then, is God?"

But here Misha appeared and drove us out. From that day Grisha came to me often, and I told him my thoughts, which horrified him, and he counseled humility:

"But why do people suffer so?" I asked.

"For their sins," he answered.

To him everything came from the hands of God — famine, fire, violent death and floods — everything.

"Can it be that God is the sower of misfortune on earth?" I asked.

"Remember Job, insane one," he whispered to me.

"Job has nothing to do with me," I answered. "I in his place would have said to God, 'Do not frighten me, but answer me clearly: Where is the way that leads to Thee? Am I not Thy son, made in Thy image? Don't lower Thyself to repulse Thy child.'"

Often Grisha wept at the foolishness of my audacity, and embracing me, he said:

"My dear brother, I am frightened for you — terribly frightened. Your words and your reasonings are from the devil."

"I do not believe in the devil, for God is all-powerful."

Then he became even more excited. He was a pure and tender man, and I loved him.

CHAPTER X

IT was at this time that I performed the penance. After my day's work I went to the church, where Brother Nikodime opened the door for me and locked me in, disturbing the stillness of the temple with the loud rattle of iron. I waited at the door till the last reverberation died away on the flagstones, then walked up quietly to the Crucifix and sat down upon the floor before it, for I was too weak to stand. Every muscle in my body ached from toil, and I had no desire to read the Acathistus.

I sat down, clasped my knees and gazed about me with sleepy eyes and thought about Grisha and about myself. It was summer, and the nights were hot and close, but here, in the semi-darkness of the church, it was pleasantly cool. The lamps under the holy pictures twinkled and winked at each other, and the little blue flames tugged upward as if they wished to fly toward the cupola, or higher still, to heaven itself, to the stars of the summer night. The quiet crackling of the wicks could be heard, each with its own peculiar sound, and half asleep, it seemed to me that the church was filled with a secret, unseen life, which, under the flickering of the lamps, held communion with itself. In the warm stillness and darkness the faces of the saints floated meditatively, as if something unsolved were before them. Ghost-like shadows passed before my face and the delicate, sweet odor of oil and cypress wood and incense surrounded me. The gold and the bronze of the holy images appeared duller and simpler, the silver shone warm and friendly, and everything melted and swam fusing into a torrent large and wide as in a dream.

Like a thick, sweet-smelling cloud, the church swung and swam to the low whispering of an indistinct prayer. I swung with it in a row of shadows, until a soft drowsiness took me up from the ground.

Before the ringing of the bell for early mass, the silent Brother Nikodime would enter and wake me, touching me lightly on the head.

"Go, in God's name," he would say, and I would answer:

"Pardon me, I have fallen asleep again."

Then I would go out swaying, and Nikodime would support me and say hardly audibly:

"God will pardon you, my benefactor."

Nikodime was an insignificant looking little old man, who hid his face from all and called every one his "benefactor." Once I asked him:

"Say, Nikodimushke, are you silent because of a vow?"

"No," he answered; "but just so." Then he sighed. "If I had anything to say, I would say it."

"Why did you leave the world?"

"Because I left it."

If you questioned him further, he did not answer

at all, but looked into your face with guilty eyes, and said in a whisper:

"I don't know why, my benefactor."

At times I thought to myself: "Perhaps this man, also, had sought an answer at one time."

And I wanted to run away from the monastery.

But here another gentleman appeared, starting up suddenly like a rubber ball against a fence. He was a strong, short, bold fellow, with round eyes like an owl's, a bent nose, light curls, a bushy beard and teeth which shone in a continual smile. He amused all the monks with his jokes and his shameless stories about women. At night he had them come to the monastery, smuggled in vodka without end, and was marvelously handy at everything. I looked at him and said:

"What do you seek in a monastery?"

"I? Things to gobble."

"Bread is given to those who work."

"That," he answered, "is a commandment from the peasants' God, but I am a man from the town and have also served two years in the Council, and can count myself as one of the authorities."

I tried to understand this jester, for I had to see all the springs which moved different kinds of people.

As I became more used to my work, Misha grew lazier, went off somewhere or other, and although it was more difficult for me alone, still it was more pleasant. People came freely to the bakery and we talked.

Mostly we were three — Grisha, I and jolly Seraphim. Grisha would be excited and threatened me with his hands; Seraphim would whistle and shake his curls and smile. Once I asked him:

"Seraphim, you vagabond, do you believe in God?"

"I will tell you later," he answered. "Wait about thirty years. When I am in my sixties, I suppose I will know exactly what I believe. At present I understand nothing and I don't want to lie."

He would tell us about the sea. He spoke about it as about a great miracle, using marvelous words, now quiet and loud; now with fear, and with love. And he glowed all over with joy which made him look like a star. When we listened to him we were silent and even heavy at heart at his stories of this vast, live beauty.

"The sea," he said with passion, "is the blue eye of earth which looks out to the far heaven and meditates on infinite space. On its waves, which are as alive and sensitive as the soul, is reflected the play of the stars and their secret path; and if you watch for a long time the ebb and the flow of the sea, then the sky, too, appears like a far-off ocean, and the stars like islands."

Grisha listened, all pale, and smiled quietly, as if a moonbeam were playing on him, and he whispered sadly:

"And before the countenance of this mystery and beauty we only barter — nothing more."

THE CONFESSION

At other times Seraphim would tell us about the Caucasus. He pictured to us a land gloomy and exquisite, like a fairyland, where hell and heaven embraced, and were at peace, both equal and both proud in their majesty.

"To see the Caucasus," Seraphim said in ecstasy, "that means to see the pure countenance of the earth, on which without inconsistency there unite in a smile the delicate purity of the childlike soul and the proud audacity and wisdom of the devil. The Caucasus is the touchstone of man. Weak spirits are ground to dust there and tremble before the power of the earth; but the strong, on the other hand, feel their strength grow and become proud and exalted like the mountain whose diamond-studded summit sends down its rays into the depths of the celestial wilderness. And this summit is the throne of the thunder.

Grisha sighed and asked in a low voice:

"And who points out the path to the soul? Should one be in the world or go away from it? What should one accept and what reject?"

Seraphim smiled distractedly and luminously.

"The glory of the sun is neither augmented nor diminished because you do not look at the sky, Grisha. Don't bother about that subject, my dear friend."

I understood Seraphim, but not entirely. I asked him, a little hurt:

"And as to people — what do you think about them? Why are they here?"

He shrugged his shoulders and smiled.

"People — are like weeds. There are various kinds among them. For those who are blind the sun is black; for those who are not happy with themselves, God is an enemy. Besides, people are young. To call three-year-old Jack, Mr. So-and-so is early a bit and doesn't quite fit."

His mouth overflowed with such quotations. They dropped from his lips like leaves from an apple tree, just as with Savelko. If you asked him anything, he immediately overpowered you with his puns, as if he were strewing flowers on a child's grave. His evasions made me angry, but he, the young devil, only laughed. At times I would say to him, irritated:

"You are loafing here, you idle dog, eating bread for nothing."

"That is the way it is with us," he answered. "He who eats his own bread remains hungry. Look at our peasants. All their life they sow wheat, yet dare not eat. You're quite right. To work is not my specialty. You get sore bones from work, but never rich and healthy; just lie in bed and shirk and you get fat and wealthy. And even you, Matvei, would rather steal than forego a meal."

I argued with him, but toward the end I myself began to laugh.

He was simple and straightforward, and that attracted me very much. He never made any pretensions, but said simply:

"I am nothing but a little insect, and not very harmful at that. I only ask for bread that I be fed."

THE CONFESSION 113

I saw that his whole make-up was very much like Savelko's and I marveled how men could keep their clear spirits and their happy frame of mind in this maelstrom of life.

Seraphim, next to Grisha, was like a clear day in spring compared to a day in autumn. Nevertheless, they grew more close to each other than to me. I was a little vexed at this. Soon they both went away together, Grisha having decided to go to Olonetz, and Seraphim said to me:

"I will accompany him. Then I will rest a week and return to the Caucasus. You should come along with us, Matvei. In tramping you will find more quickly what you are seeking, or you will lose what you have in excess, which, perhaps, is just as well. They can't bribe God away from the earth."

But I could not go along with them, for at that time I was having my interviews with Mardarie, and I was especially curious about this ascetic. I saw them off with great sadness, and my quiet evenings and my happy days went with them.

CHAPTER XI

MARDARIE, the penance monk, lived in a pit in the stone wall behind the altar. In ancient times this hole was a secret place where the monastery treasure was hidden from robbers, and there had been a secret passage to it direct from the altar. The stone vault from this pit had been taken away, and now it was covered with thick, wooden planks, and underneath it was built a kind of light cage with a little window in the ceiling. There was a grating with a railing around it, through which the pilgrims looked at the ascetic. In a corner was a trap-door, from which spiral steps led down to Mardarie. It made one dizzy to go down them. The pit was deep, twelve steps down, and only one ray of light fell in, and this one did not reach the bottom but melted and faded away in the damp darkness of this underground dwelling. One had to look long and steadily through the grating to see somewhere in the depths of the darkness something still darker which looked like a large rock or a mound. That was the ascetic, sitting motionless.

To go down to him the warm, odiferous dampness caught one, and for the first few seconds nothing could be seen. Then from the gloom would rise an altar and a black coffin, in which sat, bent over, a

THE CONFESSION

little, gray-haired old man in a dark shroud, decorated with white crosses, hilts, a reed and a lance, which lay helter-skelter and broken on his dried-up body. In the corner a round stove hid itself, and from it a pipe crawled out like a thick worm, while on the brick walls grew green scales of mildew. A ray of light pierced the darkness like a white sword, then rusted and broke apart.

On a pile of shavings the ascetic swayed back and forth as a shadow, his hands resting on his knees and fingering a rosary. His head was sunk on his breast and his back was curved like a yoke.

I remember that I went up to him, fell on my knees and remained silent. He, too, was silent for a long time, and everything about us seemed glutted with dead silence. I could not see his face, but only the dark end of his sharp nose. He whispered to me so that I could hardly hear:

"Well?"

I could not answer. Pity for this man who lay alive in his coffin oppressed and overcame me. He waited a little while, and then again asked me:

"What is it? Speak."

He turned his face toward me. It was all dark, no eyes were to be seen; only white eyebrows and a mustache and beard, which were like mildew on the agonized and motionless countenance which was effaced by the darkness. I heard the rustling of his voice:

"You argue up there. Why do you argue?

You should serve God humbly. What is there to argue about with God? You should simply love God."

"I love Him," I answered.

"Well, perhaps. He punishes you, but you must make believe that you see nothing and say, 'Praise be unto thee, O Lord.' Say that always, and nothing more."

It was evident that it was difficult for him to speak, either from weakness or because he was unused to it. His words were hardly alive and his voice was like the trembling of the wings of a dying bird.

I could not ask the old man anything, for I was sorry to disturb the peace of his death-waiting, and I feared to startle something; so I stood there motionless. From above the sound of bells leaked down, rocking the hair on my head, and I desired ardently to lift up my head toward the sky and gaze at it, but the darkness pressed down heavily on my neck and I did not move.

"Pray," he said to me, "and I will pray for you."

He became silent again. All was quiet, and a terrible fear made my flesh creep and filled my breast with icy coldness. A little later he whispered to me:

"Are you still here?"

"Yes."

"I can't see. Well, go, and God be with you. Don't argue."

I went out quietly. When I reached the earth above and breathed the pure air, I was drunk with

THE CONFESSION 117

joy and my head swam. I was all wet as if I had been in a cave; and he, Mardarie, had been sitting there now the fourth year!

I was to have five interviews with him, but I kept silent through them all; I could not speak. When I went down to him he listened, and then asked me in his unnatural voice:

"Some one came — the same one as yesterday?"

"Yes. It is I."

Then he began to mumble, with interruptions:

"Don't offend God — what do you need? You need nothing. Perhaps a little piece of bread. But to offend God is a sin. That comes from the devil. The devils, they lend a hand to every one. I know them. They are offended and they are malicious. They are offended — that is why they are malicious. So don't get offended, or you will resemble the devil. People offend you, but you should say to them: 'Christ save you,' and then go. Everything is vanity. The main thing is yourself. Let them not take your soul away. Hide it, so that they cannot take it away."

He sowed his quiet words, and they spread themselves over me like ashes from a far-off fire. They were not necessary to me, and they did not touch my soul. It seemed to me I saw a black dream, which I could not understand and which wearied me very much.

"You are silent," he said thoughtfully. "That is good. Let them do what they want, but you keep quiet. Others come to me and they talk — they talk very much. But I cannot understand what they want. They even talk about women. What is that to me? They talk about everything. But what they say about everything, I cannot understand. But you are right to keep silent. I also would not speak, but the Abbot up there said: 'Console him; he needs to be consoled.' Well, all right. But I myself would much rather not talk.

"Oh, God, forgive them all! Everything was taken from me — only prayers remained to me. Whoever tortures you, take no notice of him. It is the devils who torture you. They tortured me, too. My own brother, he beat me, and my wife gave me rat's poison. Evidently I was only a rat to her. They stole all I had from me, then said that I set fire to the village. They wanted to throw me into the fire. And I sat in prison. Everything happened to me. I was judged — sat some more. God be with them. I pardoned every one — I was not guilty, yet I pardoned. That was for my own sake.

"A whole mountain of injury lay on me. I could not breathe. Then I pardoned them and it went away. The mountain was no more. The devils were offended and they went away. So you, too, pardon every one. I need nothing. It will be the same with you."

At the fourth interview he asked me:

"Bring me a crumb of bread. I will suck it. I am weak. Pardon me, in Christ's name."

My heart ached with pity for him. I listened to his ravings and I thought:

" Why is that necessary, O Lord, why? "

But he still rustled his dry tongue:

" My bones ache. Night and day they draw. If I sucked a crumb it would be better perhaps; but this way my bones itch. It disturbs me — it disturbs my prayers. It is necessary to pray every second, even in one's dreams. If not, the devil immediately reminds one. He reminds one of one's name and where one lived, and everything. There he sits on the stove. It doesn't matter to him if it is hot — sometimes red hot. He is used to it. He sits himself there, a little, gray thing, opposite me, and just sits. I cross myself and do not look at him, and he gets tired. Then he crawls on the wall like a spider, or sometimes he floats in the air like a gray rag. He can do anything, my devil. He gets bored with an old man, but he has got to watch me, he has orders to.

" Of course, it is not pleasant for him to watch an old man. I am not offended with him. The devil doesn't do it of his own free will, and I am used to him. ' Well,' I say to him, ' I am tired of you,' and I don't look at him. He is not bad or evil, only he continually reminds me of my name."

Then the old man lifted his head and said loudly:

" They called me Michail Petrov Viakhiref."

And then he sank down in his coffin again and whispered:

"Thus the devil tempts me. Oh, you devil! Are you still here, brother? Go, and God be with you."

I could have cried with anger that day. What was the use of this old man? What beauty was there in his deed? I could not understand it. All day and many days afterward I thought of him, and I felt that a devil mocked me and made grimaces at me.

The last time that I went to him I filled my pockets with soft bread, and I brought that bread to him, with pain and anger against all mankind. When I gave it to him he whispered:

"Oh, it is still warm. Oh!"

He moved in his coffin. The shavings creaked underneath him while he hid his bread, whispering:

"Oh, oh."

The darkness and the mildewed wall — everything around us moved, reechoing the low groans of the ascetic —"Oh."

Four times a week they brought him food. Of course, he was starved.

This last time he said nothing to me, only sucked the bread. He evidently had not a tooth left in his head.

I stood there for some time. Then I said:

"Well, pardon me, in Christ's name, Father Mardarie. I am going now, and I won't return again. Let me thank you."

"Yes, yes," he answered eagerly. "It is I who thank you; it is I who thank you. But don't tell the monks about the bread. They will take it away.

THE CONFESSION

They are jealous, the monks are. No doubt the devils know them, too. The devils know everything and everybody — say nothing about it."

Soon after this he became ill and died. They buried him with solemnity. The Bishop came from the city with all his clergy, and they held a Cathedral Mass. Afterward I heard that under the tombstone of the old man a little blue fire burns of itself at night.

How pitiful it all was and how disgraceful to man!

CHAPTER XII

SOON after this my life changed entirely. Even while Grisha was here an ugly incident happened to me. Once I went into the ante-room and caught Misha in an act which gave the lie to his constant and disgusting denunciation of women as unclean. It was inexpressibly disgusting to me, for I remembered all the filth which he spoke about women; I remembered his hatred of them; and I spat and escaped to the bakery, trembling with wrath and shame and bitterness. He followed me, fell on his knees, and begged me not to tell.

"I know that she torments you at night, too. The power of the devil is strong."

"You lie," I said. "Go to all the devils, you pig. And you bake bread, you dog!"

I insulted him, for I could not contain myself.

If he had not soiled all womankind with his dirty words, I would not have minded it so much.

But he crawled before me and begged me not to tell.

"Well," I said, "can one speak about such things? It is too shameful. But I don't want to work with you. Tell them to give me other work."

I insisted on that.

At this time people were not yet alive or clear to me, and I strove only for one thing: to keep myself apart.

Misha became ill and lay in the hospital. I worked as of old and was given two assistants to help me.

Three weeks passed, when suddenly the steward called me and told me that Misha had recovered but did not want to work with me because of my obstinate nature; and therefore in the meantime I would be ordered to dig stumps out of the wood. This work was considered a punishment.

"Why?" I asked.

Suddenly the handsome monk, Father Anthony, entered the office, stood modestly aside and listened. The steward continued to explain to me:

"Because of your obstinate nature and your impudent opinions about the brothers. At your age and in your condition, it is foolish; unbearable; and you must be punished. But the Father Superior, in his goodness, said that we should take you over to the office for easy work. And that is how it may turn out."

He spoke for a long time, in a singsong voice and without feeling; and I saw that it did not come from his conscience, but that he dragged one word after another from duty.

Father Anthony leaned against a bench, looked at me, stroked his beard and smiled with his beautiful eyes as if he were joking with me about something.

I wished to show him my character and said to the steward:

"I don't seek to be raised, nor do I wish to accept humiliation, for I do not deserve it, as you know, but I want justice."

The steward grew red in the face and beat the ground with his stick.

"Keep silent, insolent one!"

Father Anthony bent to his ear and said something.

"It is impossible," answered the steward. "He is to take his punishment without a murmur."

Anthony shrugged his shoulders and turned toward me. His voice was low and warm:

"Submit, Matvei."

He conquered me with his two words and his caressing look. I bowed to the steward and to him, and then I asked the steward when I must go to the wood.

"In three days," he answered. "But these three days you must go to the dungeon — that's what."

If Anthony had not been there I certainly would have broken the steward's bones. But I took Anthony's words as a sign of the possibility to get near him, and for this I was ready to cut off my right arm — anything.

They sent me down to the dungeon. It was a hole underneath the office, in which it was impossible to stand or lie down; one had to sit. Straw was thrown on the floor, but it was wet from dampness. And it

THE CONFESSION

was quiet as a grave, not even mice were there; and such darkness that the hands disappeared. If you put your hands before your face they were not visible.

I sat there and was silent, and everything in me seemed poured from lead. I was heavy as stone, and cold as ice.

I clinched my teeth for I wished to hold back my thoughts; but they flamed up within me like coals and burned me. I could have bitten somebody, but there was no one to bite. I caught my hair with my hands, swayed back and forth like the tongue of a bell, and shrieked and raved and roared within:

"Where is Thy justice, O Lord? Do not the lawless play with it? And do not the strong trample it in their evil, drunken power? What am I before Thee? A lawless sacrifice or a keeper of Thy beauty and justice?"

I recalled the arrangement of the life in the monastery. It stood before me, ugly and cynical.

And why did they call the monks the servants of God? In what way were they holier than laymen? I knew the difficult peasant life in the villages. They lived starved and wretched. They drank, they fought, they stole, they committed every sin. But was not His path unseen? And they had no strength to struggle for righteousness; nor time. Each one was attached to the soil and tied to his house with a strong chain — the fear of starvation. What could one ask of them?

But here men lived free and satisfied. Here books and wisdom were open to them. But which one of them served God? Only the weak and the bloodless, like Grisha, remained faithful to God, who to the others was only a protector of sins and a source of lies. I remembered the evil lust of the monks for women and all their offenses of the flesh, which even the animals disdained — and their laziness and gluttony; their quarrels over the distribution of the funds, when they cawed maliciously at one another like ravens in a cemetery.

Grisha told me that no matter how much the peasants worked for the monastery, their indebtedness grew continually. I thought of myself: "Here I have already spent a long time and what has my soul profited? I have received only wounds and sores. How has my intelligence been enriched? Only by the knowledge of all kinds of baseness and of loathing for man."

Around me was silence. Even the sound of the bells, by which I could have measured time, did not reach me, and there was neither day nor night for me. Who dared to take away the sun from man?

The rank darkness oppressed me, and my soul was consumed by it. There was nothing left to light my path. The faith which was dear to my heart, the justice and omniscience of God, sank and melted away.

But like a bright star the face of Father Anthony flashed before me, and all my thoughts and feelings circled around it like a moth around a flame. I conversed with him, and complained to him, and asked him questions, and saw his two caressing eyes in the darkness.

I paid dearly for those three days and I went out of the hole blinded, my head feeling as if it were not my own, and my knees trembling. The monks laughed at me.

"What," they said, "you took a good soul-bath, eh?"

At night the Abbot called me, made me kneel before him, and gave me a long lecture.

"It is written that I shall crush the teeth of the sinner and bend his back in the yoke."

I was silent and controlled my heart. The peacemaker, Father Anthony, stood before me, and stilled my evil mouth with his affectionate look. Suddenly the Abbot softened.

"We value you, you fool," he said. "We think of you. We have noticed your zeal in work and wish to reward your intelligence. I even place before you a choice of two duties. Do you want to work in the office, or do you want to be a lay brother to Father Anthony?"

I felt as if I had been revived with warm water. I was stifled with joy and could hardly speak:

"Permit me to be a lay brother."

He frowned, became thoughtful, and looked at me curiously.

"If you go to the office," he said, "I will take away

the stump digging; but if you go as a lay brother, I will increase the work in the woods."

"Permit me to be a lay brother."

He asked me sternly:

"Why, you fool! The work is easier in the office, and more respectable."

I insisted. He bowed his head and thought a while.

"I permit it. You are a strange fellow, and one should not lose sight of you. Who knows what fires you will light — who knows? Go in peace."

I went to the wood. It was spring then, cold April. The work was hard, the wood an ancient one. The main roots went deep into the earth; the side ones were big. I dug and dug, and chopped and chopped; tied the trunk and made the horse pull out the stump. He tried with all his strength, but only broke the harness. Already by noon my bones felt broken and my horse trembled and was covered with foam. He looked at me out of his round eyes, as if he wished to say: "I cannot, brother; it is hard."

I petted him and slapped his neck. "I see," I said. And again I dug and chopped and the horse looked at me, his hide trembling and his head nodding. Horses are intelligent, and I am sure that they perceive all the senseless actions of man.

At this time I had an encounter with Misha, which came near ending badly for both of us. Once I went to my work after the noon-day meal, and had already reached the wood when suddenly he overtook me, club in hand, his face wild, his teeth showing, and panting like a bear. What did it mean?

I stopped and waited for him. He did not say a word, but brandished his club at me. I bent in time, and struck him below the belt with my head. I threw him down, sat on his chest, and took away his club.

"What is the matter with you?" I asked him. "What's this for?"

He struggled underneath me and said hoarsely:

"Get out of the monastery!"

"Why?"

"I can't look at you. I'll kill you! Get out of here!"

His eyes were red. The tears that came out seemed red, and his lips were covered with foam. He tore at my clothes; he scratched and pinched me, anxious to reach my face. I shook him lightly and arose from his chest.

"You wear the garb of a monk," I said, "and yet you are capable of such vileness, you brute! Why?"

He sat in the mud and demanded, obstinately:

"Get out of here! Don't make me lose my soul!"

I did not understand him. Finally I made a guess, and asked him low:

"Perhaps, Misha, you think I told some one about your wretched sin? It is not so. I told no one about it."

He arose, swayed, held on to the tree and looked at me with his wild eyes.

"I wish you had told it to the whole world!" he roared. "It would be easier for me! I could repent before others and they would forgive me. But you, scoundrel, despise every one. I do not want to be under obligations to you, you proud heretic. Get out, or I'll have the sin of blood on me!"

"If that is the way it is," I said, "go away yourself, if you have to. I won't go — that is sure."

He again jumped on me, and we both fell into the mud, getting dirty like frogs. I proved to be the stronger, and arose, but he still lay there, weeping and miserable.

"Listen, Misha," I said. "I am going away a little later. Now I can't. I am not staying out of spite, but because I have to. I have got to be here."

"Go to your father, the devil," he groaned, and gnashed his teeth.

I went away from him, and a little while later he was ordered to go to the monastic inn in the city, and I never saw him again.

CHAPTER XIII

WHEN my penance was finished I stood before Anthony, dressed in new clothes. I remember this period of my life from the first day to the last; everything, even to each word, was burned into my soul and cut into my flesh.

He led me to his cells quietly, and taught me in detail how and when and in what way I was to serve him.

One room was arranged with book-cases, full of worldly and religious books. "This," he said, "is my chapel."

In the center of the room stood a large table, near the window an upholstered armchair, and toward one side of the table a divan covered with rich tapestry. In front of the table there was a chair with a high back, covered with pressed leather.

A second room was his bedroom. It had a wide bed, a wardrobe filled with cassocks and linen, a wash stand with a large mirror, many brushes and combs and gaily colored perfume bottles. And on the walls of the third room, which was uninviting and empty, were two closed cupboards, one for wine and food and the other for china, pastry, preserves and sweets.

Having finished this inspection, he led me to his library and said:

"Take a seat. So, this is the way I live. Not like a monk, eh?"

"No," I answered; "not quite according to rule."

"Well, you condemn every one. I suppose you will condemn me soon, too."

He smiled, haughty as a bell tower.

I loved him for his beautiful face, but his smile was disagreeable to me.

"I do not know whether I will condemn you," I said. "I certainly would like to understand you."

He laughed low, in a base, which was offensive to me.

"You are illegitimate?" he asked.

"Yes."

"You have good blood in your veins?"

"What is good blood?" I asked.

He laughed, then answered impressively.

"Good blood is something from which proud souls are made."

The day was clear, the sun shone in through the window, and Anthony sat entirely covered by its rays. Suddenly an unexpected thought flashed through my head and pierced my heart like the bite of a snake. I jumped from my chair and stared hard at the monk. He, too, arose, and I saw that he picked up a knife from the table and played with it, asking:

"What is the matter with you?"

"Are you not my father?" I asked him.

His face became drawn, immovable and blue,

THE CONFESSION

as if it were carved from ice. He half closed his eyes so that the light went out of them, and said, almost in a whisper:

"I think — not. Where were you born? When? How old are you? Who is your mother?"

And as I told him how I was abandoned he smiled and put the knife back on the table.

"I was not in the district at that time," he answered.

I became embarrassed and uncomfortable. It was as if I had begged for charity and been refused.

"Well," he said, "and if I had been your father, what then?"

"Nothing," I answered.

"Exactly. That is the way I think about it. We are living together in a place where there are no fathers and no children in the flesh, only in the spirit. On the other hand, we are all abandoned on this earth — that is, we are brothers in misery, which we call life. Man is an accident in life, do you know that?"

I read in his eyes that he was making fun of me. I was still laboring under the unpleasant impression which my strange and incomprehensible question had aroused in me, and I would have liked to explain the question to him or to forget it altogether. But I made matters worse by asking:

"Why did you take that knife in your hand?"

Anthony gazed at me and then laughed low:

"You are a bold questioner. I took it because

I took it, and why I really do not know. I like it; it is a very pretty thing."

And he gave me the knife. It was sharp and pointed, with a design in gold laid on the steel, and a silver handle, with red stones.

"It is an Arabian knife," he explained to me. "I use it for cutting pages of books, and at night I put it under my pillow. There is a rumor abroad that I am rich and there are poor people living about me, and my cell is out of the way."

The knife as well as the hands of Anthony had a rich, peculiar perfume, which almost intoxicated me and made my head swim.

"Let us talk a little more," Anthony continued in his low, deep, soft voice. "Do you know that a woman comes to see me?"

"So I heard."

"It is not true that she is my sister. I sleep with her."

"Why do you talk of these things to me?" I asked.

"So that you will be shocked once and for all and not continue to be surprised. You like worldly books?"

"I have never read them."

He took from the book-case a little book bound in red leather and gave it to me.

"Go, prepare the samovar and read this," he said, in a tone of command.

I opened the book, and on the very first page I

found a picture — a woman naked to her knees and a man in front of her, also naked.

"I will not read this," I said.

Then he turned to me and said sternly:

"And if your spiritual superior orders you to? How do you know why this is necessary? Go."

In the annex where my room was I sat down on my bed, overcome by fear and sadness. I felt as if I had been poisoned; I was weak and trembling. I did not know what to think; I could not understand. From where did the thought come that he was my father? It was a strange idea.

I remembered his words about the soul: "The soul is made of blood." And about man: "That he is an accident on earth." All this was so plainly heretical. I remembered his drawn face at my question.

I opened the book again. It was a story about some French cavalier and about women. What did I want with it?

He rang for me and called. I came in, and he met me in a friendly manner.

"Where is the samovar?"

"Why did you give me this book?"

"So that you would know what sin is."

I became happy again. It seemed to me I understood his object; he wished to educate me. I bowed low, went out, prepared the samovar eagerly and brought it back into the room, where Anthony had already prepared everything for tea. And as I was going out he said:

"Remain and drink tea with me."

I was grateful to him, for I wanted to understand something very much.

"Tell me," he said, "how you have lived and why you came here."

I began to tell him about myself, not hiding from him my most secret impulse, not a thought which I could remember. And he listened to me with half-closed eyes, so engrossed that he did not even drink his tea.

Behind him the evening looked in at the window, and against the red sky the black branches of the trees made their outline.

But I talked all the time and gazed on the white fingers of Anthony's hands, which were folded on his breast. When I had finished he poured out a little glass of dark sweet wine for me.

"Drink," he said. "I noticed you when you prayed aloud in the church. The monastery doesn't help much, does it?"

"No; but in you I place great hope. Help me. You are a learned man; you must know everything."

"I only know one thing: You go up the mountain, reach the top, and fall — you fall to the very depth of the precipice. But I myself do not follow this law because I am too lazy. Man is a worthless thing, Matvei; but why he is worthless, is not clear. Life is exquisite and the world enchanting. So many pleasures are given to man, and man is worthless. Why? This is a puzzle I cannot solve, and I do not even wish to think about it."

Vespers rang. He started and said:

"Go, and God be with you. I am tired, and I must attend service."

Had I been wiser I would have left him that very day, for then I would have preserved a pleasant memory of him. But I did not understand the meaning of his words.

I went to my room, lay down, and noticed the little book which lay at my side. I struck a light and began to read it out of gratitude for my superior. I read how the cavalier I mentioned above deceived husbands, climbing to their wives at night through the windows, and how the husbands spied on him; how they wished to pierce him with their swords and how he escaped.

And all this was very stupid and unintelligible to me; that is, I understood well enough that a young fellow might enjoy it, but I could not understand why it was written about, and I could not fathom why I had read such nonsense.

And again I began to think: "How did I suddenly come upon the thought that Anthony was my father?" This thought ate my soul as rust eats iron. Then I fell asleep.

In my dream I felt that some one touched me. I jumped up. He stood near me.

"I rang and rang for you," he said.

"Forgive me," I said, "in Christ's name. I have worked very hard."

"I know," he answered. But he did not say, "God forgive you."

"I am going to the Father Abbot. Make everything ready, as it should be. Ah, you have read the book! It is too bad you have begun it. It is not quite for you. You were right; you need another kind."

I prepared his bed. The linen was thin, the cover soft; everything was rich and new to me; and a delicate, pleasant odor emanated from all.

And so I began to live in this intoxicating world, as in a dream. I saw no one but Anthony. But even he seemed as if he were in a shadow and moved in shadows. He spoke in a friendly tone, but his eyes mocked. He seldom used the word God; instead of God he said soul; instead of devil, nature.

But for me the meaning of his words did not change. He made fun of the monks and of the church orders. He drank very much wine, but he never staggered in walking, only his forehead became a bluish-white and his eyes glowed with a dark fire, and his red lips grew darker and drier.

It happened often that he came back from the Abbot at midnight or even later, and he woke me and ordered that I bring him wine. He sat and drank, spoke to himself in his low voice long and uninterruptedly, sitting there sometimes till matins were called.

It was difficult for me to understand his words, and I have forgotten many of them, but I remember how at first they frightened me, as if they had suddenly opened some terrible abyss in which the whole face of the earth was swallowed up. Often a feeling of emptiness and misery came over me because of his words, and I was ready to ask him:

"And you, are you not the devil?"

He was gloomy, spoke in a tone of command, and when he was drunk his eyes became even more mysterious, sinking far into his head. On his face a smile twitched continually, and his fingers, which were thin and long, opened and closed and pulled at his blue-black beard. A coldness emanated from him. He was terrifying.

As I have said, I did not believe in the devil, and I knew that it was written that the devil was strong in his pride; that he fought continually; that his passion and his skill lay in tempting people.

But Father Anthony in no way tempted me. He clothed life in gray, showed it to me as something insane, and people for him were only a herd of crazy swine who were dashing to the abyss with varying rapidity.

"But you have said that life is beautiful," I said.

"Yes, if it recognizes me it is beautiful," he answered.

Only his laugh remained with me. He seemed to me to gaze upon everything from his corner as if he had been driven away from everywhere and was not even hurt at being driven away.

His thoughts were sharp and penetrating, subtle like a snake, but powerless to conquer me, for I did not believe them, although often I was ravished by their cleverness and by the great leaps of the human mind.

At times, though this happened seldom, he became angry with me.

"I am a nobleman!" he shouted. "A descendant of a great race of people! My fathers founded Russia! They are historical figures, and this lout — this dirty lout dares to interrupt me! The beautiful dies, only the worms remain, and only one man of a distinguished family among them."

His expressions did not interest me. I, too, perhaps, came from a distinguished family. But surely strength did not lie in ancestry, but in truth, and though the evening will surely not come again, the morrow comes.

He sat in his armchair and talked, his face bloodless.

"Again the monks have won from me, Matvei. What is a monk? A man who wishes to hide from his fellow men his own vileness and who is afraid of its power over him. Or, perhaps, a man who is overcome by his weakness, and flees from the world in fear, that the world may not devour him.

Such monks are the better and more interesting; but the others are only homeless men, dust of the earth, or still-born children."

"What are you among them?" I asked.

I might have asked this ten times or more straight to his face, but he answered me always in this way:

"Man is a child of accident on this earth, everywhere and forever."

His God, too, was a mystery to me. I tried to ask him about God when he was sober, but he only laughed and answered with some well-known quotation.

But God was higher to me than anything that was ever written about Him.

I asked him when he was drunk how he saw God then. But even drunk, Anthony was firm.

"Ah, you are cunning, Matvei," he answered. "Cunning and obstinate. I am sorry for you."

I, too, was sorry for him, for I saw his solitude and I valued the abundance of his thoughts, and I was sorry that they were being sown at random in his cell. But though I was sorry for him, still I persisted firmly in my questions, and once he said, unwillingly:

"I no more see God than you, Matvei."

"Though I do not see God," I answered, "still I feel Him and do not question His existence, but only try to understand His laws, upon which our earth is based."

"As for the laws," he said, "look in the book on

Canonical Rights, and if you feel God then — I shall congratulate you."

He poured out some wine, clinked glasses with me and drank. I noticed that, though his face was as grave as that of a corpse, the beautiful eyes of the gentleman mocked at me. The fact that he was a gentleman began to lessen my feelings for him, for he unfolded his birth to me so often that he made me boil with anger.

When he was somewhat drunk, he liked to speak about women.

"Nature," he would say, "has kept us in an evil and heavy bondage through woman, its sweetest allurement; and had we not this carnal temptation, which saps out the best from the soul of man, he could have attained immortality."

Since Brother Misha had spoken about the same theme, though more heatedly, I was disgusted by this time with such thoughts. Misha had renounced woman with hatred and defamed her furiously; but Father Anthony adjudged her without any feelings and tiresomely.

"Do you remember," he said, "I once gave you a book? If you read it you must have seen how woman in her whole make-up is cunning and full of lies, and debauched to the very bottom."

It was strange, and it hurt me to hear man, born of woman and nourished with her life, besmirch and trample upon his own mother, denying her everything but the flesh; degrading her to a senseless animal. At times I expressed my thoughts to him, though vaguely; not so distinctly. He became outraged and shouted.

"Idiot! Was I talking about my own mother?"

"Every woman is a mother," I answered.

"There are some," he shouted, "who are only loose women all their lives."

"Well," I answered, "there are some who are hunchbacked; but that is not the law for all."

"Get out of here, fool!"

Evidently the officer was not dead in him.

Several times when I asked about God, we wrangled with each other. He angered me with his sly wit, and one evening I went at him with all my might. My character grew bad, for I passed through great suffering at this time. I circled around Anthony like a hungry man around a locked pantry; he smells the bread through the door, and it only tends to madden him. And the night to which I refer, his evasions enraged me. I caught up the knife from the table and cried:

"Tell me everything you believe or I will cut my throat, come what may!"

He became frightened, grabbed my hand, wrenched the knife from me and grew very much excited — not at all like himself.

"You should be punished for this," he said, "but no punishment ever helps fanaticism."

And then he added, and his words were like nails beaten into my head:

"This is what I will tell you: only man exists. Everything else is an opinion. Your God is a dream of your soul. You can only know yourself, and even that not certainly."

His words shook me like a storm and ravaged me. He spoke for a long time, and though I did not understand everything, I felt that in this man was no sorrow or joy or fear, or sensitiveness, or pride. He was like an old church-yard priest, reading the mass for the dead, near a tomb. He knew the words well, but they did not touch his soul. His words were frightful to me at first, but later I understood that the doubt in them was without force, for they were dead.

It was May, the window was open, and the night in the garden was filled with a warm perfume of flowers. The apple trees were like young girls going to communion — a delicate blue in the silver moonlight.

The watchman beat the hours, and in the stillness the bronze resounded lugubriously.

Before me sat a man with a face of stone, calmly emitting bloodless words — words which vanished and were gray like ashes. They were offensive and painful to me, for I saw brass where I had expected gold.

"Go now," said Anthony to me.

I went into the garden, and when early mass was rung I entered the church, went into a dark corner

THE CONFESSION

and stood there, thinking, what need of God had a man who was half dead?

The brothers assembled. One would say it was the moonlight which broke the shadows of night into a thousand fragments and which noiselessly crawled into the temple to hide.

From this time something incomprehensible happened. Anthony began speaking to me in the tone of a gentleman, dry and crossly, and he never called me to him in a friendly way. All the books which he had given me to read he took away. One of them was a Russian history which had many surprises for me, but I got no chance to finish it. I tried to fathom in what way I had offended this gentleman of mine, but I could not.

The beginning of his speech was engraven in my memory and lived uppermost in my mind, though not troubling my other thoughts: "God is the dream of your soul," I repeated to myself. But I did not feel the necessity of debating this; it was an easy thought.

Soon a woman came to him. It was late at night. Anthony rang for me and cried:

"Quick — the samovar!"

When I brought it in I saw a woman sitting on the divan, in a wide pink dress, blonde disheveled curls hanging over her shoulders, and a little pink face, like a doll's, with light-blue eyes. She seemed to me modest and sad.

I placed the dishes on the table, and Anthony hurried me all the while.

"Do it quicker — hurry."

"He is aflame," I said to myself.

I liked his love affairs, for it was pleasant to see how skilful Anthony was even in love — a thing which is not very difficult.

As for myself, love left me cold at this time, and the looseness of the monks kept me away from it. But what kind of a monk was Father Anthony?

The woman was pretty in her way, a delicate little thing, like a new toy.

In the morning I went into the room to set it to rights. But he was not there, having gone to the Abbot. She sat on the divan, her feet under her, uncombed and half dressed. She asked me what I was called. I told her. Then she asked me if I had been in the monastery a long time, and I answered that question also.

"Don't you get bored here?"

"No," I answered.

"That's strange — if it's true."

"Why should it not be true?" I asked.

"You are so young and good-looking."

"Is the monastery only for cripples?"

She laughed and put out a bare foot from the divan. She looked at me and let herself be seen immodestly; exposed, her arms bare to the shoulder and her gown unfastened at the breast.

"You do that in vain," I thought. "You should keep your charms for your lover."

And the little fool asked me:

"Don't women bother you?"

"I don't see them," I answered. "How can they bother me?"

"What do you mean by 'how'?" And she laughed.

Anthony appeared in the door and asked angrily:

"What is this, Zoia?"

"Oh," she cried, "he is so funny — that one!" And she began to chatter and tell how "funny" I was.

But Anthony did not listen to her, and commanded me sternly:

"Go and unpack the trunks and the bags. Then take part of the provisions to the Abbot."

Even before dinner both of them had taken enough wine, and in the evening, after tea, the woman was entirely drunk, and Anthony, too, seemed more drunk than usual. They drove me from one corner to the other — to bring this, to carry that; to heat the wine, then to cool it.

I ran about like a waiter in a drinking place, and they became more and more free before me. The young lady was hot and took off some of her clothes, and the gentleman suddenly asked me:

"Matvei, isn't she pretty?"

"Pretty enough," I answered.

"But look at her well."

She laughed, drunk.

I wanted to go out, but Anthony called out, wildly:

"Where are you going? Stay here! Zoiaka, show yourself naked!"

I thought I had not heard rightly, but she pulled off a gown she had on and stood upon her feet, swaying. I looked at Anthony and he looked back at me. My heart beat loudly, for I pitied this man. Vulgarities did not quite fit him, and I was ashamed for the woman. Then he shouted:

"Get out of here, you lout!"

"You are a lout yourself!" I retorted.

He jumped up, overthrowing the bottles on the table. The dishes fell to the ground with a crash; something began to flow hastily, like a lonely stream. I went out into the garden and lay down. My heart ached like a bone that is frozen. In the stillness I heard Anthony cry out:

"Out with you!"

And a woman's voice whined:

"Don't you dare, you fool!"

Soon the harnessing of horses was heard in the courtyard, and their dissatisfied neighing and stampings on the dry earth. Doors were slammed, the wheels of a carriage rattled, and then the large gates creaked.

Anthony walked through the garden, calling low:

"Matvei, where are you?"

His tall figure moved among the apple trees and he caught at the branches and let fall the perfumed snow of flowers, muttering:

"Oh, the fool!"

And behind him, dragging along the ground, was his thick, heavy shadow.

I lay in the garden until morning, and then went to Father Isador.

"Give me back my passport. I am going away."

He was so startled that he jumped up.

"Why? Where?"

"Somewhere — in the world. I don't know where," I answered.

He began to question me.

"I will not explain anything," I said.

I went out from his cell and sat down near it on the bench underneath the old pine tree. I sat there on purpose, for it was the bench on which those who were driven away, or went of their own free will, sat, as if to announce the fact of their departure.

The brothers passed me, and looked at me sideways; some even spat at me. I forgot to say that there had been a rumor that Anthony had taken me as his lover. The Neophytes envied me and the monks envied that gentleman of mine. And they slandered both of us.

The brothers passed, saying to each other:

"Ah, they have driven him away; thanked be the Lord!"

Father Assaf, a sly and malicious old man, who acted as the Abbot's spy, and was known in the monastery as a half-witted hypocrite, attacked me with vile words, so that I said to him:

"Go away, old man. If not I will take you by the ear and put you away."

Although he was half-witted, as I said, he understood my words.

The head of the monastery called me to him and spoke in a friendly tone:

"I told you, Matvei, my son, that it would have been better to have entered the office, and I was right. Old men always know more. Do you think with your obstinate nature that you could act as a servant? Here you have shamefully insulted the revered Father Anthony."

"He told you that?"

"Who, then? You have not said anything."

"Did he tell you that he showed me a naked woman?"

The Father Abbot made a cross over me from holy fright and said, shaking his hands:

"What is the matter with you? What is the matter with you? God be with you! What kind of a woman? That is some dream of yours, coming from the flesh; a creation of the devil. Oh, oh, oh! You should think of your words. How can a woman be in a monastery of men?"

I wanted to calm him.

"Who, then, brought you the port wine, and the cheese, and the caviar last night?"

"What are you saying? Christ save you. How can you think up such things?"

It was disgusting and enough to drive one insane.

CHAPTER XIV

AT noon I crossed the lake, sat down on the bank and gazed at the monastery where I had slaved for over two years.

The wood spread out before me with its green wings and disclosed the monastery on its breast. The scalloped white walls, the blue head of the old church, the golden cupola of the new cathedral and the striped red roofs stood out clearly from the splendid green. The crosses glowed, shining and inviting, and above them the blue bell of heaven sounded the joyful peace of spring, while the sun rejoiced in its victory.

In this beauty which inflated the soul with its keen splendor, black men in long garments hid themselves and rotted away, living empty days without love, without joy in senseless labor and in mire.

I pitied them and myself, too, so that I almost wept. I arose and went on.

Perfume was over all, the earth and all that lived sang, the sun drew forth the flowers in the field and they lifted themselves up toward the sky and made their obeisance to the sun. The young trees whispered and swayed, the birds twittered and love burned everywhere on the fruitful earth which was drunk with its own strength.

THE CONFESSION

I met a peasant and greeted him, but he hardly nodded. I met a woman and she evaded me. And all the time I had a great desire to speak with people, and I would have spoken to them with a friendly heart.

I spent the first night of my freedom in the woods. I lay long, gazed up at the sky and sang low to myself and fell asleep. In the early morning I awoke from cold, and walked on, racing to meet my new life as if on wings. Each step took me farther away, and I was ready to outrun the distance.

The people whom I met looked suspiciously at me and stepped aside. The black dress of the monk was disgusting and inimical to the peasants, but I could not take it off. My passport had expired, but the Abbot made a note under it which said that I was a novice of the monastery of Savateffsky and that I was on my way to visit holy places.

So I directed my steps to these places together with those wanderers who fill our monastery by hundreds on holidays. The brothers were indifferent or hostile to them, calling them parasites and robbing them of every penny they had. They forced them to do the monastery work and imposed on them and treated them with contempt. I was always busied with my own affairs and seldom met the newcomers. I did not seek to meet them, for I considered myself something quite extraordinary and placed my own inner self above everything else.

I saw gray figures with knapsacks on their backs and staffs in their hands creeping and swaying along the roads and paths, going not hurriedly but depressed, with heads bent low, walking humbly and thoughtfully, with credulous, opened hearts. They flowed together in one place, looked about them, prayed silently and worked a bit. If a wise and virtuous man happened to be there they talked with him low about something, and again spread out upon the paths going to other places with sad steps.

They walked, old and young, women and children, as if one voice called them, and I felt from this crossing and recrossing of the earth a strength arise from the paths which caught me also, and alarmed me and promised to open my soul. This restless and humble wandering seemed strange to me after my motionless life.

It was as if earth herself tore man from her breast and pushed him forth, ordering him imperiously, "Go, find out, learn." And man goes obediently and carefully, seeks and looks and listens attentively, then goes on farther again. The earth resounds under the feet of the searchers and drives them farther over streams and mountains and through forests and over seas, still farther wherever the monasteries stand solitary, offering some miracle, and wherever a hope breathes of something other than this bitter, difficult and narrow life.

The quiet agitation of the lonely souls surprised me and made me human, and I began to wonder,

THE CONFESSION

"What are these people seeking?" Everything about me swayed, frightened and wandering like myself.

Many like myself sought God, but did not know where to go and strewed their souls on the paths of their seeking, and were going on only because they did not have strength enough to stop, acting like the seed of the dandelion in the wind, light and purposeless.

Others unable to shake off their laziness carried it on their shoulders, lowering themselves and living by lies, while still others were enthralled by the desire to see everything, but had no strength in them to love.

I saw many empty men and degraded rascals, shameless parasites, greedy like roaches. I saw many such, but they were only the dust behind the great crowd filled with the desire of finding God.

Irresistibly this crowd dragged me along with it.

And around it like gulls over the sea various winged people circled noisily and greedily, who astonished me with their monstrous deformities.

Once in Bielo-ozer I saw a middle-aged man with a haughty mien. He was cleanly dressed and evidently a man of means.

He had seated himself in the shade of a tree, and had pieces of cloth, a box of salve and a copper basin near him, and kept crying out:

"Orthodox, those with sore feet from overstraining, come here; I will heal them. I heal free because of a vow I have taken upon myself in the name of the Lord."

It was a church holiday in Bielo-ozer and the pilgrims had flocked there in great numbers. They came up to him, sat down, unwound the wrappings on their feet, while he washed them, spread salve on the wounds and lectured them.

"Eh, brother, you are not over-wise. Your sandal is too large for your foot. How can you walk like this?" The man with the large sandal answered in a low voice, "It was given to me in charity."

"He who gave it to you has pleased God, but that you should walk in it is your own foolishness, and there is nothing great about your deed. God will not count it to your credit."

Well, I thought, here is a man who knows God's meanings.

A woman came up to him, limping.

"Oh, young one," he called out, "you have no corn, but the French sickness, permit me to tell you. This, Orthodox, is a contagious disease. Whole families die from it, and it is hard to get rid of." The woman became confused, rose and went away with her eyes lowered, and he continued calling:

"Come here, Orthodox, in the name of St. Cyril."

People went up to him, unwound their feet and groaned, and said "Christ save you!" while he washed them.

I noticed that his refined face twitched as in a

THE CONFESSION

cramp and his skilful hands trembled. Soon he closed up his pious shop and ran off somewhere quickly.

At night a little old monk led me to a shed, and there I saw the same man. I lay down next to him and began to speak low:

"How is it, sir, that you spend the night together with these common people? To judge by your clothes, your place is in the inn."

"I have taken an oath to be among the lowest of the low for three months. I want to fulfil my pious work to the very end, and let myself be eaten up by lice with the rest of them. I really cannot bear to see wounds — they make me sick; still, no matter how disgusting it is to me, I wash the feet of the pilgrims every day. It is a difficult service to the Lord, but my hope in His mercy is great."

I lost my desire to speak to him, and, making believe I had fallen asleep, I lay thinking, "his sacrifice to God is not over great."

The straw underneath my neighbor rustled. He arose carefully, knelt down and prayed, at first silently, but later I heard his whispered words:

"Oh, thou, St. Cyril, intercede before God for me, a sinner, and make Him heal me of my wounds and sores as I have healed the wounds of men. All-seeing God, value my labors and help me. My life is in Thy hands. I know that my passions were violent, but Thou hast already punished me enough. Do not abandon me like a dog, and let not Thy people drive me away, I beg of Thee, and let my prayers arise toward Thee like the smoke of incense."

Here was a man who had mistaken God for a doctor. It was unbearable to me, and I closed my ears with my hands.

When he had finished praying he took out something to eat from his bag and chewed for a long time, like a boar.

I have met many such people. At night they creep before their God, while in the day they walk pitilessly over the breasts of men. They lower God to do the duty of hiding their vile actions, and they bribe him and bargain with him.

"Do not forget, O Lord, how much I have given Thee."

Blind slaves of greed, they place it high above themselves and bow down to this hideous idol of the dark and cowardly souls and pray to it.

"O Lord, do not judge me in Thy severity nor punish me in Thy wrath."

They walk upon earth like spies of God and judges of men, and watch sharply for any violation of the church laws. They bustle and flock together, accusing and complaining. "Faith is being extinguished in the hearts of people; woe unto us!"

One man especially amused me with his zeal. We walked together from Perejaslavlja to Rostoff, and the whole way he kept crying out to me, "Where are the holy laws of Feodor Studite?"

He was well fed, healthy, with a black beard and

THE CONFESSION 159

rosy cheeks; had money, and at night mixed with the women in the inns.

"When I saw how the laws were violated and the people depraved," he said to me, "all the peace of my soul went from me. I gave my business, which was a brick factory, to my sons to manage, and here I am, wandering about for four years, watching everything, and horror fills my soul. Rats have crawled into the Holy Sacristy, and have gnawed with their sharp teeth the holy laws, and the people are angry with the church, and have fallen away from her breast into vile heresies and sects. And what does the church militant do against this? It increases its wealth and lets its enemies grow. The church should live in poverty, like poor Lazarus, so that the people might see what true holiness poverty is, as Christ preached it. The people on seeing this would stop complaining and desiring the wealth of others. What other task has the church but to hold back the people with strong reins?"

Those sticklers for the law cannot hide their thoughts when they see its weakness, and they shamelessly disclose their secret selves.

On the Holy Hill a certain merchant, who was a noted traveler and who described his pilgrimages in holy places in clerical papers, was preaching to the crowd humility, patience and kindness.

He spoke warmly, even to tears. He entreated and he threatened, and the crowd listened, silent and with bowed heads.

I interrupted his speech and asked him "if open lawlessness should be suffered also."

"Suffer it, my friend," he cried; "undoubtedly suffer it. Christ himself suffered for us and for our salvation."

"How then," I answered, "about the martyrs and the fathers of the church? For instance, take St. John Chrysostom, who was bold and accused even kings."

He became enraged, flared up at me and stamped his feet. "What are you chattering there, you blunderer? Whom did they accuse? Heathens!"

"Was Eudoxia a heathen, or Ivan the Terrible?"

"That is not the point," he cried, waving his arms like a volunteer at a fire. "Do not speak about kings, but about the people — the people, that's the important thing. They are all sophisticated, and have no fear. They are serpents which the church ought to crush; that is her duty."

Although he spoke simply, I did not understand at this time what all this anxiety about the people was, and though his words caused me fear, I still did not understand them, for I was spiritually blind and did not see the people.

After my discussion with this writer several men came up and spoke to me, as if they did not expect anything good from me.

"There is another fellow here; don't you want to meet him?"

THE CONFESSION 161

Toward vespers a meeting was arranged for me with this young man in the wood near the lake. He was dark, as if blasted by lightning. His hair was cut short, and his look was dry and sharp; his face was all bone, from which two brown eyes burned brightly. The young man coughed continually and trembled. He looked at me hostilely and, breathing with difficulty, said: "They told me about you — that you scoff at patience and kindness. Why? Explain."

I do not remember what I said to him, but as I argued I only noticed his tortured face and his dying voice when he cried to me: "We are not for this life, but for the next. Heaven is our country. Do you hear it?"

A lame soldier, who had lost his leg in the Tekinsky War, stood opposite him and said gloomily: "My opinion, Orthodox, is this: Wherever there is less fear there is more truth," and turning to the young man he said: "If you are afraid of death that is your affair, but do not frighten the others. We have been frightened enough without you. Now you, red-head, speak."

The young man vanished soon after, but the people remained — a crowd of about half a hundred — to listen to me. I do not know with what I attracted their attention, but I was pleased that they heard me, and I spoke for a long time in the twilight, among the tall pines and the serious people.

I remember that all their faces fused into one

long, sorrowful face, thoughtful and strong-willed, dumb in words but bold in secret thoughts, and in its hundred eyes I saw an unquenchable fire which was related to my soul.

Later this single face disappeared from my memory, and only long after I understood that it was this centralization of the will of the people into one thought which arouses the anxiety of the guardians of the law and makes them fear. Even if this thought is not yet born or developed, still the spirit is enriched by the doubt in the indestructibility of hostile laws — whence the worry of the guardians of the law. They see this firm-willed, questioning look; they see the people wander upon the earth, quiet and silent, and they feel the unseeing rays of their thoughts, and they understand that the secret fire of their dumb councils can turn their laws into ashes, and that other laws are possible.

They have a fine ear for this, like thieves who hear the careful movements of the awakened owner whose house they have come to rob in the night, and they know that when the people shall open its eyes life will change and its face turn toward heaven.

The people have no God so long as they live divided and hostile to one another. And of what good is a living God to a satisfied man? He seeks only a justification for his full stomach amid the general starvation around him.

His lone life is pitiful and grotesque, surrounded on all sides by horror.

CHAPTER XV

ONE time I noticed that a little, old, gray man, clean like a scraped bone, watched me eagerly. His eyes were set deep in his head, as if they had been frightened back. He was shriveled up, but strong like a buck and quick on his feet. He used to sidle up toward people and was always in the center of a crowd. He marched and scrutinized each face as if looking for an acquaintance. He seemed to want something from me but did not dare ask for it, and I pitied his timidity.

I was going to Lubin, to the sitting Aphanasia, and he followed me silently, leaning on his white staff. I asked him, " Have you been wandering long, Uncle? "

He grew happy, shook his head and tittered.

" Nine years already, my boy, nine years."

" You must be carrying a great sin," I said.

" Where is there measure or weight for sin? Only God knows my sins."

" Nevertheless, what have you done? " I laughed and he smiled.

" Nothing," he answered. " I have lived on the whole as every one else. I am a Siberian from beyond Tobolsk. I was a driver in my youth and later had an inn with a saloon and also kept a store."

"You've robbed some one." The old man started.

"Why, what is the matter with you? God save me from it."

"I was only joking," I said. "I saw a little man trotting along, and I thought to myself, how could such a little man commit a big sin." The old man stopped and shook his head.

"All souls have the same size," he answered, "and they are all equally acceptable to the devil. But tell me, what do you think about death? You have spoken in the shelters about life, always about life. But where is death?"

"Here somewhere," I answered.

He threatened me with his finger jokingly and said: "It is here. That's it, it is always here."

"Well, what if it is?" I asked.

"It is here," and rising on his tiptoes he whispered into my ear, "Death is all powerful. Even Christ could not escape it. 'Let this cup pass from me,' He said, but the Heavenly Father did not let it pass. He could not. There is a saying, 'Death appears and the sun disappears,' you see."

The little, old man began to talk like a stream rushing down a mountain. "Death circles around us all and man walks along as if he were crossing a precipice on a tightrope; one push with Death's wing and man is no more. O Lord, by Thy force Thou hast strengthened the world, but how has He strengthened it if death is placed above everything? You can be bold in thought, steeped in learning, but

THE CONFESSION 165

you will only live as long as death permits you." He smiled, but his eyes were full of tears.

What could I say to him? I had never thought of death and now I had no time.

He skipped along beside me, looking into my face with his faded eyes, his beard trembling and his left hand hid in the bosom of his cloak. He kept looking about him as if he expected death to jump out from some bush and catch him by the hand and throw him into hell.

I looked at him astonished.

Around us all life surged. The earth was covered with the emerald foam of the grass, unseen larks sang, and everything grew toward the sun in many colored brilliant shouts of gladness.

"How did you get such thoughts?" I asked my traveling companion. "Have you been very sick?"

"No," he said. "Up to my forty-seventh year I lived peacefully and contentedly, and then my wife died and my daughter-in-law hanged herself. Both were lost in the same year."

"Maybe you yourself drove her to the noose."

"No, it was from her own depravity that she killed herself. I did not bother her, though even if I had lived with her, it would have been forgiven in a widower. I am no priest, and she was no stranger to me. Even when my wife was alive I lived like a widower. She was sick for four years and did not once come down from the stove. When she died I crossed myself. 'Thank God,' I said, 'I am free.' I wanted to marry again when suddenly the thought occurred to me I live well, I am contented, but yet I have to die. Why should it be so? I was overcome. I gave everything I had to my son and began my wandering. I thought that on the road I would not notice that I was going to the grave, for everything about me was gay and shining and seemed to lead away from the graveyard. However, it is all the same."

"Your heart is heavy, Uncle?" I asked him.

"Oh, my son, it is so terrible I cannot describe it. In the daytime I try to be among people that I may hide behind them. Death is blind, perhaps it might not see me or make a mistake and take some one else, but at night, when each one remains unprotected, it is terrible to lie awake without sleep. It seems to me then that a black hand sweeps over me, feeling my breast and searching, 'Are you here?' It plays with my heart like a cat with a mouse and my heart becomes frightened and beats. I get up and look about me. There are people lying down, but who knows whether they will arise? It happens that death takes away in crowds. In our village it took a whole family, a husband, a wife and two daughters who died of coal smoke in the bath house."

His mouth twitched in a vain effort to smile, but tears flowed from his eyes.

"If one would only die within a little hour, or in

THE CONFESSION

sleep, but first there comes sickness to eat one away little by little."

He frowned and his face contracted and looked like mildew. He walked quickly, almost skipping, but the light went out of his eyes, and he kept muttering in a low voice, neither to me nor to himself: " Oh, Lord, let me be a mosquito, only to live on the earth! Do not kill me, Lord; let me be a bug or even a little spider! "

" How pitiable! " I thought.

At the station, among people, he seemed to revive again, and he talked about his mistress, Death, but with courage. He preached to the people. " You will die," he said; " you will be destroyed on an unknown day and in an unknown hour. Perhaps three versts from here the lightning will strike you down."

He made some sad and others angry, and they quarreled with him. One young woman called out: " You have nothing the matter with you, and yet death bothers you."

She said it with such anger that I noticed her, and even the old man stopped his eulogy on death.

All the way to Lubin he comforted me, until he bored me to death. I have seen many such people who run away from death and foolishly play hide-and-seek with it. Even among the young there are some struck by fear, and they are worse than the old. They are all Godless; their souls are black within, like the pipe of a stove, and fear whistles through them even in the fairest weather. Their thoughts are like old pilgrims who patter on the earth, walking without knowing whither and blindly trampling under foot the living things in their path. They have the name of God on their lips, but they love no one and have no desire for anything. They are occupied with only one thing: To pass on their fears to others, so that people will take them up, the beggars, and comfort them.

They do not go to people to get honey, but that they may pour into another soul the deadly poison of their putrid selves. They love themselves and are without shame in their poverty, and resemble crippled beggars who sit on the road on the way to church and disclose their wounds and their sores and their deformities to people, that they may awaken pity and receive a copper.

They wander, sowing everywhere the gloomy seeds of unrest, and groan aloud, with the desire to hear their groans reecho. But around them surges a mighty wave — the wave of humble seekers for God and human suffering surrounds them many colored. For instance, like that of the young woman, the little Russian, who had talked up to the old man. She walked silent, her lips compressed, her face sunburnt and angry, and her eyes burning with a keen fire. If spoken to she answered sharply, as if she wanted to stick you with a knife.

"Rather than getting angry," I said to her, "you

THE CONFESSION 169

had better tell me your trouble. You might feel better afterward."

"What do you want of me?"

"I don't want anything; don't be afraid."

"I am not afraid; but you are disgusting to me."

"Why am I disgusting?"

"Stop insisting or I will call the people." And so she struck out at every one — old and young, and women, too.

"I do not need you," I answered. "I need your pain, for I want to know why people suffer."

She looked at me sideways and answered, "Go to others. They are all in need, the devil take them."

"Why curse them?"

"Because I want to."

She seemed to me like one possessed.

"For whom are you making this pilgrimage?" I asked.

A smile spread over her face. She slackened her pace and she talked, though not to me:

"Last spring my husband went down the Dneiper to float lumber, and he never came back. Perhaps he was drowned, or perhaps he found another wife — who knows? My father-in-law and mother-in-law are very poor and very bad. I have two children — a boy and a girl — and how was I to feed them? I was ready to work — to break myself in two working — but there was no work. And what can a woman earn? My father-in-law scolded. 'You and your children are a millstone around our necks, with your eating and drinking.' My mother-in-law nagged, 'You are young yet; go to the monastery; the monks desire women, and you can earn much money.' I could not stand the hunger of the children, and so I went. Should I have drowned them? I went."

She talked as in her sleep, through her teeth and indistinctly, and her eyes cried out with the pain of motherhood.

"My son is already in his fourth year; his name is Ossip and my daughter's name is Ganka. I beat them when they asked for bread; I beat them. I have wandered a whole month and I have earned four rubles. The monks are miserly. I would have earned more at honest labor. Oh, those devils! What waters can wash me now?"

I felt I ought to say something to her, so I said: "On account of your children, God will forgive you."

Here she cried out at me. "What is that to me? I'm not guilty before God! If He doesn't forgive me, He doesn't have to, and if He forgives me, I myself cannot forget it. It cannot be worse in hell. There the children will not be with me."

I excited her in vain, I said to myself. But already she could not restrain herself.

"There is no God for the poor. When we were in Zeleniklin on the banks of the Amur, how we celebrated mass and prayed and wept for aid! But did He aid us? We suffered there for three years, and those who did not die from fever returned paupers. My father died there, my mother had her leg broken by a wheel and both my brothers were lost in Siberia."

Her face became like stone. Although her features were heavy, she had a serious beauty about her and her eyes were dark and her hair thick. All night up to early morning I spoke with her sitting on the edge of the wood behind the box of the railroad watchman. I saw that her heart was all burned out, that she was no longer capable of weeping, and only when she spoke of her childhood did she smile twice, involuntarily, and her eyes became softer.

I thought to myself as she spoke, " She's ready to kill. She will murder some one yet or she will become the loosest of the loose. There is no outlet for her."

" I do not see God, and I do not love people," she said. " What kind of people are they if they cannot aid one another. Such people! Before the strong they are lambs and before the weak — wolves, but even the wolves live in packs but people live each one for himself and an enemy to his neighbor. I have seen and see much, and may they all go to ruin! To bear children and not to be able to bring them up! Is that right? I beat mine when they asked for bread; I beat them!"

In the morning she arose to sell her body to the monks, and going away she said to me spitefully, " What is the matter with you? We slept near each other and you are stronger than I am, and yet you did not take advantage of the bargain."

I felt as if she had slapped my face.

"You do wrong in insulting me," I answered.

She lowered her eyes and then said, "I feel like insulting every one, even those who are not guilty. You are young and you are worn out and your temples are gray. I know that you, too, suffer, but as for me, it is all the same, I pity no one. **Good-by.**"

And she went away.

CHAPTER XVI

IN the six years of my wandering I have seen many people made bad by sorrow. An unquenchable hatred for every one burned within them, and they were blind to everything but evil. They saw evil and bathed in it as in a hot bath, and they drank gall like a drunkard wine, and laughed and triumphed.

"Ours is the right," they cried. "Evil and unhappiness are everywhere; there is no place to escape."

They fell into mad despair and, inflamed by it, led depraved lives and soiled the earth in every way, as if to revenge themselves on her that she gave them birth. They crawled without strength on the paths of the earth, and remained slaves of their own weakness to the very day of their death. They elevated sorrow to godhood and bowed before it, and desired to see nothing but their own sores and hear nothing but the outcries of their own despair.

They were to be pitied, for they were as though mad; but how repulsive to the soul they were, with their readiness to spit their gall into every face and pollute the sun itself with their spittle if they could.

There were others, who were crushed by sorrow and frightened by it, who remained silent and tried to hide their small and slave-like lives, but who did not succeed and only served as clay in the hands of the strong, to plaster up the chinks in the walls of their own fortress.

Many faces and expressions have become engraved on my mind. Bitter tears were shed before me, and more than once I was deafened by the terrible laughter of despair.

I have tasted of all the poisons and drunk of a hundred rivers, and many times I myself wept the bitter tears of impotence. Life seemed to me a terrible delirium. It was a whirlwind of frightened words and warm rain of tears; it was a ceaseless cry of despair, an agonized convulsion of the whole earth suffering with an upward struggle, unattainable to my mind and to my heart.

My soul groaned, "No; that is not the right."

The streams of sorrow flowed turbidly over the whole earth, and with unspeakable horror I saw that there was no room for God in this chaos which separated man from man. There was no room to manifest His strength, no spot to place His foot. Eaten up by the vipers of sorrow and fear, by malice and despair, by greed and shamelessness, all life was falling into ruin and man was being destroyed by discord and weakening isolation.

I questioned: "Art Thou not truly, O Lord, but a dream of the soul of man, a hope created by despair in an hour of dark impotence?"

I saw that each one had his own God, and that his God was neither more noble nor more beautiful than

His worshipers. This revelation crushed me. It was not God that man sought, but the forgetfulness of sorrow. Misfortune torments man and drives him in all directions. He escapes from himself; he wishes to avoid action; he is afraid to work in harmony with life, and he seeks a quiet corner where he can hide himself.

I did not find in man the holy feeling of seeking God nor a striving to rejoice in the Lord. I saw nothing but fear of life, a desire to overcome sorrow. My conscience cried out: "No; that is not the right!"

It happened more than once that I met a man who seemed deep in serious thought and had a good, clean light in his eyes. If I met him once or twice, he was the same; but at the third or fourth meeting I would see that he was bad or drunk, and that he was no longer modest, but shameless, vulgar and blasphemed God, and I could not understand why the man was spoiled or what had broken him. All seemed blind to me, and to fall easily by the wayside.

I seldom heard an exalted word. Too frequently men spoke strange words out of habit, not understanding the benefit nor the harm which was locked up in their thoughts. They gathered together the speeches of the pious monks or the prophecies of the hermits and the anchorites, and divided them among each other, like children playing with broken pieces of china. In fact, I did not see the man, but fragments of broken lives, dirty human dust, which swept over the earth and was blown by various winds onto the steps of churches.

The people circled in vast numbers around the relics of the saints or the miracle-making ikons, or bathed in the holy streams, and sought only self-forgetfulness. The church processions were painful to me. Even as a child the miraculous ikons had lost their significance for me, and my life in the monastery had destroyed any vestige of respect that was left. At times I felt that man was a gigantic worm, crawling in the dust of the roads, and that men urged each other on by a force which I could not see, calling to each other, "Forward! Hurry!"

And above them, forcing their heads to the ground, floated the ikon like a yellow bird, and it seemed to me that its weight was far too heavy for them.

Those possessed fell in heaps in the dust and mud under the feet of the crowd, and they struggled like fish in the water, and their wild cries were heard. But the crowds passed over these palpitating bodies, stamped them and kicked them under foot, and cried out to the image of the Virgin, "Rejoice, Thou queen of heaven!"

Their faces were distorted and wild with straining, damp with sweat and black with dirt; and this whole procession of man, singing a joyless song with weary voices and marching with hollow steps, insulted the earth and darkened the heavens.

The beggars sat or reclined on the sides of the

THE CONFESSION

road, under the trees and stretched themselves out like two gay ribbons — the sick, the crippled, the wounded, the armless, the legless and the blind. Their worn bodies crept over the earth, their mutilated arms and legs trembled in the air and pushed themselves before people to excite their pity. The beggars moaned and wailed, their wounds burned in the sun, while they asked and begged a kopeck for themselves, in the name of God. Many of them were eyeless, while in others the eyes burned like coals and pain gnawed the flesh without respite, and they resembled some horrible growth.

I saw man persecuted. The force which drove him into the dust and the dirt seemed hostile to me. Whither did it drive them? No; that is not the right!

Once I was in the exquisite city of Kiev, and I was struck by the beauty and the grandeur of this ancient nest of the Russians. There I had an interview with a monk who was supposed to be very wise. I said to him:

"I cannot understand the laws upon which the life of a man is based."

"Who are you?" he asked me.

"A peasant."

"Can you read and write?"

"A little."

"Reading and writing is not for such as you," he said sternly.

I saw in truth that he was a seer.

"Are you a Stundist?" he asked me.

"No."

"A-ha! Then you are a Dukhobor?"

"Why?"

"I gather it from your words."

His face was pink like flesh and his eyes were small.

"If you seek God," he said to me, "then it is for but one reason — to abase Him." He threatened me with his finger. "I know your kind. You will not read the Credo a hundred times. Well, read it, and all your foolishness will vanish like smoke. I would send all you heretics to Abyssinia, to the Ethiopians in Africa. There you would perish alive from the heat."

"Were you ever in Abyssinia?" I asked him.

"Yes," he answered.

"And you didn't perish?"

The monk became enraged.

Another time, near the Dneiper, I met a man. He sat on the banks opposite Lafra and he threw stones into the water. He was about fifty, bald, bearded, his face covered with wrinkles, and his head large. At that time I could tell by the eyes if a man was in earnest or not, and I walked up to him and sat down at his side. It was toward evening. The turbid Dneiper rolled its waters hurriedly. Behind it rose the mountains, gray with temples, where the proud golden heads of the churches shimmered in the sun, the crosses glistened and the windows sparkled like precious gems. It appeared that the earth opened its lap and showed her treasure to the sun in proud bounty.

The man next to me said in a low voice, and sorrowfully:

"They should cover Lafra with glass and drive all the monks away from it and permit no one to enter, for there is no man worthy to walk amid such beauty."

It was like a fairy tale told by some wise, great man, which came true there upon the banks of the river, where the waves of the Dneiper, rushing down from afar, splashed up against the Lafra with joy at the sight of it. But its surprised surging could not drown the quiet voice of man. With what force it commenced, with what strength it was built up! Like a faint dream, I remembered Prince Vladimir, and the Church fathers, Anthony and Theodosia, and all the Russian heroes; and I was filled with regret.

The innumerable chimes on the other side of the bank rang out loudly and joyfully, but the sad thoughts about life fell more distinctly on my ears. We do not remember our birth. I came to seek the true faith, and now I found myself wondering, "Where is man?"

I could not see man. I saw only Cossacks, peasants, officials, priests, merchants. I could find no one who was not tied up with some daily and ordinary affair. Each one served some one, each one was under some one's orders. Above the official was another official, and so they rose, till they vanished from the eyes in an unattainable height. And there God was hidden!

Night came on. The water in the river became bluer and the crosses on the churches lost their rays. The man still threw stones in the water, but I could no longer see the ripples which they made.

"Three years ago," he said, "we had a riot in Maikop on account of a pestilence among the cattle. The dragoons were called out to fight us, and peasants killed peasants. And all because of cattle. Many were killed. I thought to myself then: 'What is this faith of the Russians, if we are ready to kill each other on account of a few oxen, when God said to us, "Thou shalt not kill." ' "

The Lafra disappeared in the darkness, and like a vision reentered the mountain. The Cossack searched for stones in the sand around him, found them and threw them into the river, and the water splashed loudly.

"Such is man," the Cossack said, lowering his head. "The laws of God are like spiritual milk, but they come down to us skimmed. It is written, 'With a pure heart you will see God.' But how can your heart be pure if you do not live according to your own will? Without one's freedom there is no true faith, but only a fictitious one."

He arose, shook himself and looked about him. He was a square-built fellow.

THE CONFESSION

"We are not free enough before God; that is what I think."

He took his cap and went away, and I remained alone, as if glued to the earth. I wished to grasp the meaning of the Cossack's words, but I could not. Still, I felt that they were right.

The warm southern night caressed me, and I thought to myself:

"Is it possible that only in suffering is the human soul beautiful? Where is the pivot around which this human whirlwind moves? What is the meaning of this vanity?"

In winter I always went south, where it was warmer; but if the snow and the cold caught me in the north, then I always entered a monastery. At first the monks did not receive me in a friendly way, but when I showed them how I worked they accepted me readily. They liked to see a man work well and not take any money.

My feet rested, while my arms and my head worked. I remembered all that I saw during the summer, and I desired to draw out of it some clean food for my soul. I weighed, I extracted, I wanted to understand the reasons for things, and at times I became so confused that I could have wept.

I felt overfed with the groans and the sorrows of the earth, and the boldness of my soul vanished and I became morose, silent, and an anger arose in me against everything.

From time to time dark despair took hold of me,

and for weeks I lived as if in a dream or blind. I desired nothing and saw nothing.

I began to wonder if I should not stop this wandering and live as every one else, and stop puzzling over my riddles, and subject myself humbly to conditions of things which were not of my making.

My days were as dark as the night, and I stood alone on the earth, like the moon in heaven, except that I gave no light. I could stand apart from myself and watch myself. I saw myself on the crossways, a healthy young fellow, who was a stranger to every one, and whom nothing pleased, and who believed in no one. Why did he live? Why was he apart from the world?

My soul became chilled.

CHAPTER XVII

I ALSO went to nunneries for a week or two, and in one of them, on the Volga, I hurt my foot with an ax one day while chopping wood. Mother Theoktista, a good little old woman, nursed me.

The monastery was not large, but rich, and the sisters all had a prosperous and dignified appearance. They irritated me, with their sweetness and their honied smiles and their fat crops.

Once, as I stood at vespers, I heard one of the women in the choir sing divinely. She was a tall young girl, with a flushed face, black eyes, stern looking, her lips red, and her voice was sure and full. She sang as if she were questioning something, and angry tears mingled with her voice.

My foot became better and, as I was already able to work, I was preparing to leave the place. While I was shoveling the snow from the road one day I saw the girl coming. She walked quietly, but stiffly. In her right hand, which was pressed against her breast, she carried a rosary; her left hung by her side like a whip. Her lips were compressed, she frowned and her face was pale. I bowed to her, but she threw her head backward and looked at me as if I had done her harm at some time. Her manner enraged me. Moreover, I could not bear the sight of this young nun.

"Well, my girl," I said, "it is not easy to live."

She started and stopped.

"What did you say?" she asked.

"It is hard to master one's self," I said.

"Oh, the devil!" she said suddenly in a low voice, but with great anger. And with that her black figure disappeared quickly, like a cloud on a windy day.

I cannot explain why I said that to her. At that time many such thoughts jumped into my head and flew out like sparks into any one's eyes. It seemed to me that all people were liars and hypocrites.

Three days later I saw her again on another road. She angered me still more. Why did she cover herself all in black? From what was she hiding? When she passed me I said to her:

"Do you wish to escape from here?"

The girl trembled, threw back her head and remained standing, straight as an arrow. I thought she would cry out, but she passed me, and then I heard her answer distinctly:

"I will tell you to-night."

I was terrified, but I thought perhaps I had not heard correctly. Still, though she had spoken low, her words came as clearly to me as from a bell. At first they amused me; then I became confused, and later I calmed myself, thinking that perhaps the bold hussy was joking with me.

THE CONFESSION

When I had hurt my foot, they had brought me into the infirmary and I occupied a little room under the staircase, and that room I occupied all the time I stayed at the monastery. That night as I lay in my cot I thought it was time I stopped my wandering life, and that I ought to go to some city and there work in a bakery. I did not wish to think about the girl.

Suddenly some one knocked very low. I jumped up, opened the door, and an old woman bowed and said:

"Follow me, if you please."

I understood where, but I asked nothing and went, threatening her inwardly.

"Is that the way it is, my dear? You will see how I will surprise your soul."

We crossed corridors and came to the place. The old woman opened a door and pushed me forward, whispering, "I will come to take you back."

A match flared up for a moment and in the darkness a familiar face lit up, and I heard her voice say:

"Lock the door."

I locked it.

I felt along the wall till I reached the stove, leaned up against it and asked:

"Will there be no light?"

The girl gave a little laugh. "What kind of a light?" she asked.

"Oh, you wanton!" I thought to myself, but remained silent.

I could hardly make out the girl. She was in the dark, like a black cloud in a stormy sky.

"Why don't you speak?" she asked. Her voice was masterful.

She must be rich, I thought, and I collected myself and said:

"It is for you to speak."

"Were you serious when you asked me about my running away from here?"

I stopped to think how I could best insult her, but then, like a coward, I answered quietly:

"No. It was only to test your piety."

Again she lit a match. Her face stood out clearly and her black eyes gazed boldly. It was unpleasant for me.

I got used to the darkness and saw that she stood, tall and black, in the middle of the room, and her bearing was strangely straight.

"You need not test my piety," she whispered hotly. "I did not call you here for that, and if you do not understand, go away from here."

Her breast heaved and there was something serious in her voice — nothing loose.

In the wall opposite me was a window, and it looked like a path which had been cut out of the darkness into the night. The sight of it was disagreeable to me.

I felt uncomfortable, for I understood that I had made a mistake, and it became more and more painful to me, so that my limbs trembled.

THE CONFESSION 187

She continued talking.

"I have nowhere to run away to. My uncle drove me here by force, but I can live here no longer. I shall hang myself."

Then she became silent, as if lost in an abyss.

I lost myself entirely, but she moved nearer to me and her breath came with difficulty.

"What do you wish?" I asked her.

She came up to me and put her hand on my shoulder. It trembled, and I, too, shook all over. My knees became weak and the darkness entered my throat and stifled me.

"Perhaps she is possessed," I thought to myself.

But she began to sob as she spoke, and her breath came hot on my face.

"I gave birth to a son, and they took him away from me and drove me here, where I cannot live. They tell me that my child is dead. My uncle and aunt say it, my guardians. Perhaps they have killed him. Perhaps they abandoned him. What can one know, my dear friend? I have still two years to be in their power before I reach my majority, but I cannot remain here."

The words came from her inmost heart, and I felt guilty before her. I was sorry for her, and also a little afraid. She seemed half insane. I did not know whether to believe her or not.

But she continued her whispering, which was broken by sobs:

"I want a child. As soon as I am with child,

they will drive me away from here. I need a child, since the first one died. I want to give birth to another, and this time I will not let them take it away from me, nor let them rob my soul. I beg pity and help from you. You, who are good, aid me with your strength, help me get back that which was taken from me. Believe me, in Christ's name, I am a mother, not a loose woman. I do not want to sin, but I want a child. It is not pleasure I seek, but motherhood."

I was in a dream. I believed her. It was impossible not to believe when a woman stood on her rights and called a stranger to her, and said openly to him:

"They have forbidden me to create man. Help me."

I thought of my mother, whom I had never known. Perhaps it was in this same way that she threw her strength into the power of my father. I embraced her and said:

"Pardon me. I have judged you wrongly. Forgive me in the name of the Mother of God."

While lost in self-forgetfulness in accomplishing the holy sacrament of marriage, an impious doubt arose in my mind.

"Perhaps she is deceiving me, and I am not the first man with whom she is playing this game."

Then she told me her life story. Her father was a locksmith and her uncle was a machinist's apprentice. Her uncle drank and was cruel. In summer

THE CONFESSION

he worked on steamboats, in winter on docks. She had nowhere to live, for her father and mother were drowned while there was a fire on a boat, and she became an orphan at thirteen. At seventeen she became the mother of a child by a young nobleman.

Her low voice flowed through my soul, her warm arms were around my neck, and her head rested on my shoulder. I listened to her, but the serpent of doubt gnawed at my heart.

We have forgotten that it was a woman who gave birth to Christ and followed him humbly to Golgotha. We have forgotten that it was woman who was mother of all the saints and of all the heroes of the past. We have forgotten the value of woman in our vile lust and have degraded her for our pleasure and turned her into a household drudge. And that is why she no longer gives birth to saviors of life, but only bare, mutilated children, the fruit of our own weakness.

She told me about the monastery. She was not the only one who was sent in there by force. Suddenly she said to me, caressingly:

"I have a good friend here, a pure girl, from a rich family. And, oh, if you would only know how difficult it is for her to live here. Perhaps you could make her with child also. Then they would drive her forth from here and she would go to her godmother."

"Good God!" I thought, "another one in misery!"

And again my faith in the omniscience of God and the righteousness of his laws was broken into. How could one place man in misery that laws might triumph?

Christa whispered low in my ear: "If only you could help her also!"

Her words killed my doubts and I was ready to kiss her feet, for I understood that only a pure woman, who appreciated the value of motherhood, could speak like that.

I confessed my doubts to her. She pushed me from her and wept low in the darkness, and I dared not comfort her.

"Do you think I had no qualms or shame in calling you?" she said to me reproachfully. "You, who are so strong and handsome? Was it easy for me to beg a caress from a man as if it were alms? Why did I go to you? I saw a man who was stern, whose eyes were serious, who spoke little and had little to do with young nuns. Your temples are gray. Moreover, I do not know why, I believed you to be true and good. But when you spoke to me that first time so unkindly, I wept. 'I was mistaken,' I thought to myself. But later, thank God, I decided to call you."

"Forgive me," I said to her.

She kissed me. "God will forgive you."

Here the old woman knocked on the door and whispered:

THE CONFESSION

" It is time to part. They will ring matins soon."
When she led me along the corridors she said:
" Will you give me a ruble? "

I could have struck her.

I lived about five days with Christa. It was impossible to stay longer, for the choir singer and the neophyte began to bother me too much. Besides, I felt the need of being alone to reflect on this incident.

How could they forbid women to bear children if such was their wish, and if children have been and always will be the harbingers of a new life, the bearers of new strength?

There was another reason for my having to fly. Christa showed me her friend. She was a slim young girl, with blonde curly hair and blue eyes and resembled my Olga. Her little face was pure, and she looked out upon the world with profound sadness. I was drawn toward her, and Christa urged me on.

But this was a different matter. Christa was no longer a girl; but Julia was innocent, and her husband should also be innocent.

I had no longer faith in my purity nor did I know what I really was. It did not matter with Christa, but with the other my self-doubt had the power to interfere. Why, I do not know, but it had that power.

I said good-by to Christa. She wept a little and asked me to write to her; said she would want to let me know when she was with child, and I gave her an address. Soon after I wrote her. She answered with a letter of good news, and I wrote her again. She was silent.

About a year and a half later, in Zadona, I received a letter. It had lain a long time in the post-office. She told me that she gave birth to a child, a son; that she called him Matvei; that he was happy and healthy; that she lived with her aunt, and that her uncle was dead. He had drunk himself to death.

"Now," she wrote, "I am my own mistress, and if you will come you will be received with joy."

I had a desire to see my son and my accidental wife, but by this time I had found a true road for myself and I did not go to her.

"I cannot now," I wrote. "I will come later."

Afterward she married a merchant who sold books and engravings, and went to live in Ribinsk.

In Christa I saw for the first time a person who had no fear in her soul and who was ready to fight for herself with all her strength. But at that time I did not appreciate the great value of this trait.

After the incident with Christa I went to work in the city; but life there was distasteful to me. It was narrow and oppressive. I did not like the artisans. They gave their souls nakedly and openly into the power of the masters. Each one seemed to cry out by his action:

"Here, devour my body! Drink my blood! I have no room on this earth for myself!"

It was unpleasant for me to be with them. They

drank, they swore at each other over a bagatelle, they sang their sad songs and burned at their labor night and day, and their masters warmed their fat marrows by them.

The bakery was close and dirty; the men slept there like dogs, and vodka and passion were their only pleasures. When I spoke to them about the false arrangement of our life they listened, grew sorrowful and agreed with me. But when I said that we had to seek God, they sighed and my words flowed past them.

At times, for some unknown reason, they made fun of me, and did it with malice.

I do not like cities. The incessant noise and traffic are unbearable to me, and the city people, with their insane business, remained strangers.

There were drinking places enough, and a superabundance of churches. The houses rose like mountains, but to live in them was difficult. The people were many, but each one lived for himself; each one was tied to his work, and his life ran along on one thread, like a dog on a string.

I heard weariness in every sound. Even the chimes rang out without hope, and I felt in my whole soul that things were not created for this. It was not right.

At times I laughed at myself. What kind of a leader is this that has arisen among you? But though I laughed, it was not with joy, for I saw only error in everything, and since I could not understand, it was all the more oppressive to me. I sank into the depths.

At night I remembered my wandering and freer life, especially my nights in the open fields. In the fields the earth is round and clear and dear to your heart. You lie on her as in the palm of a hand, small and simple like a child, clothed in a warm shadow and covered by the starry sky, floating with it past the stars. You feel your tired body filled with a strong perfume of plants and flowers, and it seems to you that you lie in a cradle, and that an unseen hand rocks it and puts you to sleep. The shadows float past and brush the tops of the plants, there is a murmuring and whispering around you, and somewhere a marmot comes out from its hole and whispers low.

Far off on the horizon a dark form arises. Perhaps it is a horse in the night. He stands for a second, then vanishes into the sea of warm darkness. Then something else arises, now in another place, another form. And so the whole night long, the guardians of earthly sleep, the loving shadows of the summer nights, silently come and go in the fields.

You feel that near you, in the whole sphere, all life has drawn back, resting in a light slumber. And your conscience hurts. Yet you continue to crush the plants with the weight of your body. A nightbird flies noiselessly, a piece of earth is broken off and becomes alive, and winged with its desires, seeks to fulfil them. Mice rustle through the grass; sometimes a small, soft thing runs quickly across your hand. You start, and you feel still deeper the abundance of life; that the earth itself is alive underneath you, is near to you and closely related to you. You hear her breathe, and you wonder what is the dream she is having, and what strength is quietly being born in her breast. How will she look upon the sun to-morrow? In what way will she rejoice him, his beautiful and beloved one?

You lie on her breast and your body grows and you drink the warm, perfumed milk of your dear mother, and you see yourself completely and forever the child of the earth. With gratitude you think of her, "Oh, my beloved earth!"

Unseen torrents of wholesome strength pour from the earth and streams of spicy perfumes float in the air. The earth is like a censer to the heavens, and you both the fire and the incense. The stars burn ardently that they may show all their beauty before the rising of the sun, and love and sleep fill and caress you. The bright light of hope passes warmly through your soul. "Somewhere there exists a sublime God."

"Seek and thou shalt find." That is well said, and we should not forget these words, for in truth they are worthy of the human mind.

CHAPTER XVIII

AS soon as spring came to the city I started out to tramp to Siberia, for I had heard that country highly praised, but on my way I was stopped by a man who strengthened my soul for the rest of my life and showed me the true path to God.

I met him on the road between Perm and Verkhotur.

I was lying on the edge of a wood and had built a fire to boil water. It was noon, very hot, and the air was filled with a rosinlike woody smell, oily and sappy. It was difficult to breathe. Even the birds felt hot, and they hid themselves in the depth of the wood and sang there happily while they arranged their lives.

It was quiet on the edge of the wood. It seemed to me that everything would soon melt underneath the sun and that the trees and the rocks and my own stultified body would flow in a many-colored, thick stream upon the earth.

A man was approaching, coming from the Perm side, singing in a loud, trembling voice. I raised my head and listened. I saw a little pilgrim, in a white cassock, with a tea-kettle at his belt and a calf-skin knapsack and a sauce-pan on his back. He

THE CONFESSION

walked briskly and nodded and smiled to me from afar.

He was the usual pilgrim. There are many such, and all of them are harmful. Making pilgrimages is a paying business for them. They are boorish and ignorant and are inveterate liars and drunkards, and are not beyond stealing. I disliked them from the bottom of my heart.

He came up to me, took off his cap, shook his head, and his hair danced drolly, while he chattered like a magpie.

"Peace to you, young man. What heat! It is twenty-two degrees hotter than hell."

"Are you long from there?" I asked.

"About six hundred years."

His voice was vibrant and gay, his head small, his forehead high, and his face was covered with fine wrinkles, like a spider-web. His gray beard looked clean and his brown eyes shone with gold, like a young man's.

"He is a merry dog," I thought to myself.

But he continued chattering. "The Urals; there is where you find beauty! The Lord is a great master in decorating the earth. He knows how to arrange the woods and the trees and the mountains well."

He took his tramping gear off, moving quickly and briskly. He saw that my kettle was boiling over and he lifted it off the fire, and asked like an old comrade:

"Shall I pour out my tea, or will we drink yours?"

Before I had time to answer, he added: "Well, let's drink mine. I've got good tea. A merchant gave it to me. It's expensive."

I smiled. "You're spry," I said to him.

"That's nothing," he answered. "I am nearly dead from the heat. But wait till I'm rested. Then I will crease out your wrinkles for you."

There was something about him which reminded me of Savelko, and I wanted to joke with him. But in about five minutes I listened to his words openmouthed. They were strangely familiar; yet unheard-of, and it seemed to me that my own heart, not he, was singing the joy of the sunny days:

"Look! Is this not a holiday? Is it not paradise? The mountains rise toward the sun, rejoicing, and the woods climb to the summits of the hills, and the little blades of grass under your feet strive winged up toward the light of life. All sing psalms of joy, but you, man, you, master of the earth, why do you sit here, morose?"

"What strange bird is that?" I asked myself. But I said to him, trying to draw him out:

"But what if I am filled with unhappy thoughts?"

He pointed to the earth. "What is that?"

"The earth."

"No. Look higher."

"You mean the grass?"

"Higher still."

"The shadow?"

"It is the shadow of your body," he said, "and your thoughts are the shadow of your soul. What are you afraid of?"

"I am afraid of nothing."

"You are lying. If you are not afraid, your thoughts would be bold. Unhappiness gives birth to fear, and fear comes from lack of faith. That is the way it is. Drink some tea."

He poured tea into the cups and spoke without interruption:

"It seems to me that I have seen you before. Were you ever in Valaan?"

"I was."

"When? No, it was not there. It seems to me that you were red-headed when I saw you there. You have a striking face. It must have been in Solofki that I saw you."

"I was never in Solofki."

"You were never there? That is too bad. It is an ancient monastery and very beautiful. You ought to go there."

"Then you never saw me before?" I said, and it hurt me to find it so.

"What is the difference?" he cried out. "If I didn't see you before, I see you now; and at that time the other one must have resembled you. Isn't that just the same?"

I laughed. "What do you mean, 'just the same'?"

"Why not?"

"Because I am I, and the other one is the other one."

"Are you better than he?"

"I don't know."

"I don't know either."

I looked at him and was overcome with impatience. I wanted him to speak and speak without end. He poured out his tea and continued talking hastily:

"Yes, the other one was a one-eyed fellow, and it made him wretched. All the lame and the crippled, whether in body or in mind, are the essence of egoism. 'I am crippled,' they say, or 'I am lame; but you people, don't you dare notice it.' He was that kind of a fellow. He said to me, 'All people are rascals. When they see that I have one eye they say to me, "you are one-eyed." That is why they are scoundrels.' 'My dear boy,' I said to him, 'you are a scoundrel and a rascal yourself, and perhaps a fool also. You can take your choice. Understand this: The important thing is not how people look at you but how you look at people. That is why, my friend, we become one-eyed or blind — because we look at other people, hunting for their dark spots and put out our own light in their darkness. If you would light up the other's darkness with your light, the world would be pleasant for you. Man sees no good in any one else but himself, that is why the whole world is a wretched wilderness for him.'"

He laughed and looked at me, and I listened to him

THE CONFESSION

as one who is lost in the wood at night and hears a far-off bell and is afraid that he made a mistake; that perhaps it is only the cry of an owl.

I understood that he had seen much; that he had overcome much in himself. But it seemed to me that he did not think much of me, that he was joking with me, and that his young eyes made fun of me. Since my experience with Anthony I seldom trust a man's smile any longer.

I asked him who he was.

"I am called Jehudiel. I am a cheerful idiot for others and a good friend to myself."

"Are you from the clergy?"

"I was a priest for some time, but was unfrocked and was put in a monastery at Suzdal for six years. You want to know why? Because I preached sermons in church which the people, in the simplicity of their souls, interpreted too literally. They were whipped for it and I was convicted. And thus the affair ended. What did I preach? I don't remember now. It was a long time ago, eighteen years, and one can forget in that time. I have had various thoughts but none of them ever came to anything."

He laughed and in each wrinkle of his face the laughter played. He looked about him as if the mountains and the woods were created for him.

When it became cooler we went on farther together, and on the way he asked me about myself.

"Who are you?"

Again, like that time before Anthony, I wished

to place my former days before my eyes and to look upon their checkered face. I spoke about my childhood, about Larion and Savelko, and the old man laughed and shouted.

"Eh, what good people! The Lord's fools, what! Those were dear, true flowers of the Russian soil, real God-loving ones."

I did not understand this praise and his joy looked strange to me, but he could hardly walk from laughter. He stopped, threw his head back and shouted and called straight up to heaven, as if he had a friend there with whom he wished to share his joy. I said to him kindly:

"You resemble Savelko somewhat."

"Resemble!" he cried. "It is always good," he said, "to resemble some one. Eh, dear boy, if only the orthodox church had not ruined us ages ago, how different it would be for the living ones on the Russian soil now."

His speech was dark to me.

I told him about Titoff. He seemed to see my father-in-law before his eyes and he expressed himself freely about him.

"Such a rascal! I have seen many such. They are rapacious bugs, but foolish and cowardly."

When he heard my story about Anthony, he became thoughtful and then said:

"So, that was a doubting Thomas. Well, not every Thomas is a genius. Some of them are stupidity itself."

THE CONFESSION

He drove a bumble-bee from him and lectured it. "Go away, go away from here. Such impoliteness, to fly straight into the eyes. The devil take you!"

I listened to his words attentively, missing nothing. It seemed to me that they were children of deep thought. I spoke to him as before a confessor, except that I hesitated in mentioning God. I was afraid, and I regretted something. God's image had become tarnished in my soul at this time, and I wanted to polish it from the dust of the days, and I saw that I cleaned up to the hollow places and my heart shuddered with pain.

The old man nodded his head and encouraged me.

"Never mind; don't be afraid. If you keep silent you only lie to yourself, not to me. Speak. Regret nothing. For if you destroy, you will create something new."

He responded to my words like an echo and I became more and more at ease with him.

CHAPTER XIX

NIGHT overtook us.

"Stop," he said, "let us find a place to rest."

We found a shelter underneath a large rock which had been torn away from its mother mountain, and the brush grew upon it, weaving itself into a dark carpet underneath. We lay down in its warm shadow and built a fire and boiled tea. I asked him:

"Father, what were you telling me?"

He smiled. "I will tell you everything I know. Only don't seek for assertions in my words. I don't want to teach, but only to relate. Only those people assert who are afraid of the paths of life, for whom the growth of truth is dangerous. They see that truth burns ever more brightly since men have lit its flames more and more in their hearts, they see it and are afraid. They quickly take a little truth, as much as is advantageous to them, and press it together into a small roll and cry to the whole world: 'Here is truth; pure spiritual food, and for all ages unchangeable,' and they sit, the cursed ones, upon the face of truth and strangle it, clutching at its throat, and hinder the growth of its strength in every possible way — they are enemies to us and to all beings. I can say one thing: that is the way it is to-day; but

THE CONFESSION

how it will be to-morrow I don't know. For you see, to-day there is no true, lawful master in life. He has not come yet. I do not know how he will arrange things when he comes; what plans he will establish and what suppress, and what temples he will cause to be built. The apostle Paul once said, 'All is for the best,' and many have accepted these words. But they who have confirmed them are without strength, for they have remained in one place. The stone is without strength. Why? Because of its immobility, brother. It is not right to say to man, 'stand here,' but always, 'go farther and farther.'"

For the first time in my life I heard such speech and it sounded strange to me. Here was a man who negated himself while I tried to ratify myself.

"Who is this master?" I asked. "The Lord?"

The old man smiled. "No," he answered. "It is some one nearer us. I do not want to name him. It is better that you yourself divine it. They believe strongest in Christ who meet Him first and have Him in their hearts; and it is by the strength of their faith that they raised Him to the height of Godhood."

He held me as before a closed door, and did not open it, or tell me what was hidden behind it. Impatience and pain grew in me and the words of the old man seemed dark. From time to time sparks flashed from his words, but they only blinded me and did not light the darkness in my soul.

The night was moonlight, and black shadows surrounded us. The wood overhead crawled silently up to the mountains, and over the mountain tops, between the branches of the trees, the stars shone like lighted birds. A nearby stream murmured. From time to time an owl called in the wood, and over all the old man's words lived quietly in the night.

A strange old man! He caught a little insect which was crawling on his cheek and he held it in the palm of his hand and asked it:

"Where are you going, fool? Go, run in the grass, little creature."

I liked it, for I, too, loved all insects, and I was interested in the secret life which they led among the grass and the flowers.

I asked several questions of the old man, for I wanted him to speak plainly and more concisely, but I noticed that he evaded my problems. In fact, he jumped over them. I liked his lively face. The red reflection of the fire played lovingly over him, and everything vibrated with the peaceful joy which I so desired.

I envied him. He had lived twice as long as I, or even more, but his soul was clear.

"One man told me," I said to him, "that faith comes from imagination. What do you say?"

"I say," he answered, "that that man did not know what he was talking about, for faith is a great creative feeling. It is born from the overflow of the life-forces in man. Its strength is enormous and it incites the youthful human spirit, driving it to action, for man is bound and narrowed by his activities, and the outside world hinders him in every way. Everything demands that he produce bread and iron, but not the live treasure which is in the lap of his soul. He does not yet understand how to take advantage of this treasure. He is afraid of the uproar in his soul. He creates monstrosities and he fears the reflection of his turbid spirit. He does not understand its being and he bows to the forms of faith, to his own shadows, I might say."

I did not understand him that minute, but for some reason I became deeply enraged, and I thought to myself: "Now, I will not let you go away from this place before you answer the root of the question." I asked him sternly:

"Why do you evade the question of God?"

He looked at me, frowned and said:

"But, my dear boy, I am speaking about Him all the time. Do you not feel it?"

He stood on his knees and the fire played on him. He held my hand and spoke low and impressively:

"Who is God, the worker of miracles? Is He our Father, or is He the child of our soul?"

I remember that I started and looked about me, for I felt uncomfortable. Insanity spoke in the old man.

Dark shadows lay about and I listened, while the

murmur of the woods crept around us, drowning the weak crackle of the burning coal and the quiet sound of the river. I, too, wanted to kneel.

Then he spoke loudly, as if in argument:

"Man did not create God in weakness, no; but from an overflow of his strength. And He does not live outside of us, but within us. We have torn Him out of us in our terror at the problems of our soul, and we have placed Him above us with a desire to bind our pride, which is ever restless at this binding. I said that they have turned strength into weakness; they have hindered its growth by force. They have conceived an ideal of perfection too hurriedly, and it has resulted in harm and pain to us. Man is divided into two classes: The first are the eternal creators of God; the second are forever slaves of an overpowering desire to master the former and to reign over the whole earth. They have captured power, and it is they who maintain that God exists outside of man; that He is an enemy of the people, a judge and a master of the earth. They have disfigured the face of the soul of Christ and have falsified His commandments, for the real Christ is against them, and is against the mastering of man by his neighbor."

He spoke, and I felt that a painful tooth gnawed in my soul. I wanted to tear it out, but it hurt, and I wanted to shout, "That is not the right!"

There was a holy light in his face and he seemed intoxicated and transported with joy. I saw that

THE CONFESSION

his words were insane, but I loved the old man through the pain and the yearning in my heart, and I listened to his speech passionately.

"But the creators of God are alive and immortal, and within them, secretly and earnestly, they will create God anew. And it is about Him you are dreaming; about a god of beauty and wisdom, of righteousness and love."

His words agitated me and lifted me to my feet and gave me a weapon in my hands. Around me the light shadows shimmered and brushed my face with their wings. I was terrified, the earth swam about me, and I thought to myself:

"Perhaps it is true that the devil tempts man with beautiful words. Perhaps this sly old man is plaiting a noose for me, to catch me in the trap of the greatest sin of all."

"Listen," I said; "who are the creators of God? Who is the master? Whom do you await?"

He laughed caressingly, like a woman, and answered:

"The creators of God are the people. They are the great martyrs — greater than the ones the church has praised. They are God, the creators of miracles — the immortal people! I believe in their soul; I have faith in their strength. They are the one and certain basis of life; they are the father of all gods that have been and that will be."

"A mad old man," I thought to myself.

Up to now it seemed to me that, though slowly,

still I was going toward the heights. More than once his words were like a fiery finger that pointed to my soul, and I felt that the burn and the sting were wholesome; but now my heart became suddenly heavy, and I remained standing in the middle of the road, bitterly disappointed. Many fires burned in my breast. I suffered, yet I was incomprehensibly happy. I was bewildered and afraid.

"Is it possible," I asked, "that you are speaking of the peasants?"

He answered loudly and emphatically: "Yes; of the whole working people of the earth, of all its strength — the one and eternal source of the creation of God. Soon the will of the people will awake, and that great force, divided, will unite. Many are already seeking the means by which all the powers of the earth shall be harmonized into one, and from which shall be created the holy and beautiful all-embracing God of the earth."

He spoke loudly, as if not only I, but the mountains and the woods and all that lived, watching in the night, should hear him. He spoke and quivered, like a bird which is ready to fly, and it seemed to me that all this was a dream and that this dream lowered me.

I recalled to my mind the image of my God and placed before His face the dark rows of enslaved, confused people. Did they create God? I remembered their petty meanness, their cowardly avarice, their bodies stooped with degradation and toil, their eyes which were dulled with sorrow, their spiritual stammering and their dumb thoughts, and all their superstitions, and could they, these insects, create a new God?

Wrath and bitter laughter disturbed my heart. I felt that the old man had stolen something from me, and I said to him: "Ah, father, you have done mischief in my soul, like a goat in a garden, and this is all the result of your words. Do you dare to talk with every one like that? It is a great sin in my eyes. You should have pity for people. They seek comfort, and you go about sowing doubt."

He smiled. "I think you are on the same road as I am."

His smile was offensive to me. "It's a lie!" I answered. "I will never place man side by side with God."

"You don't have to," he said. "Do not place him there, for in that way you will put a master over yourself. I am not speaking to you about a man, but of the whole strength of the spirit of the earth — about the people."

I became enraged. This "God, creator," in rags, filthy, always drunk, who was beaten and flogged, became disgusting to me.

"Keep still," I said. "You are a crazy old blasphemer. Who are the people? They are dirty in body and in thoughts; beggars in mind and in food, and ready to sell their souls for a kopeck."

Here something strange happened. He jumped

to his feet and shouted, "Shut up!" He waved his arms, stamped his feet, and he looked as though he were ready to beat me. When he had been in a prophetic mood I stood far from him, and he seemed funny, but now the human came nearer to me.

"Shut up!" he cried. "You granary mouse! You have rotten noble's blood flowing through you, that is plain. You, who were abandoned to the people! Do you know about whom you are speaking? You are all alike. You proud, lazy land robbers! You don't know against whom you are barking, you scrofulous dogs! You have plundered and robbed the people; you have sat on their backs, and you swear at them that they don't run fast enough!"

He jumped around me and his shadow fell on me, whipping my face coldly, and I moved away from him, surprised and fearful lest he strike me. I was twice as big as he was, and ten times as strong, but somehow I had no desire to stop the man. It was evident that he forgot that night was around us, and that we were in the wilderness, and that if I misunderstood him he would lie there alone in that place, without help. I remembered how that frightened, green Archbishop swore at me that time, and crazy Misha and other people of the old faith; but here was a man who was insulting me, and his wrath burned with a different fire. The others were stronger than I, but in their words I heard fear. This man was weak, but fearless. And he shouted at me, like a child or like a mother. His wrath was strangely loving, like the first storm in spring. I was confused and did not understand the boldness of the old man, and though his anger was amusing, still it hurt me that I so enraged him. He scolded insultingly, and I did not like to be called "abandoned," but his wrath pleased me, for I understood that here was a man angered, believing truly in his own right, and such wrath does the soul good. There is much love in it, and sweet food for the heart.

I lay at his feet and he shouted at me from above. "What do you know about the people, you blind fool? Do you know their history? Read their life, and you will find them higher than all the saints, this father of ours, this greatest martyr of all — the People. Then, to your great fortune, you will understand who it is that is before you, and the strength that grows around you, you homeless vagabond, in a strange land! Do you know what Russia is? Do you know what Greece is, which is called Hellas? Do you know Rome? Do you know by whose will and by whose spirit all governments were built? Do you know on whose bones the temples were erected? Do you know with whose tongues the wise men speak? All that is on the earth and all that is in your mind was made by the People, and the nobility have only polished up that which they made."

I remained silent. I liked to see a man who was not afraid to defend his right. He sat down, damp and red in the face, and breathed heavily. I saw that there were tears in his eyes, and this surprised me, for whenever my former teachers were offended with me they did not shed tears. He cried out:

"Listen, and I will tell you about the Russian people."

"You had better rest," I said.

"Keep still," he said to me, threatening me with his hand. "Keep still, or I will kill you."

I could hardly contain myself, and laughed outright.

"Dear grandfather," I said, "you are an unspeakably marvelous old man. Pardon me, in Christ's name, if I have offended you."

"You fool! How could you offend me? But you have spoken badly about the great people, you unhappy soul. It is advantageous for the nobles to slander the people. They have to stifle their conscience, for they are strangers on this earth. But you — who are you?"

CHAPTER XX

IT was good to look at him when he talked thus. He became dignified and even stern. His voice grew calmer and deeper, and he spoke evenly and in cadences, as if he were reading from the Apostles. His face was turned upward, his eyes were round and big, and he was on his knees, but he seemed taller to me than when he stood. At first I listened to his words with an incredulous smile, but soon I remembered the Russian history which Anthony gave me, and it again opened before my eyes. He recited the marvelous fairy tale to me, and I compared this fairy tale with the book. The words tallied, but the sense was different. He came to the decline of the Kiev government.

" Have you heard it? "

" Yes, thank you."

" Well, then, know that those heroes never existed; that it was the people themselves who incarnated their exploits into characters by which to remember their great labor in the building up of the Russian soil."

Then he continued talking about the Sudzalsky land.

I remember that somewhere behind the mountains the sun rose and the night hid itself in the woods and woke the birds. Rosy masses of clouds hung over us and we lay on the dewy grass of the rock, one resuscitating the past, the other astonished, counting up the immeasurable labors of men and hardly believing the tale about the conquest of the hostile woody soil.

The old man seemed to see everything. He heard the hammering of heavy axes in strong hands; he saw the people drain the swamps and build up cities and monasteries; he saw them go ever farther along the cold rivers, into the depths of the thick forests; he saw them conquer the savage earth; he saw them render it beautiful. The princes, the lords of the people, cut and minced this earth into little pieces and fought against each other with the fists of the people whom they afterward robbed. Then from the steppes came the Tartars, but there was no defender of the people's liberty to arise from among the princes. There was no honor, no strength, no mind. They sold the people and made merchandise of them with the Khans as if they were cattle, and they bought princely power with the blood of the peasants, to have power over these same peasants. Later, when they had taught the Tartars how to govern, they sent each other to the Khans for slaughter.

The night around us was friendly and wise like an elder sistér. The voice of the old man gave out from weariness. The sun saw him, but he went still farther into the past, and showed me the truth with flaming words.

THE CONFESSION

"Do you see," he asked me, "what the people have done and what they have suffered up to the very day, when you abused them with your stupid words? I have told you mostly of that which they did through another's will, but after I am rested I will tell you on what their souls have lived and how they have sought God."

He coiled up on the rock and fell asleep like a little child. I could not sleep, but sat there as if surrounded by burning coals.

It was already morning. The sun was high and the birds were singing, full-throated. The wood bathed in the dew and rustled, meeting the day friendly and green. People walked along the road; ordinary, every-day people. They walked with bowed heads and I could not see anything new in them. They had not grown in any way in my eyes. My instructor slept and snored and I sat next to him lost in thought. Men passed by one after the other, looked askance at us and did not even bow their heads to my salute.

"Is it possible," I asked myself, "that these are the offspring of those righteous ones, those builders of the earth about whom I have just heard?"

The dream and the reality became confused in my head, yet I understood that this meeting meant very much for me. The old man's words about God, the Son of the spirit of the people, disturbed me, and I could not reconcile myself to them, not knowing any other spirit except that one which was living in me.

I racked my mind for all the peasants and the people I had known and tried to remember their words. They had many sayings, but their thoughts were poor. On the other hand I saw the dark exile of life, the bitter toil for bread, the winters of famine, the everlasting sadness of empty days, all the degradation which man has suffered and every outrage against his soul. Where could God be in this life? Where was there room for Him?

The old man slept. I wanted to wake him and shout "Speak!"

Soon he awoke, blinked his eyes and smiled.

"Ah," he said, "the sun is already near noon. It is time for me to go."

"Where will you go in such heat?" I asked. "We have bread, tea and sugar. Besides, I can't let you go. You must give me what you have promised."

Then he became thoughtful and said:

"Matvei, you should drop your wandering. It is too late, or perhaps too early for you. You have to learn. It is time for you to learn."

"Is it not too late?"

"Look at me," he answered. "I am fifty-three years old, and up to this day I learn from some little children."

"Whose children?" I asked.

"They are some children I know. You should live with them a year or two. You ought to go to the factory. It is not very far from here, about a hundred versts, where I have good friends."

"First tell me what you wanted to say, and then I shall think where I am to go."

We walked together on the path alongside the road and again I heard his clear voice and his strange words.

"Christ was the first true people's God, born from the soul of the people like the phœnix from the flames."

He trembled all over and waved his hands before his face as if he wanted to catch new words from the air, and continued shouting:

"For a long time the people carried various men on their shoulders. Without question they gave them of their labor and their freedom, placed them above themselves and waited humbly for them to see from their height the paths of righteousness on earth. But these chosen ones of the people, when they reached the height, became drunk and degraded by their power and remained above, forgetting who placed them there, and became a heavy burden on the earth instead of a joy. When the people saw that the children who were fed by their blood were their enemies, they lost their faith in them and abandoned these powerful ones, who had to fall and the power and the strength of their government decayed. The people understood that the law was not that one from a family should be raised and after having fed him on their liberty that they should live by his mind, but that the true law was that all should be raised to one height and that each one should look upon the paths of life with his own eyes; and the day when the consciousness of the inevitable equality of man arose in the people, that day was the birth of Christ.

"Many people have tried to realize their dreams of justice by creating one live being, a common lord over all, and more than once various people, urged on by this common thought, have tried to bind it with strong words that it might live forever. And when all these thoughts were mustered in one, a living God arose for them, the beloved child of the people, Jesus Christ."

That which he said about Christ, the Son of God, was near to me; but about the people giving birth to Christ I could not understand. I told him that, and he answered:

"If you wish to know, you will understand. If you wish to believe, you will know."

We tramped together for three days, going slowly; he, teaching me all the time and explaining the past to me. He recited the whole history of the people from the beginning up to the present day; he told me of the troubled times when the churches persecuted the jesters and of the merry men who awakened the people's memory with their jokes and sowed truth by them.

THE CONFESSION

"Do you understand," he asked me, "who this Savelko of yours was?"

"Yes, I understand."

"Remember that small things come from large and that the large is made up from small pieces."

We came to Stephan Verkhatour. The old man said to me:

"We must part here. My road lies with you no longer."

I did not want to go away from him, but I understood that it was necessary. My thoughts troubled me. I was agitated to the very depths and my soul was furrowed as with a plow.

"Why have you become thoughtful?" he asked me. "Go to the factory. Work there and mix with my friends. It will be no loss to you, I assure you. The people are intelligent. I learned from them, and you see I am no fool."

He wrote a little note and gave it to me.

"Go there. I wish you no harm, believe me. The people are new-born and alive. Don't you believe me?"

"Our small eyes can see much," I answered, "but is that when they see the truth?"

"Look with all your might," he cried, "with all your heart, with all your soul! Did I tell you to believe? I told you to learn and know."

We kissed and he went away. He walked lightly, like a youth of twenty, and as if some happiness awaited him. I became sad when I looked back at this bird flying away from me, Heaven knows where, to sing his song in new parts. My head was heavy; my thoughts raced like Little Russians at market in the early morning, sleepy, awkward, slow, and in no way able to make order. Everything became strangely confused. To my thoughts there was another's conclusion and to this other's conclusion my own beginning. It hurt me, yet it was funny, and I seemed all changed within.

When I went away from Verkhatour, I asked where the road led to, and they answered to the Isetsky factory. That was where the old man had wanted me to go, but I took a side road; I did not wish to go there. I wanted to go to the villages and look around me.

The people were gloomy and haughty and seemed to wish to speak with no one. They looked about cautiously, as if they were afraid some one would rob them.

"Here are the God-creators," I said to myself, looking at some pock-marked peasants. "I will ask them where this road leads to."

"To the Isetsky factory."

"What is it? Do all roads lead to that factory?" I asked myself, and wandered through villages and woods, crawling like a beetle through the grass, and seeing the factory from a distance. It smoked, but it did not lure me. I felt as if I had lost half of myself and I did not understand what

I wanted. I was unhappy. A gray, idle pain filled my soul and evil laughter and a great desire to insult everybody and myself arose in me. Suddenly, without noticing it myself, I made up my mind: "I'll enter the factory, damn it!"

CHAPTER XXI

I CAME into a filthy hell. In a hollow between mountains which were covered with stumps of felled trees, buildings arose on the earth, from the roofs of which tongues of flame shot forth. Tall chimney-stacks rose toward the sky, from which smoke and steam poured out, staining the earth with soot. There was a deafening noise of hammers, and a roar and a wild squeaking and creaking of saws shot through the smoke-laden air. Everywhere there was iron, wood, coal, smoke, steam, stench; and in this pit, filled with every kind of miscellaneous thing, men worked black as coal.

"Thank you, old man," I said to myself, "you have sent me to a nice place."

It was the first time I had seen a factory near-to. I was deafened by the extraordinary noise, and I breathed with difficulty. I went through the streets seeking for the locksmith, Peter Jagikh. Everyone I asked snarled back at me as if they had all quarreled with each other in the morning and had not yet succeeded in calming themselves. "God-creators!" I cried out to myself.

I came upon a man who looked like a bear; dirty from head to foot. His oily clothes shone with dirt

THE CONFESSION

in the sun, and I asked him if he knew the locksmith, Peter Jagikh.

" Who? "

" Peter Jagikh."

" Why? "

" I want to see him."

" Well, I am he."

" How do you do? "

" Well, how do you do? What do you want? "

" I have a note to you."

The man was taller than I, with a large beard, broad shoulders, and heavily set. His face was sooty and his small, gray eyes could hardly be seen from under his thick eyebrows. His cap was set far back on his head and his hair was cut short. He looked like a peasant, yet not entirely so. Evidently he read with great difficulty. His face was all wrinkled and his mustache trembled. Suddenly his face cleared, his white teeth shone, he opened his good, childish eyes and the skin in his cheeks smoothed out.

" Ah," he cried, " he is alive, God's bird! That's good. Go, my dear, to the end of this street and turn to the left toward the wood. At the foot of the mountain there is a house with green shutters. Ask for the teacher. He is called Mikhail. He is my nephew. Show him the note. I will come soon."

He spoke like a soldier, giving his signal on a bugle. He made the speech, waved his hand and went away.

"He is kind and funny," I thought to myself.

At the house an angular boy in a cotton shirt and an apron, met me. His sleeves were rolled up; his hands were white and thin. He read through the note and asked me:

"Is Father Juna well?"

"Yes, thank God."

"Did he tell you when he will come to see us?"

"He didn't say. Is he called Juna?"

The young man looked at me suspiciously and began to read the note again.

"How then?" he asked me.

"He said his name was Jehudiel."

The young fellow smiled. "That is a nickname which I gave him."

"Oh, the devil," I thought.

His hair was straight and long like a deacons', his face pale. His eyes were a watery blue and he looked as if he did not spring from this dirty spot.

He walked up and down the room and measured me with his eyes as if I were a piece of cloth; and I did not like it.

"Have you known Juna a long time?" he asked me.

"Four days."

"Four days," he repeated. "That's good."

"Why good?" I asked.

"Just so," he answered, shrugging his shoulders.

"Why do you wear an apron?"

"I am binding books," he said. "Soon my uncle

THE CONFESSION

will return and we will have supper. Perhaps you would like to wash yourself after your trip?"

I felt like teasing him. He was much too serious for his age.

"Do people wash here?" I asked.

He frowned. "How then?"

"I have not seen any washed ones yet," I answered.

He half closed his eyes, looked at me and answered calmly:

"People do not idle here. They work; and there is no time to wash often."

I saw that I had struck the wrong man. I wanted to answer, but he turned on his heel and went away. I felt foolish, sat down and looked about me.

The room was large and clean. In the corner there was a table set for supper, and on the walls there were shelves with books. The books were mostly secular, but there was also a Bible, the gospels and an old Slavic psalm-book.

I went out into the court and washed myself. The uncle entered, his cap still farther back on his head, and he swung his arms and held his head forward like a bull.

"Well, I will wash myself," he said. "Pump some water for me."

His voice was like that of a trumpet and both his hands together were as large as a big soup tureen. When he had washed some of the soot off his face, I saw that he had high cheek-bones and a skin like copper.

We sat down to supper. They ate, talked about their own affairs and did not ask me who I was or why I came. Still they offered me things hospitably and looked at me in a friendly way. There was something very solid about them, as if the earth was firm under their feet. I felt like shaking it for them — why were they better than I? "

"Are you Old Believers?" I asked.

"We?" the uncle replied. "No."

"Then you are orthodox?"

The nephew frowned and the uncle shrugged his shoulders and laughed.

"Perhaps we have to show him our passports, Mikhail."

I understood that I had acted foolishly, but I did not want to stop.

"I did not want to see your passports," I said. "I wanted to see your thoughts."

"Thoughts? Right away, Your Excellency. Thoughts, forward!" And he laughed like a stallion.

Mikhail, who was making the tea, said calmly:

"I know why you came. You are not the first one whom Juna has sent us. He knows people and never sends empty men."

The uncle felt my forehead with his palm and laughed:

"Please look more gay. Don't show your trumps right away, or you may lose."

THE CONFESSION

They evidently considered themselves men rich in soul and that I was a beggar compared to them. They did not hurry to quench my hungry heart with their wisdom. I became angry and wanted to quarrel, but I could find no reason; and that angered me still more. I asked at random:

"What do you mean by an empty man?"

The uncle answered: "A man who can fill up with anything you wish."

Suddenly Mikhail went up quietly to me and said, in a soft voice:

"You believe in God?"

"Yes."

But I became confused at my answer. It was not true. Did I really believe?

Mikhail asked again:

"And you respect people?"

"No," I answered.

"Don't you see," he said, "that they are created in the image of God?"

The uncle, the devil take him, smiled like a copper basin in the sun.

"With such people," I thought to myself, "one must argue sincerely and if I should fall asunder in little pieces, they will gather me up again."

"When I look upon people," I said, "I doubt the power of God."

Again it was not right. I doubted God before I ever saw the people.

Mikhail looked at me thoughtfully, with wise eyes, and the uncle walked heavily up and down the room, stroking his beard, and grunting low to himself.

It made me uneasy that I had to lower myself to lie before them. I saw my soul with remarkable clearness and my thoughts raced through me stupidly and alarmed like a frightened bee-hive. I began to drive them out of me, irritated. I wished to empty myself.

I spoke for a long time without connecting my words. I spoke at random on purpose. If they were such wise people, let them gather the sense themselves.

I became tired and asked passionately: "How can you heal my sick soul?"

Mikhail answered low, without looking at me:

"I do not consider you sick."

The uncle laughed again, and it pealed out as if a demon had come in through the roof.

"To be sick," Mikhail continued, "is when a man is not conscious of himself, but knows only his pain and lives in it. But you, it is plain, have not lost yourself. You are seeking happiness in life, and only a healthy man does that."

"But why is there such pain in my soul then?"

"Because you like it," he answered.

I gnashed my teeth. His calm was unbearable to me.

"Do you know for sure," I asked, "that I like it?"

He looked me straight in the eyes and drove his nails slowly into my breast.

THE CONFESSION

"As an honest man, you ought to recognize," he said, "that your pain is necessary to your soul. It places you above others and you esteem it as something which separates you from others. Is it not so?"

His Lenten face was dry and drawn, his eyes darkened, he stroked his cheek with his hand, while he cleaned me hard, as one cleans copper with sand.

"You are evidently afraid to mingle with people for you unconsciously think to yourself, 'Though they are ulcers, they are my own, and no one has ulcers but I.'"

I wanted to contradict him, but found no words. He was younger than I, and weaker, and I did not believe that of the two I was the more stupid.

The uncle laughed like a priest in a steam-bath.

"But this does not separate you from people. You are mistaken," Mikhail went on. "Every one thinks the same. That is why life is weak and monstrous. Each one tries to go away from life and dig his own hole in the ground and look out upon the earth from it alone. From a hole, life seems low and futile, and it suits the isolated man to see life so. I say it about those people who for some reason or other cannot sit on the backs of their neighbors to drive them where they could eat tastier food."

His speech angered and offended me.

"This vile life," he said, "unworthy of human reason, began on that day when the first individual tore himself away from the miraculous strength of the people, from the masses, from his mother, and frightened by his isolation and his weakness, pitied himself and grew to be a futile and evil master of petty desires, a mass which called himself 'I.' It is this same 'I' which is the worst enemy of man. In its business of defending itself and asserting itself on this earth, it has uselessly killed the strength of the soul, and its capacity of creating spiritual welfare."

It seemed to me that his speech was familiar to me and that the words were those which I had waited for.

"Poor in soul, the eye is powerless to create. It is deaf, blind and dumb in life, and its goal is only self-defense, peace and comfort. It creates the new and purely human only under compulsion, after innumerable urgings from without and with great difficulty. It not only does not value its brother 'I,' but hates him and persecutes him. It is hostile because, remembering that it was born from the whole from which it was broken off, the 'I' tries to unite the broken pieces and to create anew a great unit."

I listened, surprised. All this was clear to me; not only clear, but even near and true. It seemed to me that I had long ago thought the same, only without words. And now I had found words, and the thoughts arranged themselves before me like steps on a ladder, which led ever upward.

I remembered Juna's speeches and they lived before my eyes, clear and beautiful. But at the same time

THE CONFESSION

I was restless and uncomfortable, as if I were standing on a block of ice in a river in the spring.

The uncle had quietly left us alone. There was no fire in the room, the night was moonlit, and in my soul, too, there was a moonlight mist.

At midnight Mikhail stopped speaking and we went to sleep in a shed in the courtyard, where we lay in the hay. He soon fell asleep, but I went out to the gate, and sat down on some logs and gazed about me.

The moon and two large stars strode carefully across the heavens. Over the mountains against the blue sky the jagged wall of the wood could be plainly seen. On the mountains was the hewn forest, and on the earth black pits. Below, the factory greedily showed its red teeth. It hummed and smoked and tongues of fire rose over the roofs and shot upward, but could not tear themselves away and were drowned in the smoke. The air smelled burnt. It was difficult to breathe.

I thought of the bitter loneliness of man. Mikhail had spoken well. He believed his own words and I saw truth in them. But why did they leave me cold? My soul did not harmonize with the soul of this man. It stood apart, as in a wilderness.

Soon I noticed that I was thinking the thoughts of Juna and Mikhail and that their thoughts lived powerfully within me, though still on the surface, for at bottom I was still hostile and suspicious of them.

"Where am I?" I asked. "And what am I?"

I spun around in my perplexity like a top, and always faster, so that the cloud storm roared in my ears.

The whistle blew in the factory. At first it was thin and plaintive, then it became louder and masterful.

The morning looked out sleepily from the mountain and the night hurried below, taking the thin veil off the trees quietly, folding it up and hiding it in the hollows and the pits. The robbed earth stood out clear to the eye. Everything was eaten out and plundered, as if some bold giant had played in this hollow, tearing out strips of wood and giving severe wounds to the earth.

The factory was sunk in this basin, dirty, oily, covered with smoke and puffing. Dark people dragged themselves to it from all sides and it swallowed them up, one by one. "Creators of God," I thought to myself. "What have they created?"

The uncle came out into the court disheveled, stretching himself, yawning, cracking his joints, and smiling at me.

"Ah," he cried, "you are up!" Then he asked me kindly, "Or perhaps you did not go to bed at all? Well, it does not matter. You will sleep during the day. Come, let us drink tea."

At tea he said to me: "There were nights when I, too, did not sleep, brother. There was a time when I could have beaten every one I met. Even before

I was a soldier my soul was troubled, but in the service they made me deaf. An officer gave me a blow on the ear. My right ear is deaf. There was one *feldscher* who helped me, thanks to —"

It was evident he wanted to say God, but he stopped, stroked his beard and smiled. He seemed to me childish and there was something childish in his eyes. They were so simple and credulous.

"He was a very good man. He looked at me. 'What is the matter?' he asked. 'Is this human life?' I answered. 'True,' he said, 'everything ought to be changed. Peter Vasilief, let me teach you political economy.' And he began. At first I did not understand anything. But suddenly I understood the daily and eternal baseness in which we lived. Then I nearly went out of my head with joy. 'Oh, you villains!' I cried. That is the way science always suddenly unfolds itself. At first you only hear new words and then there comes a moment when everything unites and comes out into the light and that moment is the true birth of man. Marvelous!"

His face became happy and his eyes smiled softly. He nodded his shorn head and said:

"That is going to happen to you, too."

It was pleasant to look at him. The child was strong in him and I envied him.

"Thirty-two years of my life I spent like a horse. It was disgraceful. Well, I will make up for it as best I can. Only my mind is not very quick. The mind is like the hands. It needs exercise. My hands are cleverer than my head."

I looked at him and thought, how is it that these people are not afraid to speak about everything?

"But for that matter," he continued, "Mishka has brains enough for two. He has read very much. You wait till he forgets himself. The factory priest called him 'an arch heretic.' Too bad his head is not clear about God. That comes from his mother. My sister was a very distinguished woman in religious matters. From Orthodox she went over to the Old Believers, but the Old Believers did not admit her."

As he spoke he got ready to go to work. He walked from one corner of the room to the other. Everything about him shook. The chairs fell and the floor bent under him as he walked. He was funny, yet pleasant to look upon.

"What kind of people are they?" I thought. Then I said aloud: "Can I remain with you three days?"

"Go ahead," he said; "three months if you wish. You are a strange fellow. You are not in our way, thank God."

Then he scratched his head and smiled apologetically.

"The word God always comes to my mouth. It is from habit."

Again the factory whistle blew, and the uncle went

away. I went to sleep in the shed. Mikhail lay there. He was frowning sternly, and his hands were on his breast, his face was flushed. He was beardless and without mustache, his cheekbones were high; in fact, he was all bones.

"What kind of people are they?"

And with this thought I fell asleep.

CHAPTER XXII

I AWOKE. There was noise, whistling, hubbub, as if at a meeting of all the devils. I looked out into the court. It was full of youngsters and Mikhail was among them, in a white shirt, looking like a sailboat among small canoes. He stood laughing with his head on one side, his mouth wide open and his eyes twinkling. He in no way resembled the serious Lenten young man of the night before.

The children were dressed in blue, red and pink. They shone in the sun as they jumped and shouted. Something drew me toward them and I crawled out from the shed. One youngster noticed me and cried out:

"Look, fellows, here is a mo-onk!" Like fire that had been set to a heap of dry shavings, so the children jumped, wheeled about, looked at me and began to dance up and down.

"Wha-at a red one!"
"And such a hairy one, too!"
"He'll bite you!"
"Oh, don't tease him; he's strong."
"He's not a monk. He's a bell-tower."
"Mikhail Ivanich, who is he?"

The teacher became somewhat embarrassed, and they, the little devils, laughed. I did not know why I struck them as funny, but I caught the spirit from them, smiled and cried to them:

"Stop it, you mice!"

The sun was shining, a gay noise filled the air and everything about us fluttered and floated with it, blinding me with its light and wrapping me in its warmth.

Mikhail greeted me and shook my hand.

"We are going to the wood," he said. "Do you want to come along?"

It was a pleasant sight. There was one fat youngster who snatched my cap, put it on his head and flew about the courtyard like a butterfly.

I went to the wood with this band of madcaps, and the day remains engraven on my memory.

The children poured out into the street and fled to the mountain lightly, like feathers in the wind. I walked alongside of their shepherd, and it seemed to me that I had never seen such charming children before.

Mikhail and I walked behind them. He gave them orders, crying out to them; but the children refused to listen to him. They jostled, fought and bombarded one another with pine cones, and quarreled. When they were tired they surrounded us, crawled about our feet like beetles, pulled at their teacher's hands, asked him now about the grass, now about the flowers, and he answered each one in a friendly way, as if to an equal. He rose above them like a white sail.

The children were all alert, but some of them were more serious and thoughtful than their age warranted. Silent, they kept near their teacher.

Later the children again spread themselves out and Mikhail said to me, low:

"Are they created only for toil and drunkenness? Each one is a receptacle of a living soul. Each one could hasten the development of the thought which would free us from the bondage of confusion, yet they must travel along the same dark and narrow channel through which the days of their fathers flowed turbidly. They are ordered to work and forbidden to think. Many of them, perhaps all, pledge allegiance to dead strength and serve it. Here lies the source of earth's misery. There is no freedom for the growth of the human soul."

He talked while several young boys walked alongside of him and listened to his words. Their attentiveness was amusing. What could these young sprouts of life understand by his words? I remembered my own teacher. He beat the children on the head with a ruler and would come to school drunk.

"Life is filled with fear," Mikhail said, "and mutual hatred eats out the soul of man. A hideous life. But only give the children time to develop freely; do not transform them into beasts of burden, and free and alert, they will light up life both from within and without with the exquisite young fire of their proud souls and the great beauty of their eternal activity."

Their blond heads, their blue eyes, their red cheeks were around us like live flowers among the dark green pines. The laughter and clear voices of these gay birds rang out — these harbingers of new life. And all this vital beauty would be trampled down by greed! What sense was there in that? A delicate child is born rejoicing. He grows into a beautiful child, and then, as a grown-up man, he swears vulgarly and groans bitterly, beats his wife and drowns his sorrow in vodka. And as an answer to my thought, Mikhail said:

"They go on destroying the people — the one and true temple of the living God. And the destroyers themselves sinking in the chaos of the ruins, see their wicked work and cry out, 'Horrible!' They rush hither and thither and whine, 'Where is God?' while they themselves have killed Him."

I remembered Juna's words about the breaking up of the Russian people, and my thoughts followed Mikhail's words lightly and pleasantly. But I could not understand why he spoke low and without anger, as if this whole oppressive life was a thing of the past for him.

The earth breathed warm and friendly, with the intoxicating perfumes of the sap and the flowers. The birds pierced the air with their twitter, the children played about and conquered the stillness of the wood, and it became more and more clear to me that before this day I had not understood their strength, nor had I ever seen their beauty. It was good to see Mikhail among them, with his calm smile on his face. I said, smiling:

"I am going to leave you for a little. I have to think."

He looked at me. His eyes beamed, his eyelashes fluttered, and my heart answered him, trembling. I had seen little of friendship, but I knew how to value it.

"You are a good man," I said to him.

He became embarrassed, lowered his eyes, and I also was confused. We stood opposite each other, silent; then separated. He called out after me:

"Don't go too far. You will lose your way."

"Thank you."

I turned into the wood, chose a place and sat down. From the distance came the voices of the children. The thick, green wood resounded with their laughter and it sighed. The squirrels squeaked over my head, the finches sang.

I wanted to explain all to my soul; all which I knew and which I had heard these days, but everything melted within me into a rainbow, and it enfolded me and carried me on as it floated quietly along, filling my soul. It grew infinitely large, and I lost myself in it, forgetting myself in a light cloud of speechless thought.

At night I reached home and said to Mikhail that I would like to live with them some time, until I

THE CONFESSION

learned their faith. For this reason I wished Uncle Peter to find some work for me in the factory.

"Don't hurry so," he said. "You ought to rest and read some books."

"Give me your books," I said, for I trusted them.

"Take them."

"I have never read worldly books," I said. "Give me what you think I need; for instance, a Russian history."

"It is necessary to know everything," he answered, and looked at the books affectionately, as at the children.

Then I buried myself in study, reading all day long. It was difficult for me, and painful. The books did not argue with me. They simply did not wish to know me. One book especially tortured me. It spoke about the development of the world and of human life. It was written against the Bible. Everything was stated simply, clearly and positively. I could find no loophole in this simplicity, and it seemed to me that a whole row of strange powers were around me and that I was among them like a mouse in a trap. I read it twice, read it in silence, wishing to find some flaw in it through which I could escape to liberty. But I found none. I asked my teacher:

"How is it? Where is the man?"

"It seems to me, too," he said, "that this book is not true, but I cannot explain where it is wrong. Still, after all, as a guess at the plan of the world, it is very pretty."

I liked it when he answered: "I do not know; I cannot say." And I stood very close to him, for evidently in this lay his honesty. When a teacher decides to be conscious of his ignorance, it must be that he has some knowledge.

He knew much that was unknown to me and which he related to me with marvelous simplicity. Once he told me how the sun and the stars and the earth were created, and he talked as if he himself saw this fiery work, done by an unknown and wise hand. I did not understand his God, but that did not trouble me. The principal force of this world he called some kind of matter, but I placed instead of matter God, and all went smoothly.

"God is not yet created," he said, smiling.

The question of God was a standing source of argument between Mikhail and his uncle. As soon as Mikhail said God, Uncle Peter would get angry.

"He has begun it again. Don't you believe him, Matvei. He has inherited that from his mother."

"Wait, Uncle. The question of God for Matvei is the principal question."

"Don't you believe it, Mishka. Send him to the devil, Matvei. There are no Gods. It is a dark wood — religion, churches and all such things are a dark wood, where robber bandits live. It is a hoax."

But Mikhail insisted obstinately. "The God about whom I speak existed when men unanimously created Him from the stuff of their brains, to illumine the darkness of their existence. But when the

THE CONFESSION

people were divided into slaves and masters, into little bits and pieces; when they lost their thought and their will-power, God was lost, God was destroyed."

"Do you hear, Matvei?" Peter would cry out happily. "He is dead! Long live his memory!"

His nephew looked straight into his face, and lowering his voice, continued:

"The main crime which the masters of life have committed is the destruction of the creative power of the people. The time will come when the will of the people will again converge to one point, and then, again, the unconquerable and miraculous power will arise and the resurrection of God will take place. It is He whom you seek, Matvei."

Uncle Peter waved his hands like a wood-cutter.

"Don't believe him, Matvei. He is wrong."

And turning to his nephew, he stormed at him:

"You have caught church thoughts, Mishka, like stolen cucumbers from a strange garden, and you confuse people with them. When you say that the working people are called to renew life, then renew it, but don't gather up that which the priests have brought up from their holes and dropped!"

It interested me to listen to these people, and their mutual respect and equality surprised me. They argued with heat, but they did not offend each other with evil language and abuse. At times the blood would mount to Uncle Peter's head, and he would tremble; but Mikhail only lowered his voice and seemed to bend his large opponent to the earth. Two men stood opposite me, and both of them denied God out of the fulness of their sincere faith!

"But what is my faith?" I asked myself, and found no answer.

During my stay with Mikhail the thought about the place of God among people sank and lost its strength and dropped its former boldness and was supplanted by a quantity of other thoughts, and instead of the question, "Where is God?" stood other questions: "Who am I, and why? Wherefore do I seek God?"

I understood that it was senseless.

In the evenings workingmen came to Mikhail and interesting conversations took place. The teacher spoke to them about life and explained to them the laws which were bad. He knew them remarkably well and explained them clearly. The workingmen were mostly young men, dried up by the heat of the factory. Their skins were eaten by soot, their faces were dark, their eyes sorrowful. They listened with serious eagerness, silent and frowning, and at first they seemed to me morose and servile. But later I understood their life better and saw that they could sing and dance and joke with the young girls.

The conversations of Mikhail and his uncle were always on the same subjects — the power of money, the abasement of the workingmen, the greed of the masters and the absolute necessity of destroying divisions of men into classes.

But I was no workingman and no master. I was

THE CONFESSION 247

not in search of money, and they laid too much stress on capital, and thereby lowered themselves. At first I argued with Mikhail, pointing out that man's first duty was to find his spiritual birthplace and that then he would see his own place on earth, and he would find his freedom.

I spoke briefly, but with heat. The workingmen listened to my speech good-naturedly and attentively, like honest judges, and some of the elder ones even agreed with me. But when I finished Mikhail began with his quiet smile and annihilated my words.

"You are right, Matvei, when you say that man lives in mystery and does not know whether God, that is, his spirit, is his enemy or his friend. But you are not right when you say that we, who are arbitrarily bound in the chains of the terrible misery of our daily toil, can free ourselves from the yoke of greed without destroying the actual prison which surrounds us. First of all we must learn the strength of our next-door enemy and learn his cunning. For this we must find each other and discover in each other the one thing which unites each with all. And this one thing is our unconquerable, I can say miraculous, strength. Slaves never had a God. They raised human laws which were forced on them without, to Godhood, nor can there ever be a God for slaves, for He is created from the flames of the sweet consciousness of the spiritual relationship of each toward all. Temples are not created from gravel and débris, but from strong whole stones. Isolation is the breaking away from the parental whole. It is a sign of the weakness and the blindness of the soul, for in the whole is immortality and in isolation inevitable slavery and darkness and inconsolable yearning and death."

When we spoke this way it seemed to me that his eyes saw a great light in the distance. He drew me into his circle and every one forgot about me, but looked at him with happiness. At first this offended me. I thought that they misunderstood my thoughts and that no one was willing to accept any one's thoughts but Mikhail's. Unnoticed I would go away from them, sit down in a corner and quietly hold council with my pride.

I made friends with the pupils. On holidays they surrounded Uncle Peter and me like ravens around sheaves of corn. He would make some toy for them while I was bombarded with questions about Kiev, Moscow and everything I had seen. Often one of them would ask me a question which would make my eyes bulge out in astonishment. There was a young boy there called Fedia Sachkof, a quiet, serious child. Once when I was going with him through the wood, speaking to him about Christ, he suddenly said in a firm tone:

"Christ did not think of remaining a small boy all his life — for instance, a boy of my age. If He had done so, He could have lived and still have accused the rich and aided the poor, and He would not have been crucified. He would have been a small boy, and

THE CONFESSION

they would have been sorry for Him. But the way He did it, it is as if He had never been here."

Fedia was about eleven. His little face was white and transparent, and his eyes were critical.

There was another boy, Mark Lobof, a pupil of the last class. He was a thin, quick-tempered, sharp fellow, very impudent and a bully. He would whistle low, and pinch, beat and push the children. Once I saw him persecuting a small, quiet boy until the latter burst into tears.

"Mark," I said to him, "suppose he fought you back."

Mark looked at me, laughed and answered:

"He won't fight. He is gentle and good."

"Then why do you hurt him?"

"Just so," he answered.

He whistled and then added: "Because he is gentle."

"Well, suppose he is?" I asked.

"What are the gentle ones made for?"

He said that in a remarkably quiet tone, and it was evident that at twelve years old he was already sure that the gentle people were created for insults.

Each child was wise in his own way, and the more I was with them the more I thought about their fate. What did they do to deserve the wretched, offensive life which awaited them?

I reminded myself of Christa and my son, and remembering them, angry thoughts arose in my soul. Do you not forbid the women free birth of children because you fear that they might give birth to some one dangerous and inimical to you? Do you not violate woman's will because her free son is terrible to you, since he is not tied to you by any bonds? You have time and the right to bind your children whom you have brought up and equipped for the affairs of life; but you fear that nobody's child whom you have denied your supervision may grow up into your implacable enemy.

There was such a nobody's child in the factory. His name was Stepa. He was black as a beetle, pockmarked, and without eyebrows. His eyes were little and sharp, and he was quick at everything, and very gay.

Our acquaintance began with his coming up to me one holiday and saying:

"Monk, I heard you are illegitimate. Well, so am I." And he walked alongside of me.

He was thirteen, had already finished school and was working in the factory. He walked along, blinked his eyes, and asked:

"Is the earth large?"

I explained to him as best I could. "Why do you want to know?" I asked.

"I need to know. Why should I stick in one place? I am not a tree. As soon as I learn the locksmithing trade, I am going far into Russia, to Moscow, and farther still. I am going everywhere."

He spoke as if he were threatening some one. "I am coming!"

THE CONFESSION

I watched him closely after this meeting. He had a serious streak in him. He was always where Mikhail's comrades talked, and he listened and squinted his eyes as if taking aim where to send himself. He had a special way of playing tricks. He teased only those who stood near to the boss.

Once at dinner, he said: "It is dull here, monk."

"Why?"

"I don't know, but they are a rotten lot. Work and trouble, nothing more. As soon as I learn my trade I am going to get out of here, quick."

Whenever he spoke of his future wanderings his eyes became large and he glanced boldly and had the look of a conqueror, who staked his all on his own strength.

I liked this creature, and I felt something mature in his speech. "He won't get lost," I thought to myself as I looked at him.

My soul ached for my own son. How was he and what was going to happen to him on this earth?

CHAPTER XXIII

THERE was a quiet growth of new feelings within me. I felt that each man sent out to me a sharp, thin ray which touched me unseen and imperceptibly reached my heart. And I accepted these hidden rays ever more willingly.

At times the workingmen assembled in Mikhail's rooms, and then I felt that a burning cloud formed from their thoughts, which surrounded me and carried me strangely upward with itself.

Suddenly every one began to understand me more and more. I stood in their circle, and they were my body and I was their soul and their will, and my speech was their voice. And at times it was I that was a part of the body, and I heard the cry of my own soul from other mouths, and it sounded good when I heard it. But when time passed and there was silence I again remained alone and for myself.

I remembered my former communion with God in my prayers. Then I had been glad when I could wipe myself out from my memory and cease to exist. In my relationship with people I did not lose myself; instead I grew larger, taller, and the strength of my soul increased many-fold. In this, too, lay self-forgetfulness, but it did not destroy me.

THE CONFESSION

It quenched my bitter thoughts and the anguish of isolation.

I realized this mistily and vaguely. I felt that a new seed was growing in my soul, but I could not understand it. I only knew that it pulled me determinedly toward people.

In those days I worked in the factory for forty kopecks a day, carrying on my shoulders heavy trays of iron, slag and brick. I hated this hellish place, with its dirt and its noise and its hubbub, and its heat which tortured the body.

The factory had fastened itself onto the earth and pressed itself into her and sucked her insatiably night and day. It was out of breath from greed and groaned and spit out of its red-hot jaws fiery blood drawn from the earth. It cooled off, grew black, then again began to melt iron and to boil and thunder, flattening out the red iron and squirting up sparks and trembling in its whole frame, as it pulled out long strips like nerves, from the body of the earth.

The wild labor seemed to me something terrible, something bordering on the insane. This groaning monster, devastating the lap of the earth, was digging an abyss under itself, and knowing that some day it would fall into it, screeched eagerly, with a thousand voices: "Hurry! Hurry! Hurry!"

In fire and noise, under a rain of burning sparks, blackened men worked. It was no place for them. About them everything threatened to burn them by fiery death or to crush them by heavy iron; everything deafened and blinded. The unbearable heat dried up the blood, but they did their work quietly, walking about with a masterly confidence, like devils in hell, fearing nothing and knowing nothing.

They lifted small levers with strong hands, and all around and above them hands and jaws of enormous machines moved quietly and terribly, crumbling the iron. It was hard to know whose mind and whose will reigned here. At times it was man who controlled and governed this factory according to his wishes. But other times it seemed that all the people and the whole factory were subject to the devil and that he laughed aloud, triumphantly and horribly as he saw the mad and difficult rush created by greed.

The workers said to one another: "It is time to go to work." Were the men masters of their work, or did it drive and crush them? I did not know. Work seemed difficult and masterful, but the human mind was sharp and quick. Sometimes there would ring out amid this devilish noise of whirring machines a victorious and care-free song. I would smile in my heart, remembering the story of Ivan the Fool, who rode on a whale up to heaven to catch the wonder-bird, Phœnix.

The people in the factory, though they were not friendly to me, were all bold and proud. They were abusive, foul-mouthed and often drunk; yet they were free and fearless people. They were different from the pilgrims and the tillers of the soil, who offended me with their servile, confused souls, their hopeless complainings and their petty cheatings in their affairs with God and themselves. These people were bold in thought, and although they were hurt by the slavery of their labor, and grew angry with one another and even fought, yet if the bosses ever acted unfairly, thereby rousing their sense of justice, they would stand together against them as one man.

And those workingmen who followed Mikhail were always among the first, spoke louder than the rest and seemed to fear nothing. Formerly, when I did not think about the people, I did not notice men; but now as I looked upon them I wished to detect differences, so that each one might stand out separately before me. I succeeded in this and yet not entirely. Their speech was different and each one had his own face, but their faith was the same and their plans were one. Without haste, friendly and sincerely, they were building something new. Each one of them, among his fellows, was like a pleasant light; like a meadow in a thick wood for the wanderer who had lost his way. Each one drew to himself the workingmen who were wider awake than the rest, and all these followers of Mikhail were held together by one plan, and they created a spiritual circle in the factory, a fire of brightly burning thoughts.

At first the workingmen were not friendly to me. They shouted and made fun of me.

"Oh, you red-haired fly! You cloister-bug! You foul one! Parasite!"

At times they struck me, but this I could not stand,

and in such cases I did not spare my fists. Though people admire strength, still one cannot gain esteem and attention through his fists, and I would have had to bear many beatings were it not that at one of my quarrels a friend of Mikhail's, one Gavriel Kostin, interfered. He was a young metal pourer, very handsome and respected by the whole factory. Six men had come up to me and their looks boded ill for my back. But he stood next to me and said:

"Why do you provoke a man, comrades? Is he not as much a worker as the rest of us? You do wrong, and against yourselves. Our strength lies in close friendship."

He said these few words, but he said them so well and so simply, as if he were talking to children. The friends of Mikhail always made use of every incident to spread their ideas.

Kostin embarrassed my opponents and the words touched my heart also. I began to talk.

"I did not become a monk," I said, "to have much to eat, but because my soul was starved. I have lived and I have seen that everywhere labor is endless and hunger common; that everywhere there is swindle and fraud, bitterness and tears, brutality and every kind of darkness of the soul. By whom was this arranged? Where is our righteous and wise God? Does He see the infinite and eternal martyrdom of the people?"

A crowd collected about me and listened earnestly to my words. I finished and there was silence.

Finally, the head model-maker, Kriokof, said to Kostin:

"That monk there sees things deeper than you and your comrades. He has taken hold of the root of the matter."

It pleased me to hear these words. Kriokof slapped me on my shoulder and said:

"You have spoken well, brother, but all the same cut your hair by a yard. Such a mane catches the dirt and looks funny."

And some one called out:

"And is in the way in a fight."

They were joking. Evidently their wrath had passed. Where there is laughter, there is man; the animal is gone.

Kostin took me aside. "Be careful with such words, Matvei," he said. "You can get into prison for them."

I was astonished. "What!"

"In prison," he laughed.

"Why?"

"For criticizing."

"Are you joking?"

"Ask Mikhail," he said. "I have to go to work now."

He went away.

CHAPTER XXIV

I WAS very much astonished at his words. I could hardly believe them, but in the evening Mikhail confirmed them. All evening he told me about the cruel persecutions. It seemed that for such speeches as I had made thousands of people suffered death, were sent to Siberia and to the mines; yet, though the slaughter of Herod was in no way diminishing, the faithful were ever increasing in numbers.

Something grew and became clear in my soul, and the speeches of Mikhail and his comrades took on another meaning, for, first of all, if a man was ready to give up his freedom and even his life for his faith, it meant that he was a sincere believer, and he resembled the early martyrs who followed the laws of Christ.

Mikhail's words grew connected and blossomed out and came close to my soul. I do not mean to say that I understood his words at once and fathomed their depths, but for the first time that evening I felt their close relationship to my heart, and the whole earth seemed to me a Bethlehem saturated with the blood of children. I grew to understand the keen desire of the Virgin Mother when, looking upon hell, she asked of the Archangel Mikhail: "Oh, Arch-

THE CONFESSION

angel, let me suffer in this fire. Let me take part in this great agony." Only that here I did not see sinners, but righteous ones, wishing to destroy the hell upon earth, for the sake of which they were serenely prepared to undergo all suffering.

"Perhaps there are no longer holy anchorites," I said to Mikhail, "because man is not going away from the world, but toward the world."

"The true faith," he answered, "comes out in a true movement."

"Take me into this movement," I begged of him.

Everything burned within me.

"No," he answered. "Wait a while and consider it. It is still too soon for you. If you, with your character, should fall into the enemy's noose at present, you would be entangled in it uselessly and for a long time. On the other hand, you ought to go away after what you have said. There is much that is still not clear to you, and you are not free enough for our work. Its great beauty has captivated and allured you, but though it is displayed before you in its whole strength you stand before it as if you were standing in a square room from which you can see the temple being built, in all its immensity and beauty. But it is being built quietly and evenly day by day, and if you are not familiar with the whole plan, the sublime temple will disappear and vanish from your vision, and the vision, which was not deep in your soul, will vanish and the labor of building will seem beyond your strength."

"Why do you quench my ardor?" I asked him with pain. "I have found a place for myself and was happy when I saw that I could be useful."

He answered me calmly and sadly:

"I do not consider that you are capable of living by a plan which is not clear to you, and I see that the consciousness of your relation to the spirit of the working class has not yet arisen in your soul. You have been sharpened by the friction of life, and you stand in advance of the thought of the people. You do not look upon yourself as one of them, but it seems to me that you consider yourself a hero, ready to give alms to the weak from the overflow of your strength; that you consider yourself something special, living for yourself, and that in yourself is the beginning and end, and that you are not a link in the exquisite and immense unending chain."

I began to understand why he sent me back to earth and unconsciously felt that his words were right.

"You should begin wandering again," he said, "to look upon the life of the people with new eyes. Do not take books along with you. Reading will give you nothing. You do not yet believe that it is not human intelligence which is found in books, but the infinite diversity of the striving of the soul of the people toward freedom. Books do not seek to master you, but give you the weapon for emancipation; you do not yet understand how to hold this weapon in your hand."

THE CONFESSION

He spoke truly. Books were strangers to me at this time. I was used to church writings, but I could not grasp worldly thought except with great difficulty. The spoken word gave me much more than the written. The thoughts which I gathered from books lay on the surface of my soul and were quickly effaced and melted away by my fire. They did not answer my principal question: What was the law which governed God, and why, if man was made in His image, did He degrade him against His will? And, moreover, whose was this will?

Side by side with this question, not antagonizing it, lived another. Was God brought down from heaven on this earth, or was He raised from earth up to heaven by the strength of the people? And here arose the burning thought that the creation of God was the eternal work of the whole people.

My heart was cut in two. I wanted to remain with these people, yet something pulled me to go away and prove my new thought and to search for this unknown something which robbed me of my liberty and confused my spirit.

Uncle Peter urged me also: "You ought to go away for some time, Matvei. There has been some dangerous talk about your speech."

And soon things decided themselves without my control. One night a messenger came on horseback from a neighboring factory with the announcement that gendarmes were making house searches in their place and that undoubtedly they would soon be here.

"Ah, it is too soon," said Mikhail with anger.

There was a hurrying and scurrying to and fro and Uncle Peter cried to me:

"Go, Matvei, go! You have nothing to do here. You did not make the soup and you needn't eat it."

Mikhail insisted, looking straight into my face.

"You had better go away from here. Your presence will help very little and may do some harm."

I understood that they wanted to get rid of me, and it hurt me. But at this time I felt that I was afraid of the gendarmes. I did not see them, yet I feared them! I knew that it was not right to leave people in their need, but I succumbed to their will. They sent me away.

I went up the mountain to the wood through underbrush, between tree stumps. I stumbled as if I was held by my heels. Behind me a young boy hurried along, Ivan Vikof, with a great pack on his back. He was sent to hide books in the wood.

We ran forward to the edge of the wood. He found a hiding place and buried his burden. He was calm, but not I.

"Will they come here?" I asked him.

"Who knows?" he answered. "Perhaps they will come here. You must hurry."

He was an awkward boy, and he looked as if he were hacked out from an oak-tree with an ax. His head was large, one shoulder was higher than the other, his long arms were out of proportion, and his voice was sad.

THE CONFESSION

"Are you afraid?" I asked him.

"Of what?"

"That they will come and take you."

"If they only don't find what I have hidden, I don't care what they do."

He arranged the books with care in the pit, covered them over, smoothed the earth down and threw brush upon it. He sat down on the ground, and seeing that I was getting ready to go away, he said:

"Some one will come with a note for you. Wait."

"What kind of a note?"

"I don't know."

I looked out from the trees into the valley. The factory breathed heavily, like a strong man who is being choked. It seemed to me that men were being pursued in the streets and that in the darkness they ran after one another; they fought, they snarled in anger, ready to break each other's bones. And Ivan, without haste, was getting ready to go down.

"Where are you going?"

"Home."

"They will take you."

"I am not long in the movement, and they do not know me. And if they take me, there is no harm done. People come out wiser from prison."

Here some one loudly and clearly asked me: "How is it, Matvei? You are not afraid of God, and yet you fear the gendarmes."

I looked at Ivan. He was standing and gazing down thoughtfully.

"What did you say?" I asked.

"You read many books in prison."

"Is that all?"

"Isn't that enough?"

There were several lies that were rotting within me, and shameful questions shot up with piercing sparks. The night was cold, but I burned.

"I am going with you."

"You must not," Ivan said sternly. "They will certainly arrest you. This whole trouble began on account of your speech."

"How?"

"A priest in Verkhotour gave it away."

I sat down on the ground and said to myself:

"Then I have to go."

But fear took hold of me.

"Some one is running," Ivan whispered low.

I looked down from the mountain. Thick shadows were crawling over it. The sky was clouded, the moon in its last quarter now showed itself, now hid itself in the clouds. The whole earth about me moved, and from this noiseless movement something oppressive and fearful fell on me. I watched the torrents of shadows which flowed over the earth and which covered up the undergrowth and my soul with black veils.

A head moved among the brush, jumping like a ball among the branches. Ivan whistled low and said:

"It is Kostia!"

THE CONFESSION

I knew Kostia. He was a boy of about fifteen, blue-eyed, blond and weak. He had finished school two years ago. Mikhail was preparing him to be his assistant.

I understood that I was thinking about these little details on purpose, for I wanted to put my thoughts aside and stifle my shame and my fear.

Kostia arrived panting, his voice broken.

"They have arrived. They have asked for you, Monk. Here, Uncle Peter wrote a note and told me to take you to the Lobanofsky monastery. Let us go."

I rose and said to Ivan: "Good-by, brother. Greet them all for me and ask them to forgive me."

But Kostia pushed me and commanded me severely:

"Go along! Whom are you greeting? They are all taken like hens for the market."

We went along. Kostia went ahead, telling me in a low voice all that he saw below, and I followed him. But I was pulled from all sides, by my hands and the skirts of my coat, as if some one were asking me:

"Where are you going? You have entrapped people and you yourself are escaping."

I spoke aloud, to myself: "So on account of me people were lost!"

The boy answered: "Not on account of you, but on account of truth. Are you truth? What a queer fellow!"

His words were funny and he himself was small, but still they struck home. I wanted to set myself right before him, and I laid out my thoughts as a beggar lays out the crumbs from his bag.

"Yes," I said, "it is evident that a great untruth lives within me."

He muttered, answering each one of my words like a conscience:

"Why great? You must always have something greater in you than any one else."

"Those are not his words," I thought. "He has copied them from some one."

"Kostin was right when he called you a bell tower. But you are not the kind that rings only for mass, but one which rings by itself, because it was built crooked and the bells are badly hung."

He remained silent, and then he added:

"I don't like you, Monk. You are so strange."

"How?"

"I don't know. Are you really a Russian? I don't think you are good."

At any other time I would have become angry, but now I was silent. I became suddenly weak, tired unto death. Night and the wood were around us. Between the trees the gray darkness fell thickly and became dense. It was difficult to tell which was night and which was tree. The moonbeams glistened above, broke themselves upon the body of the darkness and vanished. It was quiet. All these people, beginning with Juna, bore no fear. Some were filled with anger, others were always gay, and most of them were quiet, modest people, who seemed to be ashamed to show their goodness.

Kostia walked along the path, and his blond head shone like a light before me. I recalled the youth of Bartholomew, the God-child Alexei and others. No, that was not the right!

My thoughts were like water-hens in a puddle, jumping from stump to stump.

"Have you read the 'Lives of the Saints'?" I asked the boy.

"I read them when I was little. My mother made me. Why?"

"Did you like those chosen ones of God?"

"I don't know. Ponteleimon I liked; and George also. He fought with the dragon. But I don't know what good it did the people to have dozens of them made holy."

Kostia grew in my eyes.

"If a Czar's daughter or a rich man's daughter believed in Christ and underwent martyrdom for her belief, neither the Czar nor the kingdom were ever better to the people for it? It is not spoken of in the legends that the tyrant Czars became good."

Then, after a silence, he said:

"Nor do I know of what good Christ's martyrdom was. He wanted to conquer suffering, and what came of it?"

He grew thoughtful and then added:

"Nothing came of it."

I wanted to embrace him. Pity arose in my heart for Kostia, for Christ, for all the people who remained in the village, for the whole human world. And what of me? Where was my place? Where was I going?

The darkness of the short night was lifting, and from above a quiet light came through the branches of the pine trees.

"You are not tired, Kostia?"

"I?" the small boy answered proudly. "No. I like to walk in the night. It seems to me then that I walk through wonderland. I love fairy tales."

At dawn we lay down to sleep. Kostia fell asleep quickly, as if he had dived into a river, but I circled around my thoughts like a Tartar beggar around a Christian church in winter. It is stormy and cold in the street, but it is forbidden by Mohammed to enter the temple.

I decided upon something towards morning, and when the boy awoke, I said to him:

"Forgive me that I made you walk with me for nothing. I am not going to the monastery. I don't want to hide."

He looked at me seriously and said:

"You have already hidden." Then, without looking at me, he began to wave a twig.

"Well, good-by, dear."

He bowed his head: "Good-by," he answered.

I went away, then looked back. He stood there among the trees following me with his eyes.

"Eh," he cried, " good-by!"

It pleased me that he said it with more tenderness this time.

CHAPTER XXV

LIKE one sick, I wandered for many days, full of heavy heartache. A fire raged in my soul, that quiet piece of land of mine, and lit it up like a meadow in the wood, and my thoughts now crawled ahead of me, together with my shadow; now dragged behind, like biting smoke. Was I ashamed or not? I do not remember and I cannot say. A black thought was born in my mind and fluttered about me like a bat. "They are Godless ones, not God-creators."

But heavier and broader than all my thoughts, was a hollow stillness in me, lazy and deep; a certain peace like a turbid pool, in the depths of whose heart dumb thoughts swam about with difficulty, like frightened fish who struggle but cannot rise to the light from out of the oppressive depths.

Little reached me from the outside, and I remember my meetings with men as through a dream. Somewhere near Omsk, at a village market, I woke up. A blind man sat on the road in the dust and sang a song. His guide knelt near him and accompanied him on his accordion. The old man looked up at heaven with his empty eyes and sang the words with a faraway, rusty voice, describing the past, under the reign of Ivan Vasilef, and the accordion gave out its hollow accompaniment, "U-u-u."

I sat down on the ground next to the blind man. He took hold of my hand, held it, let it go again, but did not stop singing: "Once there lived Ermak, a son of Timotheof." "A-a-a," the accordion repeated.

And around the singers a crowd collected quietly, listening thoughtfully and seriously to the story of the past, with heads bowed to the ground. A dry warmth enfolded me and I saw curiosity light up the eyes of the men, and some one asked:

"Won't he sing?"

"He will. Wait."

I had often heard these robber ballads, but I never knew whose were the words nor whose the soul mirrored there. But now all at once I understood. The ancient people spoke to me with a thousand tongues. "I pardon your great sins against me, man, for your small service."

People still looked at me with curiosity, and my spirit was aroused. The old man finished his song, and I arose and said:

"Orthodox Christians, here you have heard about a robber who plundered and robbed the people, but, afterwards, his conscience troubling him, he went away to save his soul, wishing to serve the people with his great strength. And he served them. But to-day you are living among robbers who exploit you mercilessly, and in what way do they serve the people? What good do you see in them?"

The crowd thickened around me, almost embracing

me, and their attention made my words grow strong and gave them tone and beauty, and I lost myself in my words. I only felt a close alliance to the earth and to the people. They lifted me up towards themselves, drawing me on by their silence: "Speak; speak the whole truth as you see it!"

Of course a policeman arrived and cried: "Move on!" asking what was the matter and demanding my passport.

The people melted quietly away, like a cloud in the sun, and the policeman questioned and made inquiries as to what I said. Some answered: "About God; about many things; mainly about God."

I saw a workingman standing apart. He leaned up against his wagon and gazed steadily at me, smiling tenderly. The policeman had taken hold of my collar, and I wanted to shake him off, but I saw that the people looked sideways at me, with half-closed eyes, as if they were asking: "Now, what are you going to say?"

I paled at their lack of faith. Conquering myself in time, I shook off the hand of the policeman and said to him:

"Do you want to know what I said?"

And again I began to speak about injustice in life. Again the market people gathered around me in great crowds, and the policeman was lost in them and effaced.

I recalled Kostia and the factory children, and I

THE CONFESSION

felt proud and happy. I became strong and as in a dream. The policeman whispered, many faces passed before me, many eyes burned; a warm cloud of people were around me, pushed me along, and I lay lightly among them. Some one took me by the shoulder and whispered in my ear: "Enough. Go." They pushed and pushed me, and soon I found myself in a kind of court, and a black-bearded man was on one side of me and on the other a young boy with no cap on his head. The dark man said:

"Climb over the wall."

I climbed it, then went over another. It seemed to me queer, yet pleasant.

"Eh," I thought, "is that who you are?"

The black-bearded man hurried me along. "Lively, comrade, lively!"

I asked him on the way: "Who are you?"

"One of yours," he answered.

The boy without the cap followed us silently. We crossed gardens, came to a ravine at the bottom of which a stream ran along, and found a footpath in the brush. The dark man led me by the hand, looked into my eyes and said, smiling:

"Well, good luck to you. Here, Fediok will conduct you to a good road. Go."

"You had better hurry. They might get you."

The dark man bent down, began crawling up the mountain, and Fediok and I went along by the stream.

"Who is that man?" I asked him.

"A blacksmith. An exile — for political reasons."

"I know such people," I answered.

I felt happy, but he was silent. I looked at the young man. His face was round, his nose short. His head seemed cut out from stone, and his gray eyes bulged far apart. He spoke low, walked noiselessly and held his head forward, as if he was listening or was pulled from above by some great force. He kept his hands behind his back, as my father-in-law used to.

"Are you a native here?"

"Yes, I am a farm hand at the priest's."

"Where is you cap?"

He felt his head, looked at me and asked:

"Why do you care about the cap?"

"Just so. It is night, and you will be cold."

He remained silent. Then he muttered unwillingly:

"What does it matter about the cap as long as one's head is saved?"

The ravine became deeper, the stream sounded clearer, and night rose from the underbrush.

My soul was unclear, yet I felt happy, and I wished to speak with the young man.

"Have you only one exile here?" I asked.

Here the young man opened himself as one opens an overcoat. Slowly and low, he said:

"Four. There is a nobleman from Moscow and

THE CONFESSION

three from the Don. Two of them are quiet fellows. They even drink vodka. But the nobleman and that Ratkof who was here before, speak, though in secret, with whomever they can. They have not yet begun to speak openly before the people. There are many of them here, many around us. I, from Birsky — Fedor Mitkof, am here five years. During this time there were eleven men here. In Olekhine there are eight; in Shishkof there are three."

He counted for a long time, and he reached about sixty. When he finished he became thoughtful; then began to speak, gesticulating with his finger.

"There are even some peasants among them. They all say the same thing; this life is unbearable; it stifles them. I lived in peace until I heard these words, and now I see I am not yet full grown and I must bow my head. Then, in truth, it must be that this life is stifling."

The young fellow spoke with difficulty, tearing each word from under his feet. He walked ahead of me and did not look at me. He was broad-shouldered and strong.

"Can you read and write?" I asked him.

"I once knew how, but have forgotten. Now I am studying again. It doesn't matter, I know how. When one has to, one can do everything. And I have to. If it were the noblemen who spoke about the difficulty of this life, I would not take any notice of it, for their beliefs were always different from ours. But when it is your own brothers, the poor working class, then it must be true. And moreover, some of the common people go even farther than the noblemen. That means that something social and human is beginning. That is what they always say — social, human. I am human. Then it means my way lies with them, that is what I think."

I listened to him and said to myself: "Learn, Matvei."

"What is the use of thinking about such a thing?" I said to him. "It is God's affair."

He stopped, suddenly standing stiff upon the ground, so that I almost fell upon his back. Then he turned his face towards me and asked sternly:

"Is it really God's affair? Here is what I think about it. This is why they say, 'Honor your father.' And they say the authorities are also from God. And this they confirm by miracles. But then if the old laws are changed, new miracles should have come. But where are they? There were no signs when new laws came, none whatever. Everything is as it was. In Nijni they discovered relics which performed miracles. But then a rumor arose that they were not true relics, for Seraphim's beard was gray and this one was red. The question is not the beard, but the miracle. Were there any miracles? There were, but they don't want to admit it. They call all signs false, or they say faith creates miracles. There are times when I

THE CONFESSION

want to beat them to stop their confounding my soul."

Again he stopped, and around him the night rose from the earth. The path fell more steeply, the stream flowed on more hastily, and the brush rustled, moving quietly.

"Go on, brother," I said to him, low.

He went forward. He did not stumble in the darkness but I almost fell on his back every step I took. He seemed to roll down like a stone, and his strange voice resounded in the stillness.

"If I believed them, it would be an end of everything. I am not especially kind-hearted. I had a brother in the military, and he hanged himself. My sister worked as a servant in a farmer's house near Birsky, and she gave birth to a child who is lame. It is four years old now and cannot walk. It means that a girl's life was ruined on account of a man's caprice. Where should she go now? My father is a drunkard and my elder brother has taken all the land. I have nothing."

We turned into the underbrush in the gray darkness. Now the stream went away from us into the depth, now again it flowed at our feet. Over our heads the night birds flew noiselessly, and above them were the stars.

I wanted to walk fast, but the man in front of me did not hurry and muttered to himself unceasingly, as if he were counting his words and taking their weight.

"That dark one, Ratkof, is a good man. He lives according to the new law and takes the part of the oppressed. A policeman once beat me with a club and he immediately felled the policeman to the ground. He had to sit fourteen days for it. 'How can you fight the authorities?' I asked him when he came out. He immediately explained his law to me. I went to the priest, and the priest said, 'Ah, are these the thoughts you are plaiting?' Ratkof was sent to the prison in the city. He sat three months, and I nineteen days. 'What did he say?' they asked me there. 'Nothing.' 'What did he teach?' 'He taught nothing.' I am no fool myself. Ratkof came out. 'Forgive me,' I said to him, 'I was a fool.' But he laughed. 'It was nonsense,' he said."

My guide remained silent, and then, in a new voice, and lower, he continued:

"Everything is nonsense to him. He spits blood, that is nonsense; he starves, that too is nonsense."

Suddenly he began to swear grossly, turned about and faced me, and hissed through his teeth:

"I can understand everything. My brother died — that happens in the military. My sister's case is not a rare one. But why do they torture that man to death? That I cannot understand. I go like a dog wherever he sends me. He calls me Earth. 'Eh, you Earth,' he says and laughs. But the fact that they are always torturing him, that is like a knife in my heart!"

THE CONFESSION

And again he began to swear like a drunken monk.

The ravine opened, broadened its walls down into the field, leveled them and vanished into the darkness.

"Well," said my guide, "good-by."

He pointed out to me the road to Omsk, turned back and disappeared. He was still without his cap.

When his heavy steps died in the stillness I sat down, not desiring to go farther. The night lay heavily on the earth and slept, fresh, and thick, like oil. There were no stars in the heavens, no moon, no light about. But there was warmth and light within me.

The heavy words of my guide burned within my memory. He was like a bell that had lain a long time on the earth, and had been covered by it and eaten out by rust, and though his tone was dull yet there was a new sound in it.

The village people stood before my eyes as they listened to my speech seriously and wonderingly. Their troubled faces passed before me as they dragged me away from the police.

"Is that the way it is?" I thought, marveling, and I could scarcely believe what had happened to me.

Again I thought. "This young man seeks signs and omens. He himself is a miracle. It is a miracle to preserve love for man in this horrible life. And the crowd who heard me, that, too, was a miracle, that it should not be deaf or blind, though many for a long time have tried to deafen and blind it. And a still greater miracle were Mikhail and his comrades."

My thoughts flowed calmly and easily. I was unaccustomed to it and did not expect it. I examined myself carefully, searched my heart quietly, wishing to find there anxiety and troubled doubt.

I smiled in the silent darkness and feared to move, lest I drive away the unwonted joy which filled my heart to the very brim. I believed and yet did not believe this marvelous fulness of my soul, this unexpected Godsend which I found in me.

It was as if a white bird, who was born long before, had slept in the shadow of my soul, and I had not known it or felt it. I stroked it accidentally and it awoke and began to sing quietly within me and flutter its light wings in my heart, and its hot song melted the ice of doubt and turned it into grateful tears.

I wanted to say something, to arise, to sing, to meet human beings and to embrace them. I saw before me the shining face of Juna, the kind eyes of Mikhail, the stern wit of Kostia. All the familiar, dear and new people became alive to me, united in my breast and broadened it with happiness till it ached.

So it had happened before while saying Mass at Easter, that I loved people and myself. I sat down, and thought tremblingly:

THE CONFESSION

"O Lord, is it not Thou, this beauty of beauties, this joy and this happiness?"

Darkness reigned about me, and in it were the shining faces of the Believers sitting quietly. But my heart sang unceasingly.

I stroked the earth with my hand, I patted it with my palm, as if it were a horse, which understood my caress.

I could not sit still. I arose and walked on through the night. I remembered Kostia's words. I saw before me the look of childish sternness in his eyes, and I went on, drunk with joy, walking over the earth towards the very end of autumn, gathering up into my soul its precious new gifts.

At the station in Omsk I saw emigrants, Little Russians. A great part of the earth was covered with their bodies, those friends of labor. I walked among them, heard their soft speech and asked them:

"Are you not afraid to lose yourselves, so far away?"

A man gray and bent by work, answered me:

"As long as we have a piece of land under our feet, we do not care how far it is. It is suffocating on earth when a man has to live by his own labor."

Formerly the words of pain and sorrow fell like ashes on my heart, but now they were keen sparks which lit it up, for every sorrow was my sorrow, and I too suffered from the want of liberty, as did the people.

There is no time nor place for general spiritual growth, and this is bitter and dangerous to the one who outstrips the people, for he remains alone in advance of them, and the people do not see him and cannot strengthen him with their strength; and alone and uselessly he burns himself up in the fire of his desires.

I spoke in Little Russian, for I knew this tender language.

"For ages the people have wandered over the earth, hither and thither, seeking a place where they may in freedom build up a righteous life with their own strength, and for ages you have wandered over the earth, its lawful masters, and why? Who is it that gives no room to the people, the real Czar of the earth? Who has dethroned them? Who has torn the crown from their heads and driven them from country to country, these creators of all labor, these exquisite gardeners who planted all the beauty on the earth?"

The eyes of the people burned. The human soul which was just awakened in them glowed, and my own glance also became wide and keen. I saw the question on each face and immediately answered it; I saw doubt and I fought with it. I drew strength from the hearts which were opened about me, and I united this strength into one heart.

When you speak to people some word which

THE CONFESSION

touches them as a whole, which lies buried secretly and deep in each human soul, then their eyes shine with glowing strength and fill you and carry you above them. But do not think that it is your strength which carries you. You are winged with the crossing of all strength in your heart. It surrounds you from without; you are strong by its strength just as long as the people fill you up with it; but should they go away, should their spirit vanish, you again fall back to the level of all.

So I began my teaching modestly, calling the people to a new service in the name of a new life, though I did not know how to name my new God. In Zlatout on a holiday I spoke in the square, and again the police interfered, and again the people hid me.

I met many splendid men and women. One whose name was Yashka Vladikine, a student in a theological seminary, is now a good friend of mine and will remain so for all my life. He does not believe in God, but he loves church music to tears. He plays psalms on the organ and weeps, the dear wonder-child.

I asked him laughing: "What are you howling at, you heretic, atheist?"

He cried out, tremblingly: "From joy at the knowledge of the great beauty which some day will be created. If already in this worldly and wretched life beauty has been created with the insignificant strength of individuals, what will be created on earth when the whole spiritual world shall be free and shall begin to express the order of its great spirit in psalms and music?"

He began to speak about the future, which stood out with blinding clearness to him, and he was himself surprised at his visions.

I have much to be grateful for to this friend of mine, as much as to Mikhail.

I have seen marvelous people by tens, for they send me to one another from city to city. I go as with fiery signals, and each one is kept burning by the same faith. It is impossible to enumerate the various people and to describe the joy at seeing the spiritual unity which lies in all. Great is the Russian people and indescribably beautiful is life.

CHAPTER XXVI

IT was in the government of Kazan that my heart received the last blow, the blow which finished the construction of the temple. It was at the monastery of the Seven Seas, at a procession of the miracle-working ikon of the Holy Virgin. They were expecting the return of this ikon to the monastery from the city — the day was a holiday.

I stood on a little hill above the lake and gazed about me. The place was filled with people, and the body of human beings streamed in dark waves to the gates of the monastery, and fought and struggled around its walls. The sun was setting and its autumn rays shone with bright red. The bells trembled like birds ready to fly and follow their own songs, and everywhere the bared heads of the people shone red in the rays of the sun, like double poppies.

Awaiting the miracle, near the gates of the monastery, stood a small carriage, in which lay a young girl, motionless. Her face was set as if in white wax, her gray eyes were half open, and all her life seemed to be in the quiet fluttering of her long lashes.

Next to her stood her parents. The father was

a tall man, gray-bearded and with a long nose. The mother, stout, round-faced, with uplifted eyebrows and wide open eyes, gazed in front of her. Her fingers moved and it seemed to me that she was about to give a piercing and passionate cry.

The people walked up to them, gazed upon the sick girl's face, and the father spoke in measured tones, his beard trembling:

"Orthodox Christians, I beg of you, pray for the unfortunate girl. Without arms, without legs, she has been lying thus for four years. Beg the Holy Virgin for aid. The Lord will reward you for your holy prayers. Help deliver the parents from sorrow."

It was plain that he had been carrying his daughter from monastery to monastery for a long time and that he had already lost all hope of her recovery. He poured out these same words over and over again and they sounded dead in his mouth.

The people listened to his prayers, sighed, crossed themselves, and the lids which covered the sorrowful eyes of the young girl trembled.

I must have seen about a score of weakened girls, about ten who were supposed to be possessed, and other kinds of invalids, and I was always consciencestricken and ashamed before them. I pitied the poor bodies robbed of strength and I pitied their vain waiting for a miracle. But I never felt pity to such a degree as now. A great silent complaint seemed frozen on the white half-dead face of the

THE CONFESSION

daughter and a silent and indescribable sorrow seemed to control the mother.

It was oppressive and I went away. Thousands of eyes were looking toward the distance, and like a cloud there floated toward me the warm, dull whisper: "They are carrying it."

Heavily and slowly the crowd proceeded up the mountain like a dark wave of the sea, and the golden banners burned like red foam, shooting out their sheaves of bright sparks. The ikon of the holy virgin floated and swung like a fiery bird shining in the rays of the sun. From the human body a mighty sigh arose, a thousand-voiced song: "Intercede for us, O mother of the Lord, most high."

The song was cut short by cries: "Hurry! Move faster! Hurry!"

The lake smiled brightly in the frame-work of the blue wood; the red sun melted, sinking into the wood, and the copper sound of the bells rang out gaily. Around me were anxious faces, the quiet and sorrowful whispering of prayers, eyes dimmed with tears, and the waving of many, many arms, making the sign of the cross.

I was alone. All this was sad error for me, weak despair, a weary desire for grace.

The procession marched on, their faces covered with dust, streams of sweat pouring down their cheeks. They breathed heavily, they gazed strangely as if they saw nothing, and pushed one another and stumbled along.

I pitied them. I pitied the strength of their faith which was wasted on the air. There was no end to this stream of people. A vigorous and mighty cry arose, but it was dark and sounded reproachful:

"Rejoice, O merciful one," and again, "Hurry! Hurry!"

In this whole cloud of dust I saw hundreds of black faces, thousands of eyes like stars on the milky way. I saw that those eyes were fiery sparks from one soul, eagerly awaiting an unknown joy.

The people went down as one body, pressing close upon one another, holding one another's hands and walking fast, as if the road was terribly long, but they were ready to go to what was their end without stopping.

My soul trembled with an unknown pain. Like a prayer the words of Juna rose in my memory: "The people — the creators of God."

I started forward. I rushed from the mountain to meet the people, went along with them and sang with a full throat: "Rejoice, beneficent strength of all strengths!"

They seized and embraced me, and I seemed to float away and to melt under their hot breathing. I did not know that the earth was under my feet, nor did I recognize myself. There was no time nor space, only joy, vast like the heavens. I was like a glowing coal, flaming with faith. I was unimportant yet great and resembled all who were around me at the time of our general flight.

THE CONFESSION

"Hurry! Hurry!"

The people flew over the earth irresistibly, ready to stride over all obstacles and abysses, all doubts and dark fears. I remember that the procession stopped close to me, that confusion occurred, that I was dragged near the wagon of the sick girl and heard the cries and the murmuring:

"Let us sing the Te Deum; let us sing the Te Deum."

There was great excitement. They pushed the wagon, and the head of the young girl rocked to and fro, helpless and without strength. Her large eyes gazed out with fear. Tens of eyes poured their rays out upon her; hundreds of force streams crossed themselves over her weak body, calling her to life with an imperious desire to see her rise from her bed.

I, too, looked into the depths of her eyes, and an inexpressible desire came over me, in common with all, that she arise; not for my sake, nor for her own sake, but for some special reason, before which she and I were like a bird's feather in a fire.

As rain saturates the earth with its live moisture, so the people filled the dry body of the girl with their strength, and they whispered and cried to her and to me:

"Rise, dear one, rise. Lift your arms. Be not afraid. Arise, arise without fear. Sick one, arise; dear one, lift your arms."

Hundreds of stars arose in her soul and a pink shadow lit up her death-like face, and her surprised and happy eyes opened still wider. Her shoulders moved slowly and humbly she raised her trembling arms and obediently held them up. Her mouth was open like a fledgling's about to leave its nest for the first time. A deep sigh rose around her. As though the earth were a copper bell, struck upon by a giant sviatogor with all his strength, the people trembled, and laughing cried:

"On your feet. Help her. Arise little one, on your feet. Help her."

We caught the girl, lifted her and put her on her feet, holding her lightly. She bent like an ear of corn in the wind, and cried out:

"Oh, dear one, Lord; oh, Holy Virgin!"

"Walk!" the people cried. "Walk!"

I remember their dusty faces, tearful and sweaty. Through the damp tears a miraculous strength shone out masterful, the faith in the power to create miracles.

The recovered girl walked quietly among us. Confidently she pressed her revived body against the body of the people, and smiling and pale like a flower, she said:

"Let me go alone."

She stopped, swayed, then walked. She walked as if on knives which cut her feet, but she walked alone; fearful yet bold, like a little child; and the people around her rejoiced and were friendly as to a little child. She was excited. Her body trembled. She held her hands out before her as if she

THE CONFESSION 291

were leaning against the air. She was filled by the strength of the people and she was sustained from every side by hundreds of luminous rays.

I lost sight of her at the gates of the monastery, and recovering myself, I gazed about me. Everywhere there was holiday tumult. There was a ringing of bells and the powerful talk of the people. The evening red fell brilliantly from the heavens and the lake clothed itself in the purple of the reflection. A man walked past me, smiled and asked:

"Did you see it?"

I embraced him and kissed him, like a brother after a long separation, and we found no words to say to each other. Smiling, we remained silent and separated.

. . . .

At night I sat in the wood above the lake. Again I was alone, but now forever and inseparably united to the soul of the people, the masters and miracle workers of the earth. I sat and listened to all that I had seen and known grow and burn within me in one fire.— I, too, would reflect to the world this light in which everything flamed with great significance and was clothed with the miraculous. It winged my soul with a desire to accept the world as it had accepted me.

I have no words to describe the exultation of that night, when, alone in the darkness, I embraced the whole earth with my love and stood on the height of my experience and saw the world, like a fiery stream of life-force, flowing turbidly to unite into one current, the end of which I could not see. I joyfully understood that the inaccessibility of the end was the source of the infinite growth of my soul and the great earthly beauty. And in this infinity were the innumerable joys of the live human soul.

In the morning the sun appeared to me with a new face. I saw how its rays cautiously and lovingly sank into the darkness and turned it away; how it lifted from the earth the veils of night, and there she stood before me in the beautiful and magnificent jewels of autumn; the emerald field of the great play of peoples and the fight for free play was the holy place in the procession of the celebration of beauty and truth.

I saw the earth, my mother, in space between the stars, and brightly she gazed out with her ocean eyes into the distance and the depths. I saw her like a full bowl of bright red, incessantly seething, human blood, and I saw her master, the all-powerful, immortal people.

They winged her life with a great activity and hope, and I prayed:

"Thou art my God, the creator of all gods, which thou weavest out of the beauty of thy soul and the labor and agony of thy seeking.

"There shall be no God but thou, for thou art the one God, the creator of miracles."

This is what I believe and confess.

And always do I return there where people free

THE CONFESSION

the souls of their neighbors from the yoke of darkness and superstition and unite them and disclose to them their own secret physiognomy, and aid them to recognize the strength of their own wills and teach them the one and true path to a general union for the sake of the great cause, the cause of the universal creating of God.

THE END

Printed in the United States
3179